Sara Stockbridge rose to fame in the 1980s as the muse of fashion designer Vivienne Westwood. Now she lives with her daughter in south London, writing, and acting now and then. She is working on her second novel, a ghost story set in Brixton.

HAMMER

Grace Hammer lives a sweet enough life with her children in London's dank and dirty East End, dipping the pockets of wealthy strangers foolish enough to enter there. She keeps a clean house and a tight hold on her magpie nature, restricting her interests to wallets and pocket watches. At night she dreams of shiny things. Out in the dark countryside Mr Blunt rocks in his seat by the fire, grinding his teeth. He has never forgotten his scarlet treasure, or the harlot who stole it from him. At night he dreams of slitting her lily-white throat . . .

SARA STOCKBRIDGE

HAMMER

Complete and Unabridged

ULVERSCROFT
Leicester

First published in Great Britain in 2009 by
Chatto & Windus
The Random House Group Limited
London

First Large Print Edition
published 2009
by arrangement with
The Random House Group Limited
London

The moral right of the author has been asserted

British Library CIP Data

Stockbridge, Sara, 1966 –
Hammer.
1. Jewel thieves- -England- -London- -History- -
19th century- -Fiction. 2. Female offenders- -
England- -London- -History- -19th century- -
Fiction. 3. Whitechapel (London, England)- -
Fiction. 4. Detective and mystery stories.
5. Large type books.
I. Title
823.9'2–dc22

ISBN 978–1–84782–937–5

Published by
F. A. Thorpe (Publishing)
Anstey, Leicestershire

Set by Words & Graphics Ltd.
Anstey, Leicestershire
Printed and bound in Great Britain by
T. J. International Ltd., Padstow, Cornwall

This book is printed on acid-free paper

For Max and Lelu

Prologue

Grace arrives as night falls, huge and black over her head. She had seen the smoke a mile off and supposed they had been burning the stubble that day; an acrid wisp hangs in the air over Pagham, of smouldering chaff, she fancies. There are no lights in the village as she makes her way up the lane, no one cooking, no shouting, no children. The Green Man is empty; abandoned jars stand huffily upon the bar, the clock ticks to itself above the mantel. A lonely dog barks her up the lane, whining at the end of its tether. No faces, no greetings — surprise! Coming home at last, as she had pictured it. She stands by the sleeping church, all alone, turning her head this way and that, and wonders, for a curious moment, if everyone is hiding. Past the juniper hedge she realises the tang is not fading, but coming thicker, on a soft breeze, every step. She stops short. And the clock, and the dog, and the turning earth. Her chest seems to hollow, horribly, and she picks up her feet and hurls herself up the hill, waves swelling and breaking in her ears, heart banging on her tongue. Something sharp in the lane bites through the sole of her shoe; sparks burst across the horizon as the still in the outhouse explodes.

Hellfire swallows the Hammer farmhouse, lighting the sky: a raging orb lashing jagged tongues around the black bricks, cracking screaming timber like dry ribs. It rips livid into the dark as if it would tear itself loose from the ground and cast furious Judgement down across the earth. She crosses the meadow on rubber legs. Dread smoke churns into the starry sky, gathering like doom; bats, blazing horsemen, devil hounds spiral frenzied into the night. In the distance crazy figures blow, tiny, to and fro like tumbling ashes. Demons flicker at the dead windows, spewing cinders, taking human shape, watching her drown, running through treacle. She throws herself howling on the crowd, gaping into hot faces, looking for her pa, brothers, her sweet rosy sister. May was sleeping the last time she saw her — beatific — flying, evidently, on a white horse through her favourite dream (which sounded tedious, though Grace had never said so). The good people of Pagham hold fast to her arms to stop her running into the blazing house. And they watch, rigid, as the roof caves in with a mighty groan, like an elephant dying, collapsing into a million sparks.

Grace wakes, eyes wide, upright in her bed. Sleeping breath fills the room. Someone cries, 'Thief!' in the distance. All is well. She goes back to peaceful sleep. And though she will feel something amiss in the morning she will put it down to a dream she cannot quite remember, and leave it at that.

★   ★   ★

Out in the dark countryside, in his gloomy farmhouse, Mr Blunt sits upright in his oily bed, jabbering and growling in the dark. It haunts him tonight in his sleep, as it does maybe once a year now — calling, as bright as it ever was! — leading him on, like the Pole Star twinkling through a veil of cloud, only to dissolve again, and he clenches his brutal fists, and blasts the sleeping birds from the trees.

'*Damn you, Hammer! Damn you wretched bitch!*'

Sometimes he dreams, with pleasure, of slicing her throat.

1

Jack Tallis sleeps in a warehouse at London Docks whence he ventures daily to drink himself unconscious in the Queen. He is a favourite with the local ladies, who find him captivating though he is often rude. When rejected with a contemptuous glance they giggle nervously, as if in shock, and wither back into the wall, perhaps to try their luck another evening — when he might smile charmingly, flashing his full brilliance, so that the chosen girl will feel special, though she knows he does not mean it.

Handsome! How devilish can a man be? With his dark eyes, and his insolent mouth, and the cheek of him! Flashing his winning grin! He is handsome through to the very back of his head. He shines at the lucky girl, lips curling as if they know she imagines how it would be to kiss them, tender and firm, flashing strong white teeth behind.

'Good evening, Louise.' (Or any other female name you may care for.)

She lights up like Piccadilly, a little breathless. 'Hello, Jack!'

'You are dazzling tonight, if I may be so

bold,' he says, grasping her round the waist with a rough hand and pulling her closer, pressing a knee between hers.

'Why, thank you, Jack.' She blushes sweetly and giggles.

'I must say I should like to tempt you into a darkened room with me, Louise.'

Speechless, she basks for a moment in the glow; it will be enough to keep her going until he acknowledges her existence again. This might take weeks, but such is the force of his appeal that she will be content to wait. Already his attention is elsewhere, upon Mrs Maybury, the landlady, who barred him only last week but has forgotten it already.

'What's it to be, you devil?'

'Hello, there he is! Oi, Jack!' Oh, God, that voice again, bobbing up behind him, every night of the week. It belongs to Miss Lucy Fear, whose company he has been hoping to avoid this evening. Her name may tell you all you need to know.

'Look, Sally, I found him!' She is lurching across the bar at him, shouting as she goes. 'She's been all over looking for you!' It is clearly Lucy who has been looking all over. Sally, who lives in oblivion, turns her head at the sound of her name and steadies herself to focus, which she manages with a nice blush when she sees it is Jack, even though she is pickled.

'Best please, Mrs M.'

'She wants to get hold of you, Jack!'

Lucy is prodding him now, brushing up against him. He can feel her breath on his cheek. He fights the urge to punch her loud fat face. Sally has fallen off her stool.

'Go on then, you silly girl!'

'I don't dare!'

Women flirt with Jack like clumsy children — they giggle stupidly, in a manner they imagine to be fetching, with their eyes wide like village idiots', they ask him to repeat particular words, such as 'thoroughfare' or 'thirty-three', his age, just to see the shape his lips make when he says it, and the big wide laugh that bursts like a ripe fruit, with his head thrown back as if in the throes of some passion. His dark brown eyes might cloud in the space of a blink — hard and flat — as if the charming gent to whom you were talking just a moment before had vanished, and you had never met this cold stranger.

He breaks away to sit by the wall where he cannot be cornered, next to Archie Simmons, who will talk about his bedsores, or the damp at his lodgings if he is lucky.

* * *

Grace Hammer has no reason to be in the Queen over any other public palace that dots the corner of any other street, like a rash across the Temperance map, lighting up London town: only that she was thirsty and right outside the door. This evening she is looking rather lovely, and not because she has scrubbed up nicely but because she woke up so that morning, shining like the cherry on the cake. Her assets are not racked up underneath her chin, east and west, as if in a window-box, like every other pair there. And not big either, just a nice handful. Her legs are long and strong and shapely, hidden under her skirts. Her lips curl at the corners. Grace can change like spring weather, be stern as Queen Victoria. She looks to Jack Tallis like a missing heartbeat.

He has seen her here before, in fact, across the bar; now, as then, she pays him not a flicker of attention. This evening he takes her in properly: strong hands, clean hair, her mouth, the curve from her chin to her throat. She says something to her tatty friend and laughs, showing good teeth, the whitest in Whitechapel, except maybe his own. He stares until she turns round.

They gaze at each other for several moments, delighted, and caught, share a fleeting thought — that rare thrill: There you are! After scorching him thus she looks away. He sits still for a while, stealing a glance now and then, but she doesn't look over again, so, cocksure (or putting on a good show of it), he rises from his seat to saunter arrogantly to her table.

★ ★ ★

The men of the parish envy Jack. Though he is poor he never seems to want for much. He eats well, he never wears a desperate face. His clothes are shabby but he always finds a kind lady to wash them. He will always land on his feet. He has ease, and luck, and he has long ring fingers to prove it. Only a few who have made his intimate acquaintance will know that sometimes he feels small and foolish.

She fixes him halfway across, and he falters, tripping on an invisible nail in the floor but covering it well, making her grin, and he catches the blatant thought in her eye and bats it back so that by the time he has crossed the room and sat next to her they are almost laughing, and feel that they have jumped a few steps and don't care where they start.

So he says, 'Who might you be then?' and she says, 'What's it to you?'

'I'm Jack,' he offers, tipping his hat.

9

'It's nice to meet you, I'm sure.'

'You look *fine*.'

'Is that right?'

'I've seen you here before.'

'And so?'

How startling the attraction and how strangely familiar they seem — a common element of many ill-fated connections, as Grace is well aware. They sparkle mischief, letting their mucky thoughts talk and looking at each other's lips.

'Where d'you spring from, then?'

'Round the corner.'

'And me.'

'Fancy!'

'So where do you hide?'

'Indoors!'

'That's a shame.'

'I can't see that I'm missing much.' She looks right at him as she says it, with her face quite straight, which tickles Jack Tallis. He likes a girl with prickles.

'How many have you got indoors, then?'

'Plenty to be going on with, thank you.'

'No husband?'

'Ask a lot of questions don'tcha?' Grace can't help but crack her face. She likes a man with just the right bad manners.

'Chased him away, did ya? How d'you find it on your own?'

10

'I grit my teeth.'

'I'll bet you do!'

They laugh wide together, stop, and look. She runs her fingers up his throat and grips him softly by his handsome jaw, surprising them both, and their matching lips meet. Both note that the other's breath is sweet, though laced with smoke and gin. When their mouths part they stay with their faces close together, rapt, with a little crooked smile as if they know each other well.

'I quite like you, Jack.'

'Won't you tell me your name, then?'

'No.'

Hurrying out they draw bitter glances from the usual girls. People see them go and think: What a handsome pair! Bursting with it. And all their teeth.

'Can I follow you home?'

'Not likely!'

'Will you come with me then?'

★ ★ ★

Now let us set this straight before we carry on: Miss Grace Hammer is no unfortunate creature of night. She has no need of anything this charmer may have upon his person and, indeed, has resolved already not to fleece him. She does not make a habit of stepping out down dark and lonely streets with men who have not told her where they are going, however handsome they may be, and she has a razor in her pocket, just in case.

And so she lets him lead her up Cable Street, then left, past the Dock Street Sailors' Home, past the church. The pub at the corner is bursting with noise, fights are breaking out, Irishmen are singing merry songs about their hard luck and their heartless women. Indians play dominoes on the benches outside, dark faces in shadow, bright flashing eyes. They cross Smithfield Street and go down towards Pennington along the forbidding wall of the London Docks. Grace has passed this wall only once before, though it is a mere spit due north from her front door; it seems to stretch a mile, made of countless bricks, laid by hordes of tiny men, slaving like ants on the scaffolding. She rarely sees the river, imprisoned as it is from Blackwall to the Tower. She never ventures further than this, to the end of the lane, to catch a glimpse of the dark water beyond.

* * *

The wide river Thames is England's jugular, busy like the heart. It brings in everything you could eat, drink, smoke, or wear, buy or sell from the far corners of the globe. As the city grows, so does its appetite: the ships grow larger and the hungry docks unfold, spreading towards the sea. The largest and newest is the Royal Albert Dock, past the Isle of Dogs: two miles long, built to harbour the biggest ships in the wide world — an ungodly hole in the ground, like the grave of some colossus, fallen to earth with a mighty crash. It was dug by such a dusty legion as built the great pyramids of Egypt, and killed very many of them in the process. Three unlucky men, who had nothing to do with its construction, rest in such peace as may be afforded in the concrete beneath the gigantic lock gates.

The first two — deep in the ditch! — had tried to rob the notorious Wilson betting shop, a bone-headed venture indeed, though to be fair they were new to the area, having docked just five days before. They had found the front office free of cash, which did not accord with their tip-off, and lurched upstairs, hoping to find something there, by which time the Wilson girl, who was minding the shop, had whistled across the street for the Wilson men, who came directly, with hatchets. The terrible two had found a small safe in the back room and, with a Herculean effort, had managed to heave it out of the window. It fell on to a very nice birdbath in the yard below, obliterating it, but no matter. These hapless idiots (their being referred to thus in the fairest and most amiable manner) were staring drunkenly after it, preparing to climb down somehow, when the hatchet men caught them. They ended up in the bottom of the trench the night before the concrete, in approximately five pieces each.

The third unfortunate fellow below the Royal Albert Dock gates joined them the very next day. It struck him as unfair as he went under — a harsh price to pay for a simple mistake. He had leaned just an inch too far over the edge to retrieve his watch. It had jumped from his hand as he took it from his pocket, arcing in slow motion into the wet cement; he had been meaning to get the chain fixed all week and cursed himself for putting it off. He was late and taking a short-cut to Canning Town. It was submerging slowly, looking at him with half a face, and he was sure he could reach it. He supposed the concrete was not too deep.

★ ★ ★

Below Whitechapel lurk the London Docks, tight behind fortress walls, high as the Tower, where our two tiny vagabonds scurry around

14

the perimeter, sinking into shadows. By day they swarm with hungry men, sweating blood in the warehouses, toiling under haystack bales of wool, fat barrels you could drown in, sacks of coffee, green bananas, crates of lemons; they break their backs upon the landing decks and feel lucky still to have been picked out from the crowd at the gates, like winning the tombola, even if the finger that is sacrificed most days to the jealous god of commerce should be one of theirs. (Someone ought to log these sorry digits but nobody bothers; they are clean gone, ripped smartly off in cranking chains or bitten through by turning iron teeth; they turn up now and then in the foreman's lunch.) They stack tobacco, row on row of tusks, leopard — or bearskins, tiger fur; pythons from some fetid jungle hang from the rafters to the floor.

After night falls it becomes a silent and deserted place. The barrel yard is huge and empty; the warehouses loom into the black sky beyond. The sound of lapping water comes gently across the breeze, and the groaning of stacked ships, jostling each other in the great west basin. Gulls cruise the night sky, rats come out of hiding to sniff around the storerooms.

The only human beings who inhabit this strange netherworld are Jack — who resides

15

there on the quiet, courtesy of his good friend Bill Brierley, foreman of the west dock — and the night-watchmen, of whom there are four: two for the west and two for the east and the Shadwell Basin. They are not the most vigilant guardians, preferring to take frequent tea breaks in their hut at the side of Tobacco Dock, where their beats overlap. They are supposed to patrol in pairs but split up to halve the time. They boil a little tin kettle and feel themselves very clever indeed, making rounds every hour that take them no more than seventeen minutes.

★   ★   ★

Handsome Jack Tallis stops suddenly by a small arch, hidden in the precipice of the dock wall, and looks up and down the wide ghost way, a million cobbles stretching into darkness, before sinking inside, feeling his way to the end. He presses his ear to the stout wooden door. Grace strikes a match. It flares with a tiny sizzling sound casting yellow light across their faces. Footsteps pass inside and they wait, holding their breath. He opens the lock and the heavy chain with a key that seems to have sprung from the palm of his hand, and they are through the portal into the secret world, locking it tight behind them.

The yard stretches away to the grand entrance of the wine vaults, with the clock above, the warehouses dark behind, and beyond, glimpsed between them, the sparkle of light on water. Jack grabs her hand and they scurry like rats across the vast empty yard. The watchman is almost back at his hut, his lantern fading into the distance, shaking on its chain. Grace follows Jack out by the water: deep Indian ink, rippling slowly in the moonlight. Banks of ships like sleeping dinosaurs hang in the great basin, their chains clanking softly, masts and prows stuck out like prehistoric limbs against the dark milky sky. He catches her hand and, turning her to face him, kisses her again. Arching together, moonlit, charmed rag and bone shadows.

She spots the boat first, among the great creaking hulls, just waiting with its oars tucked in, ready as if they had called for it — and in they go, water heaving beneath them, lapping like thick black jelly. Jack takes the oars and thrusts them outward into the pool.

The moon lights patterns around them, dancing out from the stern, breaking with each stroke into shards of silver. The chatter and rabble are far behind, the Queen is a dream, and the peace lies around them like a blanket. It is uncommon and blissful, and

Grace does not want to break it. She trails her hand in the water, wonders how deep it goes down. Far over on the dock wall the night-watchman's lantern casts a shaky halo but he is a speck in the distance. Jack stops rowing, oars poised in mid-air as if holding their breath, shining drops falling like chimes. They are mice in a newspaper hat, afloat on their own private sea.

'Let me try,' she says, taking the oars.

2

Jack Tallis did not have the pleasure of her company again that week or the next. He looked for her in the Queen and then the Britannia, the Alma, the Princess Alice, the Ten Bells, the Horn of Plenty and even the Saracen's Head. Had he known he had missed her by a few moments on Thursday outside Spitalfields Market and then again on Saturday at the top of Brick Lane he might have persevered, but he was not famous for sticking at it and gave up at last. He was sulking into his beer at the Frying Pan — she seemed to have disappeared from the face of the Earth, as if he had dreamed her — when the door swung open and in she came, followed by a small girl, maybe five years old, with a crisp blue bow in her hair. He almost rubbed his eyes to make sure he was seeing straight.

Grace Hammer marched straight past him up to the counter and banged her fist upon it, making the jars jump. It was midday and the regular rabble were not all in yet, so the landlord swung round ready to start, but laughed heartily when he saw it was Grace and lifted the hatch to let her through to the back room. The little girl caught Jack's eye as she followed them in, trailing by the hand from her mother's grip, fixing him to the wall with that cast-iron look he has seen already, only blue this time, right through him. Then the door closed behind them.

Jack waited, straining his ears, but heard nothing — he sat for a while feeling unaccountably awkward, as if he was watching himself. He was getting up to leave when they reappeared, and sat down quickly; there was handshaking and more joviality. The little girl ate an iced bun, looking past them at him, studying his hat and his hands, which unnerved him somehow. It seemed an awkward moment to present himself so he sank back in his seat, trying to merge with the shadow. Grace and the little girl walked out into the street. Jack drained his jug and slid after them.

★ ★ ★

Grace Hammer has four living children: Charlie, who is almost a grown man, Billy, eleven, Jake, nine, and lovely Miss Daisy, just five. The boys are a crew of fine young men with a righteous sense of justice and respect for their fellows, though they earn their daily bread and butter rifling the pockets of wealthy strangers — they are often to be found helping old Mrs Cutler to eat her meagre dinner or reading to Miss Grieve, who is dying in a cold bed. They are fiercely and utterly devoted to their little sister, though they love to tease her for their own selfish amusement.

'Who's your sweetheart Daisy? Is it Harry Harding? I saw you getting friendly on the corner.'

'Go *away*!' she shouts: a fair retort, she uses it often — for a greeting sometimes, as they enter the room, even before they have opened their mouths.

'Was you sharing secrets? Or just sugar lumps?'

Daisy does not respond in English but growls as well as any jungle creature might at such a bunch of monkeys. One day when she grows big she will be something to reckon with; for now she is small, and soft, the prettiest girl in London Town, so they laugh, and prod some more, as boys do — 'So it *is* Harry now, see! What happened to poor Joe? He was the only boy in the world last week. Ain't you gonna marry him no more?' — making her roar. Daisy beats them back and they laugh at her as they run away.

When the girls are left in peace they draw

pictures, or do chains of cut-out people, holding hands. The Hammer boys keep all the things their sister makes them — careful, knotted, twisted things of string and paper, sticks and bones, and feathers she finds in the street. There are dozens, she being an extraordinarily busy little person: sheaves of drawings and maps of the world, adorned with writing of her own design, which she will read you if you ask her nicely.

Charlie lost his father at the age of three — the only decent man Grace had found. He fell into a blast furnace at the foundry where he worked and is much missed still. Billy and Jake's father fared no better, catching tuberculosis in the outbreak of 1879 and wheezing on for a few miserable months in the Union Workhouse before kicking the bucket — a fate richly deserved as he was a useless cheat, cruel and unfaithful, though he had seemed charming at first. Grace had thought herself thoroughly cured of scoundrels until Daisy's father happened along, giving her two girls. The first was Rose, who died while still new, buried in a tiny white coffin carried by her brothers while her father mourned in the pub. The second was darling Miss Daisy, after whose conception Grace kicked him out. She had embarked already on a private life of crime and had no need of him. The family thrived thereafter; they ate well, they wanted for nothing. Grace felt herself lucky every day. Poor Mrs Ratch next door had a brute who beat her twice a week and gave her a baby every year; he spent his wages on drink and Grace could see she was starving slowly to death, trying to feed her children.

Daisy was lucky enough never to meet her father. He died under the wheels of a brewery cart not a month after he'd gone; a kindly copper brought the solemn news, which made Grace laugh and clap her hands, and ask if death had been swift and merciful, or horribly brutal; and if he had suffered, how terribly and for how long. Sergeant Manley Goodwell was shocked at Grace Hammer's cruel sentiments and wondered if she had arranged the accident — which, indeed, she would have been happy to do — but he was not to know that the dead man's favourite game was to eat his fill when there was not enough for dinner before the family were allowed to start. They had to wait around the table and watch him smack his lips and lick his fingers until there was nothing left but rind and bones and potato skins. Grace wanted to stick a fork in his eye, and we must forgive her hard heart. Reluctantly she paid for a decent funeral, which might have seemed worth every penny if she had been driving the brewery cart.

And so it is their mother who has taught the Hammer children all they know. From her the boys have learned their trade, and to read and write — which sets them in some way apart from the other ragged children in the street. She is loving, and strict as the Law, which they respect as a convention though they break it every day. They have the smartest manners in London. And though Grace has a violent temper — which last exploded on Christmas Eve of 1878, driving Billy and Jake's father bare-chested from the house, beating at his charred beard, never to be seen again — she keeps it in a box and never turns it on her children, not even Charlie with his bare cheek. She had wondered if he might be better for a slap or two until her neighbour Mrs Jacob nosed across the street one day to tell her he was getting far too clever, and to recommend correction, along those very lines: iron discipline, as she had dealt her own wilful sons. Grace wouldn't have the heart anyway. She loves him, wilful as he is.

Jake doesn't say much; she keeps a special eye on him.

Billy reads the most, easily the best behaved. She loves them all as much.

★ ★ ★

Jack didn't spot Grace and Miss Blue Eyes for a minute or two, coming out into the light of day. Blinking up Brick Lane this way and that, he clocked them outside the chapel, exchanging a word with the shoe-black. He bent to pick up an imaginary penny as she turned her head his way, and when he looked up again they were on their way down the street. He hurried after them, feeling urgent suddenly, as if it were his last chance to see her. They turned right down Church Street before he reached the corner, and for the few moments that they were out of sight a strange panic held tight to his chest, until he saw them again, walking hand in hand past the tall Christ Church. He dropped back until they crossed Commercial Street, where he dived into the crowded road after them, weaving through the traffic, and caught them up, hanging close behind. At White's Row they turned right, then left into Bell Lane. He watched from the corner as they went inside and ventured up the street a little, unusually timid, to see the door. Number twenty-eight. There it was.

Now he wasn't sure what to do next, or why he had stalked her there in such a furtive manner when he might have presented himself, with his charm and his flashing teeth, as he would any other day. Upright, he liked to see himself, not skulking in the street. He drew himself tall but felt awkward still. It seemed he must turn tail and walk away — how could he knock? He stood there stupid, feeling as if he were frozen to the spot. His next move was decided by Grace, who stepped out abruptly into the street, hands upon her hips. She stood and watched him writhe, like an earthworm in salt. Her eyes did not twinkle.

'Hello, Jack,' she said. 'Fancy meeting you here.'

★ ★ ★

Inside it was dim but for a small lamp by the bed. He was surprised by the exotic scent of tuberose, though he didn't know what it was called. Glancing around, feeling uncommonly shy, he took in the clean stove, the patchwork bedspread — and sheets! He was sure they were the only decent sheets in that street, the next and the next as well. Then a small table with books upon it, not a lonely almanac or a Holy Bible, but books, in a teetering pile, stacked by some distracted intellectual. He wondered who that might be.

A red curtain half drawn across a small

doorway revealed a second room; he could see the edge of a bed and a tin bath leaning against the wall beyond. Rows of paper dolls and some lively drawings of what he supposed were zoo creatures decorated the walls, signed in varying degrees of legibility by the artist, one Daisy Hammer. A lofty ballerina hung in pride of place, poised above the mantel on one toe with the other leg high in the air and her arms stretched out as if she was flying. All evidently the work of Miss Blue Eyes. He wondered how many others there were. Three at least, judging from all the washing. There were plates and clean cutlery, and by the stove a bucket of coal. The effect of entering the room from the world outside (apart from the frosty reception) was of stepping into an enchanted cave, in which to fall headlong and rest, receive comfort and refuge. She was certainly doing very nicely for herself, very nicely indeed. The woman in the back next door slept under a flour sack and ate apple cores and peelings from the gutter; a fact he did not know but would surely not have been surprised to discover.

'Charlie, this is Jack. Jack, this is my son, Charlie.'

Charlie was reading in the corner, sat regally upon a shabby armchair. He looked Jack up and down, in the way that young men have for male strangers who follow their mother home. 'How d'you do, Jack?' He stood up to kiss his ma.

'What you reading, darlin'?'

'Charles Dickens.'

'Oh, lovely.'

'*Two Cities*.'

'Where d'you find that?'

'Holywell Street.'

'Did you borrow it?'

'No, Ma!'

'Very nice indeed. Where are the boys?'

'Gone to look at Tommy's aunt again.'

'Haven't they buried her yet?'

'Tomorrow.'

'God bless her.'

Daisy pushed forward to be introduced to the stranger. He could see she remembered him, but was keeping it to herself for the moment.

'Hello,' she said from behind the stuffed dog she was clutching. 'Who are you?'

'Jack.'

'Can you draw animals?'

Now Jack, unknown but yet suspected by Grace Hammer, may be a chancer and a scoundrel but he is sweet with little children and they love him. He endeared himself thoroughly to Daisy and, to a lesser extent, with the young men of the family, when they

28

had tired of Tommy's aunt and returned to find this stranger. They like him much better than they allow for. By the time Grace sent him home he had been invited to the next roast dinner and asked very many questions on the subjects of football, and cards, about which he seems to know a great deal.

Grace tucked Daisy into the big bed with her scruffy stuffed dog and kissed her delicious cheek.

'When is Jack coming again?'

'I couldn't tell you, darlin', I don't know. He wasn't meant to come today.'

'Why not?'

'Because no one invited him.'

'I could invite him next time.'

'Get your face washed, Jake.'

Charlie was popping out and Billy wanted to go with him.

'Course you bloody can't. He's off to see some girl, most likely. He won't want you hanging about. Sit and read that *Family Robinson*.'

'I finished it.'

'Was it any good?'

'It's all right.'

'Well, start something else, then.'

The fire snapped; Billy shuffled through the cupboard.

'And I don't want you going to the bloody

Eagle anyway, not by yourself.'

'Yes, Ma.'

'Don't you cheek me.'

★ ★ ★

Jack Tallis lay on a sack of coffee in warehouse twelve, London Docks, smiling to himself in the dark. He drained his fine brandy, fresh from the barrel at the foot of his sackcloth bed — tomorrow he might sample the armagnac — and fell into contented slumber.

★ ★ ★

In Bell Lane Grace closed her eyes and pictured his strong hands, his face. He had a crease beside his mouth made by smiling, the particular smile that seems made just for you. He was a devil indeed. She could remember such details about him, and so vividly! What a charmer.

Out in the dark countryside Mr Blunt snoozes peacefully, with a smile upon his face. He dreams of choking her, slicing her throat.

3

Long, long ago, in a fine stately home in Hampshire, Mr Horatio Blunt liberated the magnificent ruby necklace that represented the very pinnacle of his criminal career: from a secret drawer in the Honourable Lady Stanhope's armoire that gave him no trouble at all. A big crew was assembled to strip the house down — it had thirty-seven rooms and they meant to do the job properly — organised from inside with the help of a Miss Violet Chance, who would never work as a housemaid again. Mr Charles Worth himself was rumoured to have had a hand in it, though he was entertaining the lord and lady of the house that very evening at a charity ball in Mayfair. They took the best silver, porcelain, the finest pictures — leaving pale squares on the wallpaper beside the indignant family portraits — and the jewellery.

And such jewellery! A parade of shining stones to shame the night sky, sparkling against the plush velvet lining of their cases. Precious opals, like pieces of the full moon, flashing their every colour at once, as if they could not choose. A plague of sapphires

— evidently Lady Stanhope's favourite, for not only did she have more than the Queen, but had arranged them in shade order, from the cornflower bud to the deep blue sea. And emeralds — immodestly green — ropes of pearls, exotic jet, a galaxy of diamonds: necklaces, tiaras, brooches, pins. Every drawer of the box hid a promise, bright like a brand new star, dazzling the crooked assembly, making them giddy, like girls. The heavy safe in which these treasures should have been tucked up tight arrived the next afternoon from the ironmonger, unluckily for Lady Stanhope, who greeted it with a kick and broke her toe upon it.

Outstanding among this confusion of riches were a necklace and drop earrings, boasting three brilliant-cut diamonds that Mr Blunt reckoned correctly, with a hasty glance, at three carats each, set around with emeralds and pearls, a diamond pin — small perhaps to you or I, beside its ostentatious neighbours, but rare blue, and flawless, and an opal ring as big as a brandy ball. But the best piece by far was the ruby necklace. It was exceptionally fine, which no one paused to consider, and indecently large, which they spotted straight.

As any good thief will know, a ruby is the rarest and most valuable stone. This ruby had more of a scarlet hue than crimson, a rare clear colour. It had been dug out of the ground in 1808 by a very poor man in Burma — the best find that year, the size of a good walnut — and caused great excitement among the miners, being a useful excuse to down tools for a minute or two. It went to France directly, where it was table cut, and then to England, where it was mounted in silver on a gold frame, edged by tiny brilliant-cut diamonds, as the centre drop of a magnificent necklace. Smaller rubies were set in the delicate silverwork that ran round the neck, in tiny claws among the silver leaves, worked with seed pearls and diamonds. The clasp at the back of the neck was studded with a two-carat diamond. It languished in the window display of Harvey and Gore for all of a week before it was purchased by the obscenely rich Earl Stanhope as an offering to his beleaguered wife after another of his indiscretions, and remained in the family for three generations.

In it went with the rest, as the alarm was sounded, and everything scattered. In the chaos the sack was dropped, and scrabbling in the dark for spilled jewels, so many men all around, piling great sacks of silver through the windows, tearing art from the walls, Blunt grabbed it on the sly from under a chair and ran out with it in his pocket, his arms full of the earl's fine pistol collection.

Now this, though he did not realise it at that moment, was Mr Blunt's finest hour. He could see it was something very pretty indeed but even he could not have known yet that Lady Stanhope's ruby was the most precious thing he would ever lay his eyes upon — outside the Tower of London, perhaps — never mind his fat, filthy hands. It was worth more than everything he had stolen that year together, with everything he had stolen the year before and the one before that. In the right market, at the right time. A jewel of such incomparable quality and size did not spring out of the ground every day, flashing so flagrantly red. He must keep it quiet a while, tread carefully, be patient. But what might a man do with such an asset! Start a new life, catch the right woman — she would look at him differently once he was rich. Let her refuse him then! He would escape the dead orchard, the broken roof, the damp and the howling wind. And leave his mother behind, under the holly tree, in the churchyard where she has been these twenty years last Tuesday.

It was later, on his own, gazing into its scarlet light, that Mr Blunt would see what he was holding, and the crudest man in all creation would melt a little, surrender to wonder and beauty, and his dreams begin to dawn upon it. And how could he have known he would be chasing them still as his hair turned grey? And that it was not he who held the treasure but, rather, the other way round?

★ ★ ★

The gang congregated in the woods some ten minutes later with the spoils. Blunt, along with all the rest, denied any knowledge of the ruby necklace that John and Jack Dean mentioned, and it was assumed first that they were exaggerating its splendour, and second, that it had been lost in the chase. A search of the undergrowth was dismissed on account of police activity in the area. Glimpsing torch beams criss-crossing in the distance, they made haste to their hideout.

It was a tense night that Mr Blunt spent, worrying that someone, on a sudden impulse, would demand to search the insides of his pockets. He felt it must show, that somehow he might emit a tiny involuntary signal that someone would sniff out through the folds of his overcoat. The sound of his name broke this private trance.

'Blunt, what do you say to these pearls?' He

turned his attention to them, adopting a studious attitude.

'They are fine indeed. Round and even, lustrous. The brooch is a quality trinket, much sought after.' He was surprised by how steady his voice sounded.

'And these diamonds?'

'Paste.'

'And which items invite the most interest?' Mr Blunt felt the ruby necklace almost burning through the lining of his coat.

'I reckon on the pearls, the emerald choker and this little diamond pin,' he held it up to the yellow glow of the gas, 'which, though small, is a rare blue, and quite flawless.' He rubbed his chin thoughtfully, affecting an air of detachment quite at odds with the fluttering wings in his stomach. Most of the company were wrestling with their own nerves still and yet to concern themselves with the market value of anything or its division thereof — too concerned with unidentified noises outside — so he need not have worried.

'There are, indeed, very many fine pieces in Lady Stanhope's collection. This set of table-cut sapphires, the opals — gems of unusual quality — and the citrines, though less precious, are large, well cut and perfectly clear. The settings are certainly French. Fine indeed. Uncommonly fine.'

It was agreed to take the haul to Ray Mathers's safe-house and to leave in half an hour. A tentative relief crawled up his back as Blunt watched the others twitching and peering through cracks in the wall, eardrums cocked into the black dark outside.

Barely a word was spoken as the hand crept round the clock, until Mathers Senior gave the word. They gathered themselves, like ugly children, in a crooked line. Hard-faced men of granite stared impassively at the wall; weasel eyes darted nervously about beneath Big Arthur Bolt's iron shoulders.

'Wait a minute,' someone said. 'There's summink missing.' A profound silence fell upon the company; owls called in the wood outside; a delirious moth slapped into the lamp. 'I can smell it.'

Blunt thought on reflection, much later, that it had been Snook, long and thin and bitter, who had uttered this vile suspicion, pointed like a bony finger at hapless Harold Whitbread — most likely to deflect attention from himself. Whitbread, indeed, *seemed* shifty: he blanched even in the dim lamplight.

'So can I,' said Charlie Fry.

Well, he's got something in his pocket for sure, thought Blunt. Piping up like that, all keen. Two or three of the crew weren't looking too smug suddenly either. In his guilty fog Blunt had quite forgotten the dishonourable thieves among the company and he wanted to laugh now that he remembered them. Even so, his heart seemed to bang against his ribs and he felt sure his colour had risen. He prayed silently and put his faith in the Lord God, whose mercy he really had no claim to, and the secret pocket deep in the lining of his greatcoat.

'Show us what you got, you sly bastard!' Poor crooked Whitbread, trembling, shook out his pockets, looking like a man with a rope already round his neck. Most of the crew were glad the suspicion had converged on someone else's head and stared intently at him, their eyes glinting with cruelty. He never did have the stomach for serious crime, thought Blunt. How quickly, in accordance with the laws of nature, does the pack turn on its weakest member! The circle tightened round Whitbread's shaking hands, eyes converging in a single beam, scorching his fluttering light-fingers. When his pockets were empty they turned to his boots, whence, after a short and futile struggle, a twinkling sapphire ring was brought forth. Just a small stone, really, set in gold, flanked by two little square-cut diamonds, and seen through Whitbread's eyes at that moment, most definitely not worth it. A moment passed before he started to whimper, horribly, for mercy — a thin, ghastly sound, it seemed to creep across the floor and clutch, wheedling, at their ankles, making them want to throw it off in revulsion and stamp upon it till it ceased. Had he known that his pleading would inspire not sympathy but murder he might have contented himself with a Hail Mary or two and repented his sins in time to enter Heaven, as he had always planned in such an eventuality. Someone struck him round the head, hard, with a heavy cudgel, making him squeal in panic and confusion like a stuck pig. And the Mathers mob piled in like hungry dogs, blunt weapons cracking at his head, a frenzy of sweat and muscle and raining blood.

They left him with his face covered, such as was left of it, a sticky pool under their boots, darkening red across the floor as they vanished into the night. Blunt thanked the devil for his luck and poor Whitbread for his diversion. The ruby necklace snoozed comfortably in the folds of his coat. He kept hold of himself, even after the company had parted, until he had locked his own front door behind him. Trembling, he leaned his back against it and allowed himself a quiet sigh of relief. He stood in the hall, listening, cast his eyes down the dark passage to see if the girl was there, suddenly, with tea. The house was still.

In his dusty library, with the heavy curtains drawn and every chink that might admit a view robustly secured, Blunt reached into his pocket, shaking a little. His clammy fingers found cold stone and he pulled it out, sparkling, into the candlelight, forgetting himself, blood red rays warming his face.

After more time than he could account for, when he thought of it afterwards — spent in rapturous delirium that he could not altogether recall or explain — Mr Blunt laid the necklace tenderly to bed in a secret nook, high behind the sleeping books, glancing over his shoulder all the while, heart in his throat. And there it hid, just an arm's reach through the hole behind *Bleak House* — the last book his dear mother had bought before she died — for all of nine days, until it was stolen, which served him right.

It is poetic to imagine that Grace might have left it well alone, had she known what she was stealing — a deadly thing, a burden and a curse. But, of course, it would have made no difference. She is a thief, after all: she will steal the priest's watch on her deathbed; that's how she was born.

★　★　★

You know it's not done with, says the tiny voice at the back of her head, the one that speaks at unsure moments, most often in the dark. You might walk the plank yet!

He falls out of the sky into her busy day, of pans and plates and laundry, maybe once a year now — a chill that runs down her neck, unprovoked — today, as it happens, while she is shaking out the bed. And still it makes her stop and look behind her, as if he might be there. She feels foolish and laughs at herself, but a cold hand grips her belly and the ground falls away at her feet. Then she marvels, as she does every time, at how she could forget such a thing, before she forgets it again — buried treasure, sparkling to itself in the dark — as if it had been a dream. Sometimes she imagines it rusting.

4

Though it had all gone off nicely after the inauspicious start, Jack found himself tortured with shame when he remembered being caught lurking outside the Hammer home — a moment he had relived every twenty minutes or so throughout the last few days, causing him to wince visibly. Several of his companions asked him if he was feeling quite all right, to which he replied that someone had just walked over his grave.

He spent a great deal of time wondering what on earth had possessed him to follow Grace home, and came up with no good answer, which made him all the more uncomfortable. Jack is a creature of habit, though he may vary the order in which he visits the pubs and the women he consorts with. It would not do well with him to be trailing after any one in particular and he vowed not to do it again, leaving the next time they meet to chance, though he hoped it would be soon. Thus resolved, he ordered another jar of Truman's.

* * *

Grace kept expecting Jack to pop up outside the window, which made her uneasy. How dare he trail around after her? She was furious that he knew where she lived. Grace is a secretive soul; she is happy to hide under a rock and come out when she pleases. She has a great many secrets and an instinctive dislike of anyone too forward. Miraculously Jack has not fallen within that bracket, in spite of his clumsy manners. Daisy likes him very much. She asks when they might see him next and Grace tells her there are no plans to do so.

★   ★   ★

Tuesday afternoon the Hammer family were at large in Whitechapel, enjoying the warmth of the day. They were searching, as usual, for the next dip, but to anyone in the busy thoroughfare who cared to look they were just picking along the gutter. East London in July is barely clearer than it is in any other month, and smells a good deal worse, but at least there is light and heat. Today the sun threatened to break through the veil; there was no breeze to relieve the stink and the air hung still and thick around them. The haze had defeated the weaker members of the street race and they lay in pools of beer and other stagnant fluids among the rubbish, feet stepping round them.

The family turned into the Whitechapel Road, merging into the bustle of traders and carousers, shoving and lurching, pausing to look at a monkey in a miniature ballgown performing a vigorous dance to the strains of 'The Boy I Love Is Up In The Gallery'. The boys bobbed off into the crowd at intervals, popping up here and there. Daisy kept a grip on her mother's hand. Where the throng became too thick for her little legs Grace hoisted her up and carried her on her hip.

'Can *we* have a monkey, Ma?'

'No.'

They walked on past the Horn of Plenty, where they spotted Sally Ann Dunn in her usual spot, rocking and vomiting into the gutter. She lurched up and looked around with a wild, glazed grin, toppling towards the gentleman with whom she was consorting that afternoon. She had split her lip the day before, from the look of it. Grace wondered whether she'd been thumped or fallen flat on her face on the cobbles.

Her attention was caught by an angry commotion, rising even above the clamour of the street: urgent shouting six or seven heads away, a shrill police whistle, a struggle. Someone had her Billy by the scruff of the neck and was shouting into the face of a burly copper. She grabbed Jake by the collar as he was diving in to help his brother.

'This little bastard had my wallet!'

'Put the boy down at once, sir, and calm yourself. Turn your pockets out, lad.'

Both complied with these fierce orders. Billy turned out a piece of wire, a stone, an apple and a shilling from his pockets. His ear burned.

'I saw him take it, I tell you! I saw him!'

'Well, where could it be now, sir?'

'How am I to know that? He will have passed it to an accomplice in the crowd.'

The man was agitated and undoubtedly German. His red face seemed to swell as he waved his cane, tracing wild circles before him as if to keep the riff-raff at bay, stabbing the air for emphasis. He wore a fine wool overcoat, best kid gloves, a nice pearl pin in his cravat, gold watch-chain and studs, and a powder-blue silk handkerchief just so in his breast pocket. Most definitely a tourist, stuck out like a sore thumb, come to see the dubious sights of London's fabled poor and rotting East End. So he got what he came for really, thought Grace. Her eyes flickered distractedly over the sea of faces.

Jack was in the crowd, having heard the to-do. There he is again! she thought. Can't shake him off nowadays! What a picture he was too, even better than she remembered; she caught herself gawping and stopped at once, a little irritated. He looked ready to jump in for Billy, watching with his handsome frown, wondering what to do, and she wanted to shout to him not to worry. There were no flies on Billy — he hadn't turned a hair. He was tip-top, better even than Charlie, who would have the wallet away by now: they were home and dry, you could smell the roses already.

★ ★ ★

Jack ran his eyes over the crowd and caught her watching him, a little crooked smile on her face. She gave him a right saucy wink and he wondered — while his nether regions stirred, without reference to the rest of him — why she made no move to help her son. He returned the secret signal, but without the reserve he would have liked, grinning idiotically, rather than enigmatically, as he had intended. People peered in from every side like beady-eyed museum visitors, chattering excitedly about the exhibits. A crow in a dusty black hat shoved her elbow into his ribs, digging in to get a better look, craning her scraggy neck, lined with dirt. The grimy ribbon on the back of her hat caught him in the eye as she climbed on her neighbour's foot. The crowd pushed and swelled, starting to boil; the policeman tried to calm the general mood, without success. He turned back to the German, grim-faced.

'Are you quite sure this lad had your wallet, sir?'

'How dare you question my integrity, Constable? I saw it in his filthy hand.'

The policeman, a kindly chap by the name of Frank Wallace, knew this scrap most likely had robbed the loud red man — in fact, he would have laid money on it — but he didn't take kindly to his loud red manner, laying down the law — as if it was he who was wearing the uniform. He would set him straight and no mistake. An intense dislike for the pompous balloon was unfolding in his chest, fuelled further by the irrelevant but nonetheless influential fact that it had been a German man his mother had run away with on the morning of his seventh birthday. Ice formed round his good heart.

'So you say. Only he doesn't seem to have it now, sir.'

The German took a deep lungful and drew up to his full height in readiness for a fresh torrent of rage.

PC Wallace chipped in, as officiously as he could manage, his generous moustache seeming to puff itself up like his chest. 'Would you be so good as to check your pockets, sir? If it's not too much trouble.'

The German spluttered but pulled forth from his pocket, dumbfounded, his wallet, with all his money present and correct. He gasped, open-mouthed, as if a bucket of cold water had been thrown in his face. The onlookers roared. His shame was not spared by PC Wallace, who insisted he apologise to the boy, with the support of the howling crowd, some of whom were delighted to see the underdog triumph for a change, and others who simply disliked large bombastic foreigners. Then our good constable dealt the final blow.

'I'm afraid you'll have to come along to the station, sir. This seems to me to be a clear case of public affray and disturbance. This way please.' And off they went to Leman Street, the German raging. A crowd of filthy children and drunks followed them, shouting and jeering down the street.

Billy slipped back in next to Grace. They exchanged a look — what it said Jack couldn't fathom. Grace looked as though she would burst into song.

'Come on,' she said. 'Let's go home.'

She looked for Charlie, who appeared at her elbow.

'Look!' said Daisy. 'There's Jack!'

At home Grace dumped the princess on the doorstep with a chunk of peanut brittle, and went inside with Charlie and Billy, whom she pulled in by the collar. She had been friendly enough on the way but did not invite Jack indoors or, indeed, so much as look at him as she shut the door. He kicked about with Jake for a minute or two, wondering whether to go or what. Daisy stared at him, sticky, and offered him a piece of brittle.

Indoors Grace reached into the secret pockets deep inside her skirts and drew out seven wallets, a gold watch and a handsome silver bracelet, which she threw upon the table. 'That was a bloody close call,' she said to Billy. 'What happened?'

'I was clumsy.'

'That's not like you.'

'He was looking at some girl,' said Charlie.

'Huh! Were you frightened?'

'No!'

'Good lad. You're a triumph incarnate.'

'Cheers, Ma.'

'Go on, then.'

As Billy came out to play in the street Jack caught a glimpse inside of Charlie and Grace hunched together. The boys lined up before the door with Daisy as it shut, peering at

Jack, like a row of sparrows on a chimney-stack.

The takings spilled on the table; coins and wads of notes were sorted in a flash. Grace counted swiftly, lips moving. 'A bounteous haul today. Enough for a little extra!'

5

'So, what will we wear for the Bank Holiday?' enquired Daisy, voicing her most urgent concern.

'What do you want to wear, darlin'?'

'A beautiful dress.'

Daisy Hammer, the only living daughter of a comfortable criminal, had the advantage of brand-new clothes, while her poor friend Emily, whose parents did honest work, had to suffer the hand-me-downs of her five sisters.

'Any particular colour?'

'Lilac. With ribbons and bows.'

'Well, you know what you want, don't you?'

So out they went to the West End (all except Charlie, who wanted to be on his own, though he said he was not in a bad mood). Grace always kept something by to splash in the shops, for fancy things they didn't need. What else was the object of devoting the family to a life of crime?

They took the Green bus west, the boys heading straight for the top deck, right at the front, Daisy tripping up the stairs in her haste to keep up. She positioned herself in the middle where she wouldn't miss anything, her eagle eyes scanning the vista. As they left Spitalfields behind she beamed at Grace, glowing, brimming with it. Faint sunshine ahead that seemed to come from the promised land of the West End lit her hair like butter melting. Grace promised herself to take outings more often, wrapped up in the joy of simple things that were there every day on the doorstep.

They passed the City and the Bank, and soon after the great dome of St Paul's loomed before them, dwarfing all around it like a great grey mountain, stunning even Daisy into momentary silence. She kept her eyes upon it as they passed, as if it might fall, but recovered quickly, and resumed her barrage of questions — 'Who lives in there?' 'Why does that man have his hair like that?' 'Will we see the Queen?' — directed mostly at Billy, who seemed to know about everything. They made their way slowly, wedged in traffic, down Fleet Street towards the West End, gazing at the scene around.

★ ★ ★

The majestic façades of Regent Street are an enchanting sight when you have money in your pocket to spend. Their eyes were like dinner plates as the omnibus turned up towards Oxford Circus. Even Jake stopped fidgeting to look at the broad sweep of the street. Elegant store fronts lined the curve of the thoroughfare, clean, cream, shining in the sun, running perfectly parallel on either side of the broad road, wide like the Amazon river, which Billy had come upon in the encyclopedia while looking up 'armadillo'. The sky was deeper here, the air sweeter, the clouds white! Billy wondered if it was like this every day in the West End, if they in East London were just idiots under a shadow. As they stopped in traffic his wandering eyes alighted on a wiry little man through an upstairs window, hunched at his desk beneath a tower of papers. A napkin was tucked into his collar and he was carving a piece of ham upon the desk before him. As Billy watched he sliced hard into his thumb, dropped the knife, yelped, silently, through the glass and shoved the bloody digit into his mouth. He shook his fist at the boys as they rolled away.

'What are you laughing at?' said Grace, leaning round from the front.

They alighted by Howell James & Company as if in a foreign land, mute and gazing round like marmosets, even Billy who had been once before at Christmas. They held hands so as not to lose each other. Diamonds glittered at them from a window.

53

'Look at that!' said Billy. Jake slipped between the passers-by and pressed his face to the glass; Grace held Daisy up so she could see. They gaped aghast through the glass at sparkling rocks, brilliant cut, elegant tendrils of pale gold, intertwined at the throat, dripping yellow diamonds like shining syrup. The necklace was laid on black velvet and beside were the earrings, two carats each. The family's eyes were as wide as they could go, as if it might help them see more. If they had observed themselves at that moment they would have laughed a great deal. In the next window was a tiara.

'Look, Ma, a crown! Look!'

'Yes, darlin', isn't it lovely?'

'Is it for a princess?'

'I expect so.'

'How can you be a princess?'

'You have to marry a prince.'

They admired a flamboyant brooch of flowers made from seed pearls; a citrine the size of a macaroon, a necklace and earrings set with table-cut emeralds of evil green, jet beads, opals, topaz like knuckles, clasped in golden claws. Grace led them away, up towards Oxford Circus. Their first port of call was Hamley's toy shop.

Though they had worn their best clothes that day, feeling overdressed as they waited for the bus on Whitechapel Road, Grace felt a little tawdry among the fine ladies and gentlemen of the West End, milling about at leisure. The boys had never seen so much unbroken glass. Grace kept her eye on them, though they were sworn to their very best behaviour, secured by the promise of two shillings each to spend.

'Can we buy something for Charlie?' asked Billy.

'Yes, can we?' echoed Daisy, wishing she had thought of it first. 'Because he missed the trip?'

'Yes, darlin', course we can. Shall we let Billy choose? He knows what boys like.'

They left the boys looking at fishing rods, on a strict promise to meet them in an hour, and went to see about dresses.

* * *

How wonderful it is to have a little girl, to hold her hand in yours and chatter as you wander down the street. Grace thought of her own mother, remembered walking this way. She took Daisy to Marshall & Snelgrove, grandest store on Oxford Street, taking up a whole block to itself: swish enough for a princess.

Daisy tried several dresses on. She twirled

before the mirror, charming the shop-girl, who had seemed doubtful when they had come in. Grace disarmed her with polite chatter, affecting a better accent and employing the natural air she could conjure of having some kind of status, whatever it might be, so that the girl had put her dark skirts down to Bohemian eccentricity. She was from the country herself, having been in the Smoke just two weeks, and fancied herself already a cosmopolitan lady. Her name was Tabitha Berry and one day she hoped to marry a rich man, to be a Tabitha Rothschild or a Tabitha Vanderbilt, and move in society circles. She did not yet know that, though sweet-faced enough, she had none of the requisite ruthlessness and would be back in the sticks within the year, happily hitched to a potato farmer.

Blue suited Daisy better even than lilac, though she would have looked delectable in a coal sack, to her doting mother anyhow. She chose her favourite dress the moment she put it on and did not trouble herself with a second thought about it. She wanted to wear it home but was persuaded, with the enticement of pink tissue paper, to take it wrapped. They chose a pretty little raffia hat for hand-me-down Emily, with a pair of tiny apples on the brim; and bought satin ribbon, green for Grace's eyes and blue for Daisy's.

After Grace had managed to tear Tabitha Berry and Daisy apart they joined the boys, who, to Grace's amazement, were waiting in the tea-room as instructed, quiet as church mice. They were even standing up straight. The manager was eyeing them suspiciously, looking for a reason to turf them out.

'What have you done?' she said warily.

'Nothing!'

They had bought a cricket bat for Charlie and a football for themselves, and had managed not to lose each other or venture towards shady St Giles. They did not show her the pocket-knife they had lifted in Gentlemen's Sundries. Daisy brimmed with news about her dress, to which they listened sweetly, although they had no interest in clothing. All refreshed themselves with lemonade and iced buns.

★ ★ ★

Marshall & Snelgrove was a flurry of delight, a carousel of finery and ladies shopping, buying things they had already, in the latest style, such as dinner plates or luggage or gloves. Seated at every counter in the perfume hall, where a thousand delicious scents blend into a soft cloud that wafts across the ceiling, they primped and picked and enjoyed the eager attention of the staff. This season their hats were adorned with dyed ostrich feathers, which fluttered in the perfumed air, red or blue or violet; pheasant for the country.

The family meandered through this palace of wonders, trying not to touch anything, past the crystal, the silverware, the cut glass. Grace steered them towards the door, holding her breath as they traversed the fine-china department. Rows of polished cutlery blinked ostentatiously as they went by; a giant candelabra posed in all its pompous glory, as if it were the only thing in the shop.

They never noticed the pallid stranger who fixed his eyes upon them from behind the ostrich-leather-bound address book he was pretending to study. As they went past he put it down and moved after them towards the door.

The boys were outside already when Daisy noticed the display by the entrance and stopped. It had a rural theme: branches fanned out on either side, hung with shiny artificial fruit. At its centre was a mannequin, dressed for the next season in sumptuous velvet, standing on a cushion of moss. She wore a short tweed Jacket, draped with silver fox, and a full skirt of deep berry red that matched her hat, frozen jauntily atop her upswept curls. In her gloved hands she held a fur bag and a lace handkerchief. Daisy appraised this ensemble, aping the pose, admiring the skirt, the blue glass eyes, the pink painted lips.

The stranger sidled closer, lurking behind the display. He could hear them talking. They were looking at a stuffed robin perched above the mannequin's hat, and as he crept round the plinth he glimpsed them through the branches. They never noticed him, staring, like a man who had seen a ghost. As they went out through the grand doors into Oxford Street he hurried after them.

* * *

Mr Ivor Squall is a spindly little man. He resembles an insect, with his hunched back and dark suit, cut tight and mean as befits his demeanour. In fact, his wealth is his only personal asset. His business is ostensibly bookkeeping, run from offices in Oxford Street — it launders the proceeds of his quiet export trade. He finds his offices most conveniently located for his frequent business in notorious St Giles — hive of lawless activity, just a stone's throw away — coming and going, scuttling about unnoticed. His various associates are well aware that Mr Squall has always something hidden, shifty as the woodlice in the skirting, and keep their wits about them. When he laid eyes on Grace he forgot altogether the purpose of his shopping trip, not because she caught his fancy — for Ivor Squall has none — but because a bell rang in the back of his head, from long ago.

He remembered her face as if in a dream. Compelled by this notion — under a spell — he abandoned the umbrella he had set out to purchase, and followed. There was no doubt that he knew her from somewhere. He knew he must remember where.

★ ★ ★

This was the first day all year that Grace Hammer had dropped her guard. She was not in her own manor, and in the rare delight of taking a whole day for entertainments she had abandoned her usual watchfulness. The sky was blue, the boys were behaving themselves: there was no reason to look over her shoulder.

Ivor Squall shadowed them at a discreet distance until they took the bus and, hiding at the back of the line, he slipped on unsuspected. He had been involved in many underhand things but had never actually followed anyone before, and he began to enjoy it thoroughly; as thoroughly, that is, as he could in his own miserly way — a sly tingle of excitement pinched his scrawny belly, the cloak-and-dagger thrill of his mission, though he was still unsure of its end. He stole furtive glances at the family, the little girl smiling to herself, proud of the parcel on her lap, the boys hanging out over Regent Street, pointing at things and kicking each other. The bus crawled towards Charing Cross; all the while he wrestled the clues in his head, long-ago pictures, things he thought he had seen.

He might well struggle to place her. The first and last time they had met was seventeen years to the day before. The answer buzzed around him like a fly. He realised he was staring; the little girl had noticed him and tugged at her mother's sleeve. Luckily for him, she was busy reprimanding the boys for spitting on somebody's hat. Mr Squall bent down in his seat, pretending to tie his shoelace, which took him a full minute. When he lifted his eyes above the handrail of the seat in front, the family were engaged with some new distraction, laughing among themselves. He watched more carefully this time, making a show of looking out at the view as they crossed Trafalgar Square. As the bus passed Nelson the children craned their necks to look at him, stood all alone on his great big column. The woman was smiling contentedly, taking in the scenery. A ray of sunshine crept through the clouds and she shut her eyes and tilted back her head — and then he saw it, like a flash. He almost shouted aloud with the relief of remembering.

★ ★ ★

Grace did not notice their shadow until Cheapside. She wondered where he had got on and decided to ignore him, for what else was there to do? They would get off by St Mary, beyond their stop, and walk back.

Now, perhaps Grace was unusually carefree that day — it might be, as he sat behind them, she had not enough time to get a good look. Whatever, we are witness to something rare, like a perfect eclipse of the sun: Grace Hammer misses a trick. She does not recall Ivor Squall. Not a penny drops, not a bell rings.

The City rumbled past, then Aldgate. A boy was standing on his hands outside the window when the bus stopped, a group round him watching as he walked about upside-down. A couple dropped coins into the hat between his feet. They passed St Botolph, then the rag market, and rolled past their stop.

By Church Lane he and they were the only passengers left from the West End. As Grace made ready to get off she turned to look at him again — just a little too long, with a quizzical air so fleeting he might have imagined it. He felt his face colour and his heart quail as he shrank into his seat. Then she was gone. He dared not get off after them but stole a glimpse over his slippery shoulder as the bus moved away again, to catch them rounding the corner into Osborn Street. Alighting at the next stop Ivor Squall tore back down the street as fast as his matchstick legs would allow but, of course, by the time he reached the turning they were nowhere to be seen. He recovered his weak breath and made his way home, trembling with impatience. Had he stayed on the corner for another minute he would have spied them coming out of the grocer's, with a bag of oranges.

★ ★ ★

Ivor Squall recorded every detail of his encounter, with his bookkeeper's pedantic efficiency, the very moment that he reached his office in order that he might not forget the smallest thing. He found he derived considerable pleasure from compiling this furtive intelligence and positively glowed with self-satisfaction at the prospect of passing it on to its intended recipient. Though he had nothing much to note he made a great deal of it on new paper, toying with the idea of small sketches before contenting himself with exhaustive descriptions of each member of the family in perfect lines of spider-crawl across the page, scratching away in his favourite uncomfortable seat at his plain desk that had spindly legs to match his own. He stopped only to dip his pen in the ink, as urgently as he could without splashing, holding his breath — as well as he was able with his meagre lungs, being sickly from birth — feverish as the drop trembled at the end of his nib. Ivor Squall had never yet splashed ink on his desk. Every day this became more significant and he was not ready to blot it, however whipped up he might feel. He finished carefully, as if he was writing important legal documents, and set down his pen with a weak sigh, before allowing himself to revel — as much as he might in his tight suit — in his own efficiency and his symmetrical desktop.

Then he rubbed his hands with glee and

wrote a short message addressed to Mr Horatio Blunt, with which he caught the last post.

Dear Esteemed Friend,

I trust this letter finds you in sufficient health after these long years. I send intriguing news — brooking not a moment's delay — which I venture may be of interest. This very afternoon I have uncovered information, by fortunate chance — and artful investigation — pertaining to the whereabouts of your former employee: a Miss Hammer, if I recall correctly. I hope these efforts will serve to be of satisfaction.

Yours most faithfully, Ivor Squall Esq.

On the other side of London the Hammer family reconvened and shared gifts.

'You picked the right day to go up west,' said Charlie. 'That man from the board school's been about.'

'Look at these beautiful chocolates,' said Daisy.

The subject of Jake's education had come up in conversation not two days before between Grace and her busybody neighbour

Mrs Jacob, who had raised six children — as she never tired of recounting — all of whom now lived as far away from her as was possible without leaving the country.

'Do you not think that Jake might be better at school now?' she had ventured nosily.

Grace wondered at how no one ever noticed that Billy was not at school either, most likely on account of his beautiful manners. 'Well, they do seem very crowded, Mrs Jacob. And a hotbed for typhoid.'

'A proper schooling teaches a youngster some discipline, Miss Hammer. Prepares him for a trade, perhaps. A good, decent future.'

Grace had felt her blood begin to simmer. She put a swift, graceful end to the conversation.

'Well, the last time he went he reckoned they were still learning the alphabet, Mrs Jacob. Once they've got past that I'm sure he may consider going again. And as for a trade, well, I'm sure he's spoilt for choice. I expect you'd have him up some toff's chimney, or sewing shirts, perhaps. Jake's quite happy to be out and about with me. He's a good little helper. Good day to you.'

6

Grace Hammer was an ugly baby. She was born in Pagham, near Bognor, by the Sussex seaside, on the morning of 18 July 1853, with the sun shining on rippling waves of barley. She had a comical air, as most brand-new people do, with dark spiked hair and serious navy blue eyes that seemed to focus from the moment they opened. These changed to blonde and green respectively within six weeks to devastating effect.

Within a few short years she was asserting her natural authority over the rest of her family, at least her doting parents and four older brothers, if not her sister, who was almost six and her closest playmate as well as her worst enemy. Grace remembered playing dens under the bed, but also the time she had been tricked into eating soap, which had made her sister laugh a great deal before Ma had come in and slapped her. Baby Grace grew razor-sharp wits very quickly, ready to strike the first time she clapped her eyes upon a book. It was an illustrated edition of *Tales from the Brothers Grimm*, which had sat undisturbed for a decade or more next to

Moll Flanders upon a dusty shelf at the very top of her grandmother's house. These lonely tomes had belonged to Great-grandfather Hammer, who had entertained scholarly aspirations, and, though treasured in his memory, had been forgotten due to their subsequent uselessness within the Hammer family — a practical bunch, more inclined towards husbandry and agricultural pursuits, which was certainly a good thing, for the farm ran like clockwork. If there was spare time they used it to sit about and drink cider.

Little Grace had climbed the stairs one day, finding no one to hand for games — the family having rushed out to the barn to watch the cow labour — and, standing on a chair, she reached the shelf and pulled out the first book, having not the slightest notion of such a thing. It fell open at the illustration of Rumpelstiltskin before the Queen, twisted and raging, his foot stuck through the floor! She could not imagine what had made him so angry. He had long, spindling legs and a chicken feather in his hat. She leafed through the pages and looked at the pictures and something started turning in her head.

Grace could read and write by her seventh birthday, having worked it out mostly for herself with the benefit of spells at the village school, thus surpassing her parents' academic achievements. By the time she turned eight she could cook for the family — roast pork and potatoes, mutton stew, apple cake — stood on a box, while her ma went to help with the lambing. She sheared sheep at nine, split logs at ten and ploughed the field at eleven. When she was twelve her proud father was entrusting her to manage certain affairs of the farm, among them the bookkeeping, which he found intolerable. At thirteen she ran an independent sideline selling vicious apple brandy she distilled in the barn. This paid for the books she ate. She enjoyed the works of Dumas: *The Three Musketeers* being the book she had read most frequently (though not in the French), Jonathan Swift and Edgar Allan Poe, but her favourite author was Charles Dickens. She thought him quite the sharpest man that ever scratched a page, having happened upon *David Copperfield* while perusing the shelves of the bookshop in town, affecting, with some success, an air of knowing what she was looking for while having no idea.

She had pulled it out from the row of spines and, reading a page or two, had quite lost herself, sunk into the world therein, until the shopkeeper had broken the spell at chapter three, with a touch on her shoulder, to enquire if there was anything in particular with which he could assist her. She came to with a little start, before she remembered where she was and paid for the book with urgency and much charming fluster, thus procuring a small discount.

Outside the shop she sat down upon the pavement and swallowed chapters four to eleven, neglecting her thirsty horse until it became too dark to read. She rode thereafter into Chichester every fourth Tuesday for fresh books, and her family thought her quite mad, though this did not diminish their enjoyment of her fireside readings — furnished as they were with different voices for each character (their favourite being the odious Uriah Heep, for whom Grace contorted her elastic face into an alarming mask, twisting her handsome features beyond recognition and frightening the dog) and piles of hot toast — which they ate in perfect silence, ears cocked, eyes wide, pausing mid-chew as Mr Bill Sykes battered Nancy to her dreadful death or poor Mr Guppy shone his lamp on Krook's grim remains.

Though she loved her happy family, by her fifteenth birthday Grace had tired of her surroundings and decided to leave them behind, if not permanently then at least without imminent plans to return. Upon the announcement of these plans her father, sick with the fear of unknown threats ahead, promptly and utterly forbade any such idea. So she stole from the house that very night, down a rope from the window, avoiding the creaks that lurked in the staircase and the attendant paternal ears, pricked in sleep. She dropped the last yard to the ground outside, next to the bag ready packed in the flowerbed, picked one last crimson camellia and was gone.

Now, young Grace had a soft spot for unlikely men, which was the very first worry on her poor pa's long list. This fancy had begun with the extra farmhands who came every summer. They were gypsy lads, fit and dark, up to no good. They looked wild and their arms and chests rippled in the sun; they had brown skin and strong hands and mischief crackling around them like a dirty halo. (Years later Grace Hammer would wonder why she found trouble so attractive and still have no answer.) She gazed up at them on top of the haystack and they grinned back down at her, bold like a red rag.

It was one of those lads she stole away with that night, taking him for company till Chichester, where reluctantly but with no significant guilt she gave him the slip, reasoning that he had been most pleasing at the top of the haystack, mystery intact, and that he made dull conversation and had bad breath to boot. A fresh breeze broke over her as she left with his wages, a scent of blossoming freedom.

★ ★ ★

Grace Hammer has been in proper employment only twice in her long life — the first a three-week stretch that November 1872, after hearing her ma was lost to scarlet fever. For a week she roamed desolate through Wiltshire before taking a position as housemaid in the grand house of Lord and Lady Davenport of Tisbury, being desperate and unwilling to return empty-handed to her family home, with no mother inside it.

She found little time for sad reflection as her job was cold and thankless and entirely at odds with her proud demeanour, most especially as the mistress was an imperious bitch who never uttered a please or a thank-you. She stalked round the house finding causes for complaint — a patch of dust that had been missed along the top of a door, an invisible tarnish on the silver — barking at creases in the table linen. She snapped orders at her staff in the morning without greeting them first and never addressed them by name, though two of them had been in her service for thirteen years, come Christmas — which would bring them nothing but an orange each and stiff new aprons, as had the twelve before. If that is a real live lady! thought Grace — how glad I am not to be one and determined not to try! They were woken at six every morning of the year, save Mothering Sunday (as if everyone had mothers to call on), to empty chamber-pots as dawn broke, followed by scrubbing and washing and polishing and running upstairs and down until they fell into hard beds at ten o'clock.

This employment ended abruptly after the mistress accused Grace of stealing pennies that she herself had set under the drawing-room rugs to test the honesty of the servants on the one hand and their attention to the sweeping on the other, leaving them guilty either way. When Grace remarked that if Mistress did not want to lose her money perhaps she would do better not to leave it lying about, she flew into a rage and dismissed her at once. Grace had not, in fact, stolen anything and took satisfaction in doubling back two miles down the road, cross-country, and hiding in the orchard till dusk when she scaled the wisteria and left with the mistress's favourite diamonds. Indeed, they were the finest stones in the jewellery case: a pair of drop earrings, two carats each. A little bird caught her eye in the next velvet compartment — a sweet thing, flashing tiny jewelled wings, a ruby berry in its slender beak; it sparkles at her but she isn't greedy.

★ ★ ★

Now, let us cast some light inside Miss Hammer's head, where a hundred forgotten trinkets languish in the dark — for it is true to say she is a magpie, and likes a shiny thing. It is her nature and her joy to steal a precious sparkling stone. She doesn't care to wear them, but holds them to the lamplight and turns them in her hand, bewitched; then she hides them in the dark, in secret places, strung across England like lost stars. Though she means to take them with her mostly she forgets. They call her, miles down the road, kicking stones, laughing at the sky; she never goes back. There are more ahead. She has stolen so many jewels that today she might be living in Belgravia, but she would not suit the company, or care to dress for dinner every evening. Grace would find herself downstairs, drinking with the servants and peeling the potatoes. And now she has a family she restricts herself to wallets and pocket watches, which are bread and butter — a different matter altogether — and she is pleased her sons seem not to have inherited her blind compulsion but go about thieving as a practical business — except perhaps Jake, who has buried treasure in his eyes sometimes. She keeps a tight rein on her magpie nature for she wants for nothing more than she can enjoy today, and should she surrender to it she would head for the Tower straight to steal the Crown. Just the Crown, mind, nothing else. Grace prefers to take the best thing in the box.

*   *   *

When the theft was discovered, riders were dispatched into the countryside to find the thieving hussy, who was sleeping in a hedgerow, just two miles away — having the cheek of the devil and the good sense to have left nothing behind to scent the dogs.

Lady Davenport never did recover her earrings, despite the efforts of the local men, who tired after a day or two of her demanding manner and decided that the relatively poor reward of thirty pounds could remain unclaimed. She wore out the sympathy of her visitors with her ranting — they departed with sore ears, wishing the unscrupulous, insolent girl luck, leaving Mistress Outrage to squawk at the staff instead. When she called at their houses the next day to acquaint them with the indignant details she had forgotten to mention she found no one at home.

She returned late to find the house quiet. Her best Meissen vase was gone from the mantel. The silver was missing. Someone had turned out her dressing table on the bed and made off with the rest of her jewellery. We may only imagine how our good lady's mind boggled at this heinous discovery — indeed she took several minutes to recover her breath: she gaped like a drowning fish and rubbed her eyes to make sure she was not seeing things. And where were the servants? She would see them hang for this. She discovered them locked in the cellar, drinking the armagnac to restore their shattered nerves. They could not describe the culprits, save to say they were fearsome men, gruff, four or more of them, neckerchiefs tied round their faces like olden-day highwaymen.

* * *

Three days after she had left the Davenport manor Grace arrived by means of her weary feet and fateful chance at Hatetree Farm, by Netley Marsh — a sprawling ramshackle pile at the edge of Hampshire and home to a Mr Horatio Blunt. The sky was low and thick with cloud, darkness was falling. She was spent indeed, having travelled away from the road and slept fitfully the night before, dreaming of dogs on her trail. Her steps slowed as she drew near, halting a few cautious feet from the crippled fence.

Beyond it a derelict yard, studded with bricks and bottles and broken wheels, stretched before a stone farmhouse, crouching in the gloom. Though young Grace was not much given to notions of the kind, the house seemed to watch her with one cold yellow eye, staring through the twilight, eerie silence blanketing the ground. But for her lonely breath, time itself stood still. A tortured apple tree stuck its claws up to the dead sky. The very air above this wretched homestead seemed to stall, thick and listless; she might have supposed the house abandoned but for the lighted window. Not a welcoming glow but a harbinger, burning greenish, casting slippery light. It was as clear as a sign on the gatepost that somebody lived there alone. Ghoulish creatures from the *Tales of Grimm* ran through her head. She stood by the fence as the rain started to fall, weighing the prospect of warmth and rest against her reluctance to knock at the door.

The gate creaked on its rusty hinge. She took a brave step up the tired path, brambles catching at her coat. She was not to know what the knock on the door would bring and neither was the occupant, sitting by the fire in his favourite chair. If he had he would certainly not have answered it.

The door was opened halfway after a short wait, revealing to each their first view of the other. The man seemed to fill the little porch, his coarse face leering, pork fingers in sweaty bunches. He looked to Grace as if she had disturbed him counting money.

'Good evening, sir,' she said, with all the breeze she could muster, as if she had set down at Claridges.

He took her in from head to toe before he spoke. 'Yes. What do you want?'

'I have come from the coast and I am sorely tired. I beg a bed and a rest in return for useful work, housekeeping perhaps, or whatever else you might need.'

This last part had caught Mr Blunt's imagination and stirred him somewhat — though he knew that the particular 'whatever else' that sprang immediately to mind was not what she had meant by it — so he widened the gap to let her in. She looked promising indeed: fair, despite the grime upon her skin. Without the slightest nod to civil manners he held the candle closer to inspect her, unabashed, his rude eyes raking her as if she were a fruit stall. Grace would not have been surprised if he had looked behind her ears for mould, or squeezed some piece of flesh to see if she was ripe. His hands looked clammy and the corners of his mouth were wet. His stare was greedy and repulsive, poking at her, pulling at her clothes; she clasped her shawl across her chest. Had she not been tired and cold she might well have left there and then, but the fire crackled enticingly in the grate and she longed to sit down by it.

Presently she was shown to a small room at the top of the house, bare except for a bed, a chair and a bucket, set in the corner to catch the drip above. Mr Blunt explained that she was to cook twice a day and tidy and clean, as well as run general errands, and that she might rest from all duties save cooking on Sunday. She was to confine herself to her bedroom, the kitchen or the parlour in her own time, though she might enter the library to dust. On no account was she to disturb the bedroom off the landing — which had been his dear mother's — or the outhouse, or the attic. It seemed they were indeed alone together in the house.

Grace listened patiently, thinking it best

not to divulge that she would be leaving in a day or two. For a moment she let her curiosity run up to the attic but brought herself back to hear him telling her he liked his eggs soft-boiled, with pepper. When he left her alone at last she inspected the door thoroughly for chinks or cracks and put a piece of rag in the keyhole. There was no key or bolt or other means of securing the door from inside, so she wedged a chair against it. She found a short board in the corner, held down by one nail, and eased it up with her knife. Down went Lady Davenport's diamond earrings and back went the floorboard — there they lay, together in the dark: two carats each, brilliant cut, sparkling quietly, catching tiny rays of candlelight that crept through the cracks in the floor. A mouse or two came and sniffed at them but found them quite the most inedible prospect and left them alone.

★   ★   ★

Grace woke to the sound of heavy snoring on her first morning at Horatio Blunt's residence. It seemed to shudder through the walls, flabby and thick, echoing round the house. She got up and stoked the fire, made some tea, ate several slices of a large ham she

80

found in the larder. All the while the snoring went on. She was making her way quietly back upstairs to fetch her things, having decided to leave before her host woke up, when a sparkle of light caught her eye, on the floor, a flash of red under the coat-stand. She picked it up: a delicate bird, worked in small diamonds, a brilliant-cut ruby clasped in its slender beak. The pin and settings were of white gold, with a tiny safety chain. She had seen it not four days before in Lady Davenport's jewellery box.

A cold wave swept over her, rooted to the spot with this glittering thing in her hand; the clock stopped, a tangle of questions ran through her head. The still air was shattered by an urgent hammering upon the door. Grace leaped almost out of her skin. She shrank into the back of the house, heart banging — the knocking came again, and the snoring, which had been going steadily all the while, stopped. As Mr Blunt grunted his way downstairs she was at the back door, ready to run — her only chance, and not a good one — if it was someone come for her. She could not imagine Mr Blunt had many visitors. Trembling on the back step she could hear him dusting down the caller for banging on the door so loudly, and at such an unreasonable hour of the morning when a fellow might be sleeping in. She could barely make out what the caller said but she caught 'Lady Davenport'. This was enough for Grace and she had started across the yard when she heard Mr Blunt bellow and the door slam. She froze like a deer, every nerve pricked. All was quiet. She slunk back to the door and ventured an ear across the step. She heard him pick up the poker and stab at the fire, huffing and puffing to himself. Shaking, she put on the water to boil his eggs and went into the front room. There he was, sweaty and half dressed, face bloated from sleep. His demeanour gave away nothing.

'Good morning!' she said brightly.

He scowled and scratched his groin. If he had anything to say he kept it to himself, but he looked her clean through as he dumped himself down in his chair. There he sat without speaking, staring into the fire until he had swallowed his breakfast. During this imposing silence Grace realised the brooch had disappeared. In the panic she had clean forgotten it. It was not in the kitchen or on the floor, as far as she could see. She busied herself with sweeping and tidying so that she could look more thoroughly but came up with nothing.

Later she would search her pockets, to no avail — it seemed it had flown away to its little golden nest, never to be seen again.

After a loud belch Mr Blunt pushed back his plate and turned his boorish gaze on her. She tried to look nonchalant, feeling as though she was thinking out loud.

'Where did you say you had come from?' he asked, without attempt to make his enquiry appear conversational or courteous.

'Christchurch,' she replied, as casually as possible. There was a stagnant pause. 'Who was at the door?'

'Evidently there has been a local robbery.'

'Oh?'

'Apparently, a housemaid,' — he chuckled to himself at this — 'has made off with an item of considerable value from the grand house of Lady Davenport — you may know it. Naturally Lady Davenport is keen to have it back. They gave a detailed description of the girl and asked if I might have seen such a person.' They looked at each other steadily.

'Goodness! I wonder where she might be,' said Grace at last.

'Indeed.' He lit his pipe and settled further into his greasy chair. 'You must stay here for the time being. If you leave they will pick you up within hours. And you do match her description quite remarkably.'

7

Grace could see from the first that Mr Blunt was a busy thief. New silver appeared on Monday, only to vanish on Tuesday. There were furtive comings and goings at irregular hours; shady visitors called. He was out till the small hours on Friday night, and made much explanation at breakfast of how he had come to be so late at the Swan, though she had not asked. Now Grace had an eye for an opportunity and she began to wonder what she might gain from this situation. Perhaps she would stay a while longer.

And so she made herself useful. She cooked and tidied, kept the stove burning, kept quiet. By the second week she was part of the furniture, picking up scraps of conversation as she served brandy and tea to his associates at cards — gloomy affairs in the back parlour with talk that stopped as she entered the room. She grew ears like a bat, caught crumbs of information. It seemed a grand plan was afoot, ambitious business indeed. Prospects seemed to open up before her. Lady Davenport's earrings faded a little, forgotten under the floor.

Mr Blunt's favourite supper, when in at his pig-pile for the evening, was liver and onions, which he ate with enormous relish, smacking his lips greedily, eyes fixed upon his plate. He expected this feast to be served on Monday, Wednesday and Saturday, and Grace was happy to provide it, though it meant having to witness the spectacle of its consumption, her company being required at the trough. She ate her own meals in the kitchen. Blunt would look her slowly up and down as she brought in his tray, and if she turned by the door on her way out she would catch him staring at her arse, with a lascivious smile that came back to her at dead of night and made her shudder. She dreamed of walloping him around the head with the poker. And wondered how long she would give it.

It wasn't long before Mr Blunt chanced his arm. On the twelfth day he pounced, after smoking his pipe. Grabbing her by the back of the skirts as she went by with the pail for his mustard bath, he dragged her down to the gloomy depths of his armchair.

We will not relive the details of this encounter. Suffice to say that she fought him off with a gritted smile before the bounds of decency were contravened, laughing but forcing her way out with his filthy damp hand up her skirts. Grace considered leaving that very night, but decided that the time already spent in his repulsive company should not go to waste. She resolved to stab him the next time he tried it. She must make some result of her efforts, and soon.

For the next few days she kept well clear of him, leaving the room when he entered, ignoring his requests. Dinner was dumped in front of him on a cold plate. He felt sheepish, which was quite a new sensation. Indeed, he might have forced himself upon her and could not altogether understand why he had not. She seemed to glow with some enchantment; he barely dared look at her now. Perhaps after she had calmed down he might make a better approach; he had heard that women liked flowers. Perhaps that was the way to win her affections. Catching himself, he shook his head to quiet these unlikely thoughts — they seemed to have crept in through his ear, while he was asleep perhaps: like a hex cast upon him.

★   ★   ★

The week's end brought some other matter to occupy him — he grew distracted, the atmosphere drew tight around the house. People came and went, talking in low voices: a general furtiveness seized the air. Grace sensed that the grand plan was hatching at last.

There was a knock at the door late one night as she was halfway up the stairs to her bed. She opened it to a strange little man, thin like a twig, in a tall hat.

'Good evening,' he said, with an oily smile. 'I am Ivor Squall. Is Mr Blunt within?'

★   ★   ★

Grace happened to notice that Mr Blunt spent a good deal of time in his library the following week. She hadn't had him down as much of a reader before, never having seen him so much as touch a book, or, for that matter, set foot in the library, that she could recall. He seemed nervous: he would wake in his chair with a start and look towards the door, or rise to patrol the hallway, fancying he heard an unusual noise; once or twice she found him standing guard outside the library, in silent contemplation of the brass door-knob.

Mr Blunt had inherited his extensive collection of books from his mother who, bedridden, had spent her very last bean on them. She was a caustic woman who despised her lazy, stupid son but had no one else to whom she could leave her estate. Unluckily, he had no interest in literature. In spite of this he enjoyed the library for its grand associations, visiting it once a month or so to take sherry and stalk about in a lordly manner, surveying the room with satisfaction. A couple of volumes had gone on the fire when he couldn't be bothered to chop a log.

The books stretched from wall to wall and up to the lofty ceiling, perhaps six hundred of them. Grace often browsed when he was drunk and sleeping and the house was quiet. *The Memoirs of Casanova* was a rare curiosity and she had swallowed three chapters before tiring of his conquests and deciding that, at six thick volumes, perhaps he had remembered too much. She moved on after that to *The Vampyre*, which she finished before leaving the chair, and then *Jane Eyre*, which she discarded some twenty pages in, in favour of *Candide*. Currently she was enjoying *The Last Days of Pompeii* — though she thought it rather melodramatic — but had been unable so much as to glimpse a book through the keyhole for days. Mr Blunt's new-found interest in literature was as inconvenient as it was puzzling.

★ ★ ★

Harold Whitbread had come back to haunt his murderers — all except the brothers Dean, who had not a shred of conscience between them. He had howled so terribly as they beat him to death that Blunt heard it still in his nightmares. He had seen Whitbread in the garden at night, his face battered in, smiling at him, peering in at the window through one red eye. Blunt became nervous and shifty, grew restless with the dark; he watched Grace more carefully than usual. He did not like the way she seemed — too quiet of late. He knew it must be his own anxiety; he must calm himself and try to behave as normal. The ruby necklace seemed to burn a hole in his head, throbbing at night through the library walls; he wanted rid of it. He would sell it on soon, prosper, start his new life. She would look at him differently once he was rich.

It never occurred to Mr Blunt that Grace might read; he never saw her take a book from the shelves. Why would he have spared it a thought? He had learned at his mother's knee, and had read sometimes to please her, but had not opened a book since she died of consumption. The idea that one might pull out a book from the shelf to peruse it had become an alien notion to him, as strange as taking the clock down from the wall to tell the time. This oversight would cause Mr

Blunt to curse himself whenever he thought of it thereafter, stupid as it was.

★ ★ ★

A few nights later he drank himself into a proper stupor. Grace slipped into the library for the first time in a week and sat back down with *The Last Days of Pompeii*. After it had gasped its last she breathed a sigh and put the book back in its place. She bent an ear towards the kitchen and was rewarded with snoring; looking up at the shelves, tall all around her, she wondered where she should start. By the stroke of extravagant fortune she picked on *Bleak House*.

As her fingers closed round the treasure it seemed to pulse, like a beating heart in her hand, and she covered her eyes to peek at it through her fingers. Carefully, fearfully she looked, lest she drop down dead, and slowly, slowly, she dropped her hand and held up her face to bask in its enchanted rays, helpless like Eve. Scarlet light enveloped her, intoxicating, stealing her magpie heart away.

★ ★ ★

After finishing her employment with Mr Blunt — abruptly, at dead of night and with spoils as never before in her pockets — for the first time in three long years Grace Hammer set sail for her family home. She missed them sorely and had managed to fight this down by not thinking about them, and now as she made her way back she gave in to empty longing. Her sister would be grown; her brothers would be fine, strapping men. Not half a mile on she remembered Lady Davenport's diamond earrings. She laughed at the thought of them nestling still under the board in her leaky bedroom, perhaps under Mr Blunt's very feet as he paced furiously about. A shepherd watched her go by and thought her soft in the head, cackling at the sky.

Mr Blunt woke the next morning at ten o'clock with a fearful headache. He shouted, from his prone position, for tea. The house seemed unduly quiet: not a sound came up the stairs, not the chink of a plate from the kitchen or a creak in the floor. He hauled himself from his bed, still clothed, holding his throbbing head, and made his way down the stairs. There was no fire in the stove, no kettle boiling.

'GIRL!' he shouted into the still air. The birds stopped their twitter and froze in the trees, the mice held their breath in the skirting. He stood at the door of the kitchen, scowling, the story unfurling in his head.

Slowly he went, as if trying to put off the horror, his eyes fixed on the library door. He held his breath as he turned the handle and stepped inside: nothing seemed disturbed. As he crossed the room, blind panic seized him and he hurled himself towards the shelves, ripping out *Bleak House*, plunging his hands into the empty hole, scrabbling at nothing. He let out a howl of blistering rage that scattered God's creatures a mile around.

★ ★ ★

Grace woke in a hedge with a beady-eyed robin regarding her, turning his head this way and that as if sizing her up. They considered each other a short while before she took the necklace from her pocket and held it up to catch the morning light. The ruby flashed at them, a deep red wink, like an exotic dancer lifting her veil, mesmerising them for a few moments. She hid it back in her skirts and crawled out from the hedgerow, unsnagging her hair from twigs. The bird resumed his hunt for berries.

She was quite sure that Mr Blunt would kill her if he found her so Grace kept to the hedgerows and did not stop for refreshment until she reached Havant, twenty-nine miles away. She ate steak and kidney pudding and drank a pint of beer. A little brown bird flew down and pecked at pastry crumbs on the windowsill. A slice of sunlight was casting a golden stripe on the floor, a thousand tiny flecks of dust caught in its beam.

Coming out of the King's Arms, a little sleepy from the suet in her belly, she looked across the yard and nearly jumped clean out of her skin. There he was, unmistakable even with his back turned, watering his horse. She dived back inside, heart pounding. There was no other door to leave by and as she looked around again he was walking towards it. She took a seat at the back of the room, shrinking behind the bar. Luckily it was mid-afternoon and seasonable, so the inn was busy with people drinking. She saw him enter the pub in the mirror on the back wall. She must take the red ribbon off her hat. She stole another glance as she snatched it from her head.

He was so gruff that he was served without delay and moved off to one side of the bar, striking up a conversation presently with a young girl who didn't seem to mind his attentions. Grace made her move, edging out between the people, round the other side of the bar, holding her breath as she crossed the room. A bare space lay between her and the door, she could hear his growl in the babble of the pub; out she went, wanting to run, a prickle running up her back.

Grace did not stop shaking for half an hour. She took immediate cover and did not move so she could see which way he left. His companion evidently amused him as he spent more than an hour inside; Grace was wondering if she had missed him when she heard heavy hoofs on the path. She peered through the hedge to see him riding past, towards Chichester.

Blunt had been lucky thus far to find himself on the right road. He made another stop some miles on to refresh himself and his poor weary horse. Unluckily for them, the Hammer family were well known in that part of Sussex for their business acumen and their lively parties — being part Irish. It did not take him long to find a local who claimed to know them well. After a great many drinks, much laughter and back-slapping, Mr Blunt had gathered a good deal of useful information.

★ ★ ★

A large ruddy man arrived at Pagham that afternoon, asking after the Hammer family. The good people told him nothing, feeling an instinctive mistrust towards the stranger. All except sweet imbecilic Nora Barker, the village idiot, who thought nothing of it and pointed him down the lane.

Mr Blunt skirted the village and took up a vantage-point at the edge of the wood above the Hammer farm. He bided his time until dusk, when he saw the family coming in from the fields to their dinner. Tethering his horse to a tree, he stole down the hill. He could hear laughter inside as he slunk round the house, circling it with a trail of kerosene and dry hay. It went up like a beauty.

★　★　★

After the fire Grace Hammer was a shrunken woman. She was taken in by neighbours — for a week she did not speak at all. She would not eat or, indeed, move, except to take sweet tea; otherwise she merely gazed through the window.

The ruby became an object of horror to her. It seemed to haunt her, beating under the floor, like the Tell-Tale Heart. She took it from its hiding-place one day, determined to be rid of it, and dug a hole in the lower field by the river; but when the time came to throw it in she could not seem to let it go. She stood a long while, looking at the ground, wishing she was down inside it.

The day after the funerals she went to the ruined house. It was a terrible sight: a blackened shell, scorched timber stumps stuck up against the sky, desolate in the rain. She left the next afternoon without warning, with the ruby necklace in her deepest pocket, wrapped in a charred page of Grimms' *Tales*.

8

It was only after Ivor Squall had deposited his letter safely in the post-box — stamp end first, according to his ritual, making sure it did not touch the sides — and was scurrying back to his office, wiping his fussy hands on his handkerchief, which was the only thing about him that may be called generous, that his thoughts turned to what it had all been about. He had been rather carried away with the intrigue and his own congratulations and only now did he reach back through his dusty cranium, to dig up old bones, balance old accounts he had forgotten.

It was Ivor Squall who had arranged for the disposal of goods from the Stanhope robbery, among others that had taken place that distant year at the hands of the Mathers mob; though this association had been profitable, he did not last the winter. By that November Ivor was a nervous wreck, being thoroughly afraid of most of them — he found the business troublesome, too much so for his liking, and intolerably complicated. Come December he had extricated himself and slithered off to London, where he found a little hole and went quietly about his business. Ivor trusted no one, but preferred to deal with people more his own size; he had seen none of the Mathers mob in ten years or more and he hoped to see none of them ever again — something he failed to consider fully until after his letter was safely in the post-box. He remembered with a shiver what he had heard of sorry Harold Whitbread; he had done well, he told himself, to get away. Ray Mathers's brutish face floated before his mind's eye, Big Arthur Bolt's heavy hands, and the Dean brothers, with their vulpine teeth, as clear as last week.

Any passing acquaintance of Mr Blunt that year knew the name Hammer: her disappearance had been at the forefront of Mr Blunt's concerns to an extent that one might fairly call obsessive. They had heard of nothing else. No one had managed to elicit quite why it vexed him so — he raved and tore his hair, or sat and watched the wall, as if to petrify himself — or why he wanted so urgently to find her, or should grieve so bitterly over the silver tankard that had apparently departed with her, even if it had been his beloved mother's. Most decided he must have been smitten, which in fact was true. Ivor had his own suspicions. She had left after the Stanhope robbery — abruptly, he would wager. Not for the first time he wondered what she had taken with her.

*   *   *

The thought came back to Ivor Squall the next evening as he scurried out to meet an associate in St Giles: if there was anyone at all to ask it was Emmeline Spragg. She would know the Hammer family or find them out. Even so, he had decided against it once already and, turning the idea over, rejected it again. Though Ivor Squall is straight in his own crooked way, and does a great deal of good criminal business — and much of it with Miss Spragg — he is not a man to share, unnecessarily, any extra profit that might fall from the tree, in the way of a reward, for instance. On the other hand, if it came to that, he might enquire casually, by way of conversation — he would have to make more than usual. Scheming made him itch and he decided, scratching along Fleet Street, to put it aside for the moment.

Ivor Squall cannot be expected to know that Grace Hammer is no ordinary mortal who may be traced with a few local enquiries, but rather a name that no one recalls, who has just left the room, who may not have been there at all. She is invisible even to the all-seeing eye of his associate. He may as well look for a black cat in a coal-hole, blindfold.

★ ★ ★

Miss Emmeline Spragg keeps her business as quiet as possible: she comes and goes without attention, her appearance doing nothing to announce her considerable wealth. In fact, she is often mistaken for a bundle of rags, should she be lurking in a quiet corner or crouched beside a wall. This suits her well, allowing her to hear all manner of useful information. She keeps tabs on the mobs that run London, each to their own piece, and her evil eye over the East End, where her network runs down every street, pushing sly tendrils through the keyholes and around the sleeping children — dreaming fitfully of Newgate prison, where their mothers stay for now. It winds like bindweed in at broken windows, beneath floorboards, into secret meetings, confidences: into anyone's affairs she cares to know. She has a hundred pairs of faithful eyes to cover Shoreditch, Whitechapel, Stepney, Bethnal Green, Wapping and Limehouse; and a hundred and ninety-seven pricked ears. Miss Spragg can account for only one of the lost ears — indeed she keeps it close about her person, hidden in her deepest pocket, where she squeezes it sometimes for comfort. Of the other two she knows nothing. This particular ear belonged to one Arthur Cuttle before her, who kept it cocked at the London docks, where he worked when last he had a pair. Arthur squealed to the foreman who caught him, at the back of Shadwell Basin, piling furs over the wall, and named names, like a leaky bucket — Miss Spragg's among them — at the prospect of losing his fingers on a block in the skin house, one by one. (Mr Muster, the devil's foreman, took a couple off in any event. He had meant to remove just the one but, unluckily for Arthur, he misjudged it.)

Miss Spragg had Happy Harry Harding chop the ear off — clean enough for the Queen, and flush with his scalp — leaving Arthur two fingers and an ear down on the deal. It was soft and barely cold when Harry presented it; she put it in a deep pocket and forgot about it altogether, until she saw its brother twelve weeks later, in the Alma, on the side of Arthur's head.

The ear had turned quite shiny in her pocket, and shrunk a good deal, hard and brown; she thought it charming and kept it about her from that day on, as a sort of lucky token; thus she invested it with superstitious importance, more every day, until she could not leave it behind. She has grown more attached to it than Arthur Cuttle ever was, and it is right and proper she should have it; evidently she needs it more than he, for he gets along nicely without it, and does not seem to care that it is gone. Miss Spragg and he are back on terms, and he keeps the ear he has left to the ground.

And so the wicked witch maintains the respect and loyalty of her trusty band of criminal accomplices, and runs a profitable empire, cornering the stolen-goods market east of the Tower. She never spends her money but keeps it in a tin chest, buried in a crumbling recess behind the chimney-breast. One day the wall will sink into the Thames, taking her fortune with it.

★　★　★

St Giles was not the rat-hole Ivor Squall remembered when first he knew it: it grew brighter and drier every year. This rotten log was all but torn up, the vermin scattered, to Clerkenwell, or Saffron Hill. Off Drury Lane, around Seven Dials the last dark spots remained. It was to shady Nottingham Court he made his way that evening — stronghold of the criminal element, unspoilt by sunlight or civic improvement — to the usual bolt-hole, an expedient spot upstairs at Willie the Stick's knocking shop, where Miss Spragg and he might conduct their business undisturbed. A gaggle of filthy children threw stones at him on the corner as he scuttled past. Cursing, he knocked at a mildewed door, handkerchief wrapped round his scrawny knuckles. A hatch snapped open and a beady eye poked out.

'Let me in,' said Ivor irritably, the filthy children closing in, cat-calling down the street behind him. He beetled up the dark stairs, past a dead rat on the landing. She was waiting in the back room, crouched in a gloomy armchair, black eyes glittering in the shadow. 'Good evening, Emmeline,' he said, with his best grimace.

Now, St Giles is not strictly Miss Spragg's patch — it reminds her of her mother, whom she prefers not to think about — but she would come up if she had something of particular quality that might suit Mr Squall's foreign clients. She would be in a good mood only after she was home again, with the money.

'What so, Mr Squall,' she croaked. 'You are late.'

'I do beg your pardon,' simpered Ivor.

Spragg looked him up and down as if he were a stuffed sheep. 'I do hope the exertion will be worth my while,' she said, though she had come not four miles. She pulled a bunched handkerchief from her skirts and unwrapped it in her wizened palm, holding it towards the lamp for his inspection. He peered at it gingerly, recoiling inwardly at the greasy rag. A shiny thing it was too: a jewelled cross, unusually ornate, fine yellow gold, certainly Russian. It had surely come from a church. Divine light seemed to radiate from the holy thing, incongruous in the goblin's cursed hand. He wondered that it did not scorch her with its goodness, drive her shrieking underground.

Ivor Squall does not believe in God, but allows for the possibility for his own insurance — he repents his sins once a week, in case he is hit by a bus unexpectedly and finds it is all true. His name would be marked — especially dark for this — in the book of reckoning. Reparation must be made on Sunday. His foreign client, on the other hand, would be pleased as punch.

He lifted the cross, piously, with the very tips of his fingers, and adopted a doubtful air, as if it were not up to scratch — which was a struggle to maintain as it flashed its golden light, brilliant in his face. He did manage to convey a sense of disappointment, though it fell some way short of the effect he had intended; Spragg, in any case, is no fool. She knows exactly what is what. Ivor opened his mouth, thought better of it and shut it again.

'You seem bewildered, Mr Squall.'

'Merely wondering how best to proceed, Miss Spragg.'

'Is the business not clear to you, sir? Straightforward, indeed.'

'Perfectly so.' Ivor stalled, searching for hairs to split, something to bargain the price down, though it was fixed already and he saw it was a tidy deal. 'Did we fix upon a price?' he ventured, hoping to negotiate it.

★   ★   ★

Grace, boiling the kettle for tea in Bell Lane, felt a sudden disquiet, blowing over her feet, like a draught under the door. She looked up from her trance and into the fire, to capture the thought. Who was the little man on the bus? Why did he trouble her?

★   ★   ★

In dark and desperate Miller's Court, Sally Ann Dunn leaned against the wall of the passage, her arms swinging limp by her sides, mouth hanging open. She was fighting the urge to collapse upon her favourite spot and give in to unconsciousness. The pavement blurred, swaying beneath her. Summoning all her strength and will, and remembering dimly how cold she had been in the morning the last time she had slept in the passage, she lurched upright and staggered into the darkness in the direction of her filthy bed. A fortuitous choice, indeed — perchance her guardian angel was watching, and sober.

That night a cold wind blew. A monster was abroad; he walked right past the archway, on the very paving where she might have been sleeping. He did not find the right moment to act that night, which evidently irked him, as he accomplished his task the next, finding conditions more favourable.

9

The morning of the Bank Holiday, Monday, 6 August 1888, also, incidentally and much less importantly, the forty-fourth birthday of the Duke of Edinburgh, dawned blue and bright. Sun soaked through the curtain and lit the room with the glow of a special day beginning. The Hammers leaped out of bed and into a flurry of dressing and shoe polish and ribbons. Even the boys washed in honour of the occasion. Daisy put on her new dress and everyone admired her as she turned in the middle of the room to show them, a little shy but beaming, delighted at herself with her clean rosy face and her pretty hat. It had a pansy like a tiny face and a velvet ribbon.

Grace took in the scene: the boys, all scrubbed and shiny, Daisy twirling at the centre. She must have the family picture taken. What a marvel, to capture and keep them! Breaking from this reverie she said, 'Let's go!' The family cheered. 'And keep your mitts to yourselves today, my boys,' she added, as they went out of the door.

'What do you mean 'keep your mitts to

yourselves'?' asked Daisy, who wasn't meant to hear.

'I mean be good.'

★ ★ ★

They were to meet Jack outside the Britannia at eleven — an arrangement Daisy had made — and Grace was glad to see that he had not disappointed her. There he was, freshly shaven, with a clean shirt and shiny boots. The cheeky peaked cap he had worn the first time she saw him was pushed back from his handsome face in the same distracted manner, as if he knew nothing of his devastating charm. Grace managed not to seem too eager; Daisy bounded up to him with transparent delight. After he had admired her hat and dress, and she his boots, they made their way with the milling crowd towards Victoria Park.

The Bank Holiday was a feast of merriment. Wondrous diversions were everywhere they looked and they spent the day pointing at things and trying to win coconuts. The little ones rode a donkey, ate ice cream and cockles and doughnuts and went twelve times on the merry-go-round. As Grace got down from her painted horse Jack sprang forward to help her, though there really was

108

no need, as close as he could, taking her hand, with his other round her waist; a little current passed between them for a moment, with Daisy watching in fascination and the boys nudging and giggling behind.

It was true that Jack had thought about Grace a great many times that week, and feared he was losing his head, the feeling growing every day. He could not remember the last time he had polished his boots or thought much about a woman he had already hooked, and he did not altogether like it — though he had urged the Bank Holiday to come. And he liked her better every time he saw her, he supposed — on account of his obstinate nature — because she didn't seem all that keen. When the children got back on the merry-go-round he caught her by the green ribbon round her neck, gently, and kissed her hard. A curious sensation came over him, blood flowing to his boots and his hands, an agitation. They watched Daisy go round again.

When he handed Grace hot tea with sugar she smiled at him as though she would take him to a private room. Daisy was clamouring to go on the Big Wheel — a hypnotic confection, turning above them with its pink and green seats, the footboards adorned with painted flowers.

The wheel went up slowly, stopping every few feet to let people on at the bottom. They chattered, excited, as they went higher, picked out the boys in the crowd, thrilled at the park stretching all around. When the wheel was full it started to turn at speed, flying them over the drop, and as their seat swung down to earth, Daisy felt as though she was falling and clung to her mother as though her life depended on it. 'I don't like it,' she said urgently.

Oh, bloody hell, thought Grace, it's only just started. 'It's all right, darlin', it'll stop in a minute.'

'I hate it.'

'Don't worry, girl. Look at all the things around — there's Charlie, see?' She tucked her comforting arm further round Daisy. She didn't like it too much herself. It seemed to go on and on, with the lurch of your stomach each time as you dropped down forwards, making you clench your hands and jaw though you know there is no need. What use indeed would that be should you fall, heaven forbid, or the wheel should break, or the bolt that your seat hangs on? she thought, as she did it once more.

'I hate it,' Daisy said, as they went round again.

'It's all right, baby, just sit still. Look up at the sky.'

They wandered home among the happy debris with the crowd, thinning out now in the darkness, stall lamps lighting their way. Daisy invited Jack back for a cup of tea and he duly obliged her, though Grace gave him gin instead. Jake fell asleep on the bed straight away so she took off his boots and breeches and pulled the blanket over him. Charlie wanted to go out and asked if Billy could come, which was kind, leaving, as it did, Grace and Jack to be alone. After Daisy had gone to sleep, that was, which took a full twelve minutes.

'Come here and kiss me,' he said.

'But you're ugly.'

'Don't make me come and get you!'

Grace did as she was told for only the second time since he had known her and sat on Jack's knee, one hand on his chest, just resting there while the other unbuttoned his fly. They did not tear off their garments with abandon and fuck each other senseless, as they might have liked, but slowly, under her skirt, pressing together, in silence, looking at each other all the while.

★ ★ ★

Billy was enjoying himself thoroughly at the Paragon. The Sisters De Laine were on the bill, and something called Devil Bird; and they had just seen Miss Vesta Tilley, queen of the music-hall stage. He had even been allowed a gin, which was swimming round his head. The thick smoke stank; rowdy chat and laughter filled the room. Suddenly he felt a bit sick.

Charlie had spied a pretty girl and was oblivious to Billy's discomfort. She had huge brown eyes and ruby lips like a china doll's; her hair was tied back from her flushed cheek with stray tendrils falling round her face. When she looked over he smiled bashfully, wishing he could make a more confident impression, but she smiled bashfully back. Her name was Elsie Brown and she worked at Bryant & May, which Charlie would find out later, when he dredged up the courage to talk to her, aided by a good many beers. Billy struggled with his nausea, trying not to vomit.

An Alpine Vesuvian is the best match money can buy — indeed, it is the king of matches — being sturdy and highly explosive in its own diminutive way. You can strike it in heavy wind and it will not fail you, making it an excellent companion for camping expeditions or country jaunts. Elsie cleared four hundred boxes a day through her part of the dipping table alone. She did not know it yet but the phosphorus will kill her.

*   *   *

Daisy and Jake slept peacefully on into the night, dreaming of toffee apples and the merry-go-round. The day was blighted only by terrible events in George Yard Buildings, scene of horrible murder that night as the festivities rolled into the early hours, the bloody corpse undiscovered till dawn.

*   *   *

Out in the country, near the little town of Netley Marsh, Mr Ivor Squall's letter lay upon Mr Blunt's doormat, next to an unpaid bill from his solicitor. It remained there for a week or more, gathering dust, its recipient being abroad in Berkshire, where there were many fine country houses.

10

Mrs Atkins from Hanbury Street was a fading flower, just twenty-four and without Mr Atkins now for three months or more. He had found himself unequal to the responsibilities of family life and left her to it, with their three children and her opium habit to feed (the latter taking priority as is customary in this tortured world) and a baby on the way — having been busy up until the very moment of his departure, that particular aspect of their relations unaffected by the wretchedness of the rest.

The baby, when his turn came, was very small and took several minutes to draw his first sickly breath. He seemed doomed from the start and died before the week was out, having neither hunger nor interest in living to inspire him. The others, meanwhile, suffered their betrayed and broken slap-happy mother, scratching around for their own food, lifting her head from puddles in the gutter when they found her. They would sit and guard her until she came to and cried at them for being there, hugging them too hard, and then, guilt done for another day, would scrape herself up off the pavement and back into the crowd, promising to come back in a moment with ice cream.

Daisy had spotted the Atkins girls, and remarked that they walked sadly and looked as though they were frightened and had no friends. Grace had seen their mother talking to Sally Ann in the Ten Bells and she looked much as the girls did. The next week Billy reported that there was also a small boy in the Atkins house, not more than two or three years old. He was evidently alone, left to the care of his sisters, whom Billy had seen begging in Brick Lane — their ma had not been home for two days, and they had left him as they were all hungry and he was too heavy to carry. Grace and Daisy went to Hanbury Street and found him chewing an old mutton bone, damp and reeking. They gathered him up and left a note, with their address, hoping the recipient could read it.

'His name is Tom,' said Daisy, helpfully.

'Have you seen him before?'

'Only through the window. He was playing by himself.'

'Come on, Tom. Come and have a nice bath.'

'Can we wash him?'

'Yes, we can. He seems to like us all right.'

'He smells. Can we keep him?'

'Hold your horses there, Miss Daisy. Let's wash him first and talk to his ma.'

* * *

If Tom had ever had a bath before he had forgotten it: he shrieked with fear at first and then delight as he felt the warm water. Daisy and Jake found this hilarious and they caught the giggles. They washed him sweetly with a flannel, carefully around the scabby patches, and showed him how to splash. It made a very cosy scene and Grace quietly prayed she wasn't up the duff. Then they got him out and dried him by the fire, and combed the lice out of his hair.

'Jake, can you run round to Hanbury Street and wait for his sisters to come home?'

'They're called Annie and Kate. Annie is nine and Kate is seven.'

'Thank you, Daisy. When they come home, bring them here. When Billy gets back I'll send him to wait with you.'

And so it was that the Atkins children came to stay with the Hammers. When Jake returned with the girls, wide-eyed like rabbits, she sent Billy to wait for Mrs Atkins to come home.

'Her name is Mary Jane,' said Daisy, 'but I don't know how old she is.'

Mary Jane never got home that night or the next. The landlord came to throw her out on Wednesday but went away again. The children found her dead in her bed on Thursday morning. Tom still hadn't seemed to notice she wasn't there. The thin, haunted girls came back with Billy's arms round them.

'Will you go over, Ma? I'll watch them.'

★ ★ ★

Grace found Mary Jane Atkins stone cold and stiff on her filthy bed in her boots and hat. She had choked on the vomit that had dried down her dead neck, and her face was waxen and grey. Mercifully her eyes were shut. A fly droned above them, banging into the windowpane. Grace took her possessions, such as they were: a hat with a tattered bird perched on the brim, ragged children's clothes, some shells from the seaside. She looked at Mary Jane's fingers for a wedding ring but, of course, it had gone to the pawnshop long ago. Then she stroked her, just lightly, on the arm and the cheek, to touch her before she went into the earth. Her skin was frigid, blood pooled along the back of her hands and arms, turning a purple pattern on the pale flesh. She was taken away the next morning, in a box with rope handles.

For the next three days Annie and Kate, who was the image of her mother, were ghostly figures who drifted round the Hammer home, soundless, with empty faces. Daisy exerted the full power of her hospitality, making encouraging conversation, involving them in games and anything else she thought would make them feel better. They could not be persuaded to leave the house, not for cricket or catch, or even just to sit in the street, and clung round Grace as close as they could without actually touching her. Charlie had given up his bed quite cheerfully to his brothers, who with Grace, had forgone their place in the big bed so that tiny Tom and the girls could be comfortable together. This left Charlie and Grace on the floor, which was the only place they could stretch out, and they couldn't do that for ever. Billy insisted on each of them taking a turn in his place for a night at least, his ma first on Sunday, Charlie Monday. Tuesday they made up a cot for Tom, put the girls top to toe and got back into their beds. Grace lay in the dark in the sleeping room, wondering how they would manage and what she should do for the best.

The Atkins children had not been with the Hammers a week before there was trouble. It came in the vile shape of Mirabel Trotter as she passed by the end of Thrawl Street.

She is a sly piece of work, Mrs Mirabel Trotter, like a great flabby toad lurking under a dank rock, staring out from the gloom at her dinner. She is solid, and square, with the strength of a man to match her temper. She wears a great deal of gold, all of her jewellery at once, it seems, to show off — it does nothing to enhance her appearance save to dazzle the spectator in sunlight. Although she is vulgar in this respect she has a good few impressive connections: various baronets and a duke or two, among other esteemed clients, for whom she herself is the model of discretion, and she leads an enviable life of comfort, her empire stretching across East London. In addition to her quieter interests she owns the greater part of Thrawl, and Flower and Dean Streets, chunks of Hoxton, a lodging-house or two in Bow. She has everything, in fact, except true love, which she heard about long ago and has pursued ever since, finding it elusive, which is not only, as she thinks, because she cannot buy it but also because she is so unfortunate as to lack any personal appeal whatever.

She had spotted the Atkins girls out and about and, not knowing who was looking after them, had engaged the poor innocents in conversation, from which she deduced that their mother was dead and they were staying with a local family for now. They told Grace about the fat, frightening lady in the fancy carriage who had spoken to them, though they tried not to say much; how she had watched after them down the street, waving as they hurried away. Grace knew why the old sow was sizing them up, though they might be all of eight and nine. She told them to stay away from Thrawl Street and asked the boys to keep an eye open.

Sure enough, two days later Billy came racing home, in a breathless panic.

'Annie's gone, she's been snatched.' He was near to tears, Kate by his side, her eyes like empty dinner plates. Grace grabbed her little hand. 'Where?'

'Dorset Street.'

'What in *God's* name were you doing in Dorset Street?'

'We was taking a short-cut.'

Now Dorset Street, dear reader, is no likely avenue for a quiet stroll or a short-cut to anywhere, though it runs not a hundred and fifty yards long, between Crispin and Commercial Street. It is said by some to be the most notorious street in London. Policemen rarely patrol it and only in pairs. You can find a man for the dirtiest job here;

cut-throats and thieves rub shoulders with the grimiest brasses, smoking opium and drinking their filthy London gin. Near one end is an archway that leads through to Miller's Court, which sounds cheery enough but is really a warren of mouldy rooms and passages, so neglected by sunlight that not even moss can grow on the wet walls, never mind a pot plant — if there was anybody here who might keep such a thing: hideout for the Blind Beggar mob, bitter rivals of the Nicholses, and squalid home to other shady operations and some of the most wretched girls in the parish. A century ago Dorset Street was a clean thoroughfare with fresh air, the wide blue sky and flowers growing at the windows; a century before that, a country lane. It is doomed to be the scene of dark events, though no one can know these things yet. Grace was down there like a flash.

Miss Kelly was the first voice of reason: she had spotted the children round about twelve and told them to get themselves home. Then she'd gone into Miller's Court for a minute, only just inside the archway, to see that Sally Ann was breathing — she had stumbled in a half-hour before and fallen asleep in the passage. No one wanted to move her as she had walloped Nelly Holland last time for trying to put her to bed, and her eye was still black. Coming out again she had spotted Billy racing down the street with the little one in tow, stumbling to keep up, all the commotion behind them, and Busy Liz Stride hammering with her long arms on the door of MacMurphy's lodging-house, wailing in Swedish.

★ ★ ★

Mrs Mirabel Trotter, in all her glittering gold, has plucked Annie Atkins, along with two other girls that day, from the street and they are on their way, terrified, in a plain carriage, to an address in Shoreditch. The journey is tortured and silent. She receives them at the inner door once the gate is firmly locked behind them. She tells them they will be put to work straight away at general household tasks and that they are there by order of the Metropolitan Board of Works. Two of them do not know that this is untrue.

★ ★ ★

There was one person who could help poor Annie Atkins, and Grace had wasted no time in looking for her. She searched every pub the length of the Whitechapel Road, which was no mean feat, and returned home, where Billy

122

was minding the little ones, to find Charlie and Jake on the doorstep, having scoured Commercial Street all the way to the station and back down Brick Lane, with no joy either. Trixie May Turner, lady of leisure, East End society queen, was not in the neighbourhood that afternoon. Grace wanted to sit down in the road and cry with hopelessness. It was Daisy who suggested the next step: 'You could ask Jack.'

It was true that he knew everyone. And he seemed a reliable sort, strangely enough, the kind you might turn to in times of trouble.

'That's a good idea, darlin'.' And so it was her turn to find him.

*   *   *

He turned up in the Saracen's Head, luckily at that moment not charming a lady but cracking rude jokes with Michael Robinson, the landlord. She grasped him by the elbow, a little breathless.

'Will you run an errand with me, Jack?'

As it happened, Jack knew a thing or two about Miss Trotter; not, as Grace suspected, because he frequents her brothel but because Trixie May Turner was his best friend for drinking and sometime associate. He did not divulge this information for now, expecting she would make something of it, as women in his experience are wont to do. And he happened to know that Trixie was in Canning Town and not due back until after dinner. He had never met the vile Mrs Trotter but her reputation preceded her for miles around, and he felt as if he knew her already more intimately than he would like.

He rejected Grace's plan to find Mrs Trotter and confront her — a brave idea, but foolish. Mirabel Trotter runs a tight racket and casual callers rub her up the wrong way, which nobody wants to do. Those with troublesome enquiries or pointy fingers are likely to be shown through to the yard, to be dealt with where no one can hear them. Jack was not about to go knocking on the door at Thrawl Street or her fortress in Shoreditch. Furthermore, Annie might not be at either, but at Trotter's premises in Mile End. Or — though he refrained from saying it — dead in a ditch already. He proposed instead that they visit an acquaintance of his in Limehouse, who is the best source of information on any business in the criminal world, if you can get her to talk. He drained his beer and they left at once.

★ ★ ★

Jack is a city boy, born and bred in St Olave. His great-grandmother had kept a beautiful tidy cottage in Hanbury Street in the days when Whitechapel had clean air and bird-song, and fields still skirted the district. He remembers her faintly, as if in a dream, her window-boxes the last flash of colour in their street. He may be an unsuitable choice for a consort but he can be a solid friend. He has saved many a day, rescued many a damsel in distress — and not just the young, pretty ones.

He was surprised that Grace asked for his help, having supposed that she was cast iron. They stormed down Commercial Road heading for Limehouse: scene of human degradation, lair of the wicked, axis of criminal activity. It was one of the blacker spots on East London's face, dark and grey and damp. The wood had rotted on the windows in these bleak streets, eating itself; the buildings were slipping slowly into the marsh, with the people still inside, clustering and scuttling like silverfish.

As they walked past the workhouse at the end of Thomas Street they saw a dead dog in the road.

'It's just round the corner and down the alley now,' he said.

They rounded the corner and stepped from

their grimy, stinking surroundings into a rotten place. A narrow, crooked passage, slick with condensation from the sewage on the floor, the sound of thick drops dripping. It smelled of dead things and sickness and shit. Tunnel-like alleyways led off in other directions ahead. This was Blight Street, St Anne, notorious den of thieves and miscreants.

As they picked their way through the slime they passed tiny windows, some dark and soundless, some patched with pathetic rags or greasy brown paper, with a faint light inside and the sound of crying. Just inside a half-open doorway, a baby was asleep on the floor, sucking breaths of fetid air into rattling lungs. Their footsteps squelched under them, someone shrieked in the distance. They climbed some stairs that appeared suddenly from the gloom, feeling the way, passing figures slumped unconscious or dead on the steps. Grace was certain she had stood on someone's hand. A rotten door appeared at the top and upon knocking they were admitted, after a gruff inquisition through the keyhole.

The creature who opened the door to them was more goblin than woman in appearance and demeanour. She greeted them with a smile that was neither warm nor friendly and hollow black eyes.

'Good day, Miss Spragg, how nice it is to see you,' said Jack, tipping his hat, plainly lying but doing very well at it. 'May I beg a moment of your valuable time?'

'Why, charming Mr Tallis, can it really be you after all these weeks?' she replied, with a sickening grin. 'I had quite forgotten you! What could you be wanting this fine day, I wonder? And who's this pretty piece?' She jabbed a vicious claw in Grace's direction. Grace swallowed the urge to smack her rotten teeth down her throat.

'This is my good friend Miss Jane Hanbury,' said he. 'One of her girls has been taken this morning, in Dorset Street. I'm sure you've heard something about it.'

The goblin Spragg laughed nastily, creature of hell, black-hearted. 'Oh, sure indeed, are you?' she rasped, through her fit of merriment.

'I'm sure you will think of something to say,' he said quietly, 'when you have heard me out in private.'

She looked a little uneasy suddenly and stepped aside to let them in. Her long skirts covered her feet so she seemed to glide or, rather, to scuttle along. They entered a damp passageway and ascended a flight of rotting stairs, the reek of mildew closing round them. Upstairs a fire hissed in the grate, burning green wood, like the poison tree Grace had read about in some tale or other, most likely Grimm.

'You. Wait here,' the goblin told Grace, her eyes cold, black like a spider's. She waved Jack up another flight. Grace watched their feet disappear. Footsteps crossed the floor above and faded away.

★ ★ ★

Now Jack, in fact, had nothing on Miss Spragg at all. He was blessed, however, with hypnotic eyes, the crooked gift of effortless deception as he spilled from his mother's womb. He employs it often for his own casual amusement, dropping confusion here and there like litter: a curse that his sorry victims struggle with, brows knit, until they are buried with it, doubt worrying them under the ground — so that even before the gates of Heaven, as they declare their tally before St Peter, a part of them is caught in perpetual distraction, perplexed by something they cannot remember, wondering what he meant.

Jack fixed Emmeline Spragg with his deep dark eyes.

'Do you know where Arthur Cuttle's been this last week?' he said. Not a question but a foregone conclusion that she did not and would want to. 'You might keep a special eye on him.' Pity poor Arthur Cuttle, who had nothing to do with anything underhand but loyal service to his goblin mistress.

The glassy black eyes glittered back at him in the gloom. Jack smiled affably as he watched the cogs tick behind them, chewing on his words.

As she and Jack share a fair few connections, the wicked witch was wondering who he had been talking to and what they had said — the unfortunate consequence of living as a dishonourable criminal, without loyalty even to one's own associates.

Jack adopted his best mysterious face. 'Tell me about Mirabel Trotter,' he said, 'what business she has been about this week.'

The goblin's ears pricked at the mention of Mrs Trotter. She was expecting something altogether trickier from him, and had no idea why Jack should be asking after her business. However, Mrs Trotter and Miss Spragg have their own private bone, which she is always keen to gnaw on. So, to his satisfaction, she indulged his enquiries. She wondered what to do for the best about Arthur Cuttle. And who exactly the woman downstairs might be. With the green ribbon round her neck.

★ ★ ★

Meanwhile in Shoreditch, Annie Atkins, showing more spine than we may give her credit for, is plotting her escape. Though she has been in the Shoreditch house not more than four hours she has already noticed that the keys are kept on a chain by bone-fingered Miss Craven, vile keeper of their prison, who sleeps downstairs with her glass eye open, and that the only window without bars is on the third floor: in fat Mrs Trotter's private office. She resolved to keep her eyes peeled and her spirits up. The other girls are a Maureen O'Dowd, a pretty Irish thing, and a little Polish girl called Nina, who speaks about six words of English, none of which can help her, being things like 'fire' and 'baby'. The most helpful words she has are 'Thank you', which she has no occasion whatsoever to use here. She is younger even than Annie Atkins and, like Maureen, is lost in confusion and will cry herself to sleep in the narrow beds to which they are shown that night, after the door has been bolted, while Annie lies awake, listening to their jailers carousing below.

* * *

It is rumoured that Mirabel Trotter once kept a man in her cellar for a month, chained to the wall, whom she flogged every morning until he begged, weeping, for his life and she threw him bleeding and penniless on to the street. His name was Sam Miller and he had a wife and three young children and owed Mrs Trotter twelve shillings. Foolishly, he had attempted to hide when he was unable to repay it, rather than explain his difficulties — which in truth would have made little difference to the treatment he received. She had to make an example of somebody once in a while to maintain her credibility, and that time it happened to be him.

He crawled home to find his family gone. The landlord had thrown them out a week before and, having survived upon the kindness of her neighbours for a day or two, Mrs Miller had turned to hawking the only asset she had left, believing her husband to be dead. He was a good man, not given to disappearing, she told her friends. He must have met some dreadful fate. They nodded sympathetic agreement but secretly thought not. The day before Sam Miller returned, his wife decided she could not carry on without him. She was a fragile soul and unable to bear the shame of her new situation. No one saw the family go. The next person to lay eyes on them was the lighterman who pulled them out of the Thames at Tilbury, still clinging together, little dead hands entwined in her hair.

Mrs Trotter has a finger in every pie in the criminal world. Her own mother sold her to a travelling show of wonders as she was such an extraordinarily large and odd-looking baby. She was trained to juggle and perform acrobatics in a troupe of girls, four of them, with strange faces and muscular arms, in yellow satin gowns. The Daffodil Sisters was their stage name and they went down very well all over London for a time.

After this brief but exhilarating career had run its course she made an important decision. She would never allow her circumstances to revert to their former humble state; on the contrary, she would make something important of herself — acquire position and power, pursue the high life she had tasted. This meant clearing seven hundred pounds per annum by her most conservative estimate. The only serious way to achieve such an ambition seemed to be through organised crime. Starting with minor robbery and prostitution — at which she enjoyed surprising success — she progressed to extortion and brothel-keeping, by virtue of the contacts she had made. Within a year she had twin sons by Alfie Skinner, notorious villain and scourge of Hatton Garden, kept fifteen girls on her books and protected the interests of several other local concerns for a monthly fee, helped by her associates the Wilsons and Mr Harry Harding. Thus she carved her own way through East London until she controlled a good part of it, vanquishing her enemies (not least Mr Trotter, a hapless little man with his trousers an inch or two short — she forgets why she married or, indeed, killed him: he rests peacefully under the vegetable bed at her country retreat near Harlow). She feels lonely sometimes, but she knows she will never have everything.

She and Miss Spragg tolerate each other, having separate patches. Miss Spragg's line is more in goods: she can sell anything of quality, the finer the better, having more connections than the Queen herself, an unusual circumstance for someone who looks as if they live under the ground.

★ ★ ★

Jack emerged from the lair at last. He said nothing until they had left the crumbling kingdom behind.

'What now?' she said.

'Annie's in Shoreditch. Locked up tighter than Newgate. There's only one person can help you with that.'

They happened upon Trixie May Turner at

last, after dark, propping up the bar of the Grave Maurice. She embraced them both with exuberant fondness and bought them a drink.

'You could do better!' she said to Grace.

'I can't shake him off.'

'Try rat poison.'

Jack revelled in this appreciation, knowing he was the handsomest cad in the parish. After these greetings were done they took a corner table and Trixie settled down to listen.

★ ★ ★

Trixie May Turner (which is not her real name) was born to a rich family, who disowned her, in shame and disgrace, pregnant by a bricklayer named Arthur Blakey, who was devilish charming. He stole her heart clean away, costing Trix her rightful inheritance of the family pile. Less than three minutes after she had imparted this news he was out of the door and away, never to return. This had happened twenty-three years ago last Wednesday, but though he was a distant memory that popped up less often than her birthday, Trixie could see his face still, and feel the pain, as sharp as if he had left yesterday. She had drunk like a whale at

134

first to dull the sorrow but had tired of the company and reverted to her lively self: she likes to talk, and eat well, and knows everybody.

She finances her moderately hedonistic lifestyle through a steady business in opiates, which has gone along nicely since 1872, by way of a good Asian connection and a friend at Custom House, who manages to overlook the import tax on her goods. She knows Mirabel Trotter from long ago; they dine together often, sharing a taste for good wine and caviar. They never do business, or talk about it, which is why they get on so well, restricting their badinage to matters of entertainment. Vile Mrs Trotter has been seen, on occasion, gazing rapt as Trixie talks, like a little girl watching the Queen.

★   ★   ★

Stripe Wilkins seemed to enter the room without opening the door, as he always did, and hovered silently before his mistress, waiting for the word.

'Jack Tallis was here not an hour ago,' said the goblin Spragg. 'He brought company. A tall woman, handsome, good teeth. I've not seen her before.'

He slid from the room, gone as she turned

from the grimy window, without a squeak, through the keyhole, into the slippery street.

★   ★   ★

After the matter at hand was discussed, Jack and Grace sat down to roast beef and potatoes, at Trixie's insistence; they must eat and there was nothing more to be done for now. Grace forced down her dinner and left at ten — Jack saw her to the door. His kiss was coarse; he tasted of stale beer. She shoved him back into the pub and went on her way.

London was slick with rain, black and grey. The streetlamps glowed sickly yellow on the Yorkshire stones, showing up the dirt and shit, the rotten leaves pasted flat, mixing slime and grit, sticky city.

★   ★   ★

Back in Bell Lane the family were tidying the rooms and folding their clothes as a surprise for Ma so she wouldn't have to fuss at them or shout. Jake and Tom fell asleep after pie and mash at seven o'clock. When everything was nice Billy read to Daisy in bed and Charlie stoked a nice cosy fire. Twenty minutes passed peacefully so, till poor Billy burst suddenly into tears. He was racked with

136

guilt about Annie and, though he had been holding it well all day, he cried his heart out, with Charlie's arm around him.

'Come on Billy,' he said, 'you musn't blame yourself.'

'It's all my fault' sobbed Billy.

'No it ain't.'

Daisy hugged his head and wiped away his tears. She was sure that Annie would be back at any moment.

'It'll all come out in the wash, Billy,' she said. This made him laugh a bit and she was pleased to have cheered him up. Then she tucked him into bed next to her. Charlie stayed up to see his ma home, and tried to immerse himself in a new serial, which he could not, despite having a fancy for the heroine. He had read several pages without taking in a word when Grace came home, knocking softly on the window. As he opened the door Mrs Jacob's curtain twitched across the way and prying eyes clocked Grace as she went in.

Charlie looked at her expectantly but Grace just shrugged her shoulders in a gesture of despair and exhaustion. Then she took off her boots and fell fast asleep with all her clothes on.

11

The very next day Trixie May Turner called at the Shoreditch residence of Mrs Mirabel Trotter, dining partner and acquaintance of early days, dressed in a fancy bonnet to amuse herself and anyone else who might be looking. The bell was answered by Miss Isobel Craven, fastidious housekeeper and devout reader of the Holy Bible, naturally drawn to suffering and punishment. Her hair was scraped back tightly from her gaunt face, tied in a painful knot and stuck with a sharp comb. She regarded Trixie with utter indifference, as if she had no idea who she was or what she might want, or the slightest interest in finding out. Her glass eye fixed upon something invisible beyond Trixie's left shoulder, rolling slightly in its socket, making Trixie want to laugh out loud.

'Good day,' said Trixie, haughtily. 'Would you announce me to the mistress?' Trixie knew Miss Craven quite well and loathed her thoroughly. She enjoyed getting under her tight, witless skin — being possessed of an unusual taste in amusement — so much so that she indulged this impulse every time she called at the house. The drollery mostly took Miss Craven's neurotic domestic routine as its inspiration: in light of the recent chimney-sweeping Trixie had planned something special for today.

She ascended the stairs (after being made to wait) with a flounce and a toss of her head because she knew it irked Miss Craven when she put on airs and graces. At the top was Mrs Trotter, toad woman, at the helm of her empire. She glowered from behind her desk, heavy eyebrows knitted, trying not to look as though she was pleased to see Trixie, who dissolved her with a beatific smile, a feat that only she could perform. There was truth in the rumour that Trotter preferred women for love, and no one exploited this better than Trixie, being in the unique position of her equal, from the start of their long acquaintance in the days when Trotter turned tricks in the graveyard at St Botolph. She has severed connections with all others who remember her so, thus bestowing on Trixie a singular omnipotence that she wields on occasion to her own advantage. Mrs Trotter regrets this soft spot, but is unable to resist her. And so Trixie May can flirt with the toad and extract things with charm without resort to the unthinkable. And though Mrs Trotter has been in love, as much as she is able, with

Trixie for these last fifteen years, despite getting nowhere, they are friends of a sort still.

'So,' said Trixie, brightly, dropping into the easy chair, 'what news?'

'I might ask you the same,' said Mrs Trotter, 'having heard neither hide nor hair of you all this week.'

'Oh, come now, Mirabel, don't sulk. You know I've had my hands full with Mr Worth being over.'

'I know you've been drinking yourself sick in the Grave Maurice. I have eyes at every corner, you know.'

'You sound just as my mother would if she were breathing.'

They glared at each other for a moment. Trixie lit her pipe.

'Tell me, Mirabel,' she said, after a lengthy pause — in which they waited, quite at ease, as if the other were not there, to see who would speak next, one contemplating the condition of her fingernails while the other wondered idly where to dine that evening. 'What of the new girls?'

Mirabel Trotter sat up quite straight in her French leather chair. Trixie May Turner never mentioned the girls, new or not, having a distaste for the business that she had laid upon the table long ago, with typical candour, resulting in the understanding that the subject never came up again. Why she should toss it into the air now, after twelve years or more, in such a casual manner, Mrs Trotter could not imagine.

'What of them?'

'I heard tell you've found a new one in Dorset Street.'

Mirabel Trotter took a good look at Trixie May. There was something about her this afternoon. She did not like the angle, more rakish than usual, at which she was wearing her hat, which, now she happened to notice it, sported a new peacock feather. She smelled a rat. 'That may be so,' she ventured, with what she hoped was a cryptic air.

'One Annie Atkins, if I recall correctly,' continued Trixie, smoothly, cutting directly to the point without regard for Mrs Trotter's aura of mystery. 'Unluckily you have picked upon quite the wrong girl.' She took a long draw on her pipe for effect, and looked out of the window as if composing difficult news.

Mrs Trotter held fast to her nerves.

'The problem with Annie,' said Trixie at last, 'is her royal connection.' She had been studying a hoarding outside and had not completely planned what she was to say; she wanted to reel the words back in as soon as they had escaped her lips.

They sounded so utterly far-fetched, however, that Mirabel Trotter was reluctant to dismiss them, the truth being, in her wide experience, much stranger than fiction. She waited instead for what might follow, while Trixie's mind somersaulted, paddling, like swan's feet, beneath her composed exterior, scrabbling for the next words to say. They came out by themselves, as they ever seemed to do, by virtue of her disregard for the cares of the world, a happy quality born of a broken heart.

'She happens to be the bastard child of one Robert Samms, Master of Command and most esteemed counsel — the chief courtier to Her Majesty the Queen herself, and protected therefore, though it may be at arm's length, by the might of the Crown. When Scotland Yard become involved they shall certainly find their way into your affairs, whatever your connections may be.'

Mrs Trotter digested this, weighing it, wondering how much a fool she might be, looking all the while at Trixie May Turner, who kept her gaze steady. The clock ticked on the mantelpiece. 'And what might this have to do with you?' she ventured at last.

'Nothing at all,' replied Trixie, employing her most innocent expression of concern, which she heightened further by leaning earnestly forward, stopping just short of clasping the flabby hand upon the desk. 'I am merely passing on what news I have heard, out of care for a dear friend. I am only sorry that I know nothing more.'

Mirabel Trotter looked doubtful, but not confidently so.

'Do with it as you wish,' said Trixie, rising from her chair and making for the door. 'I shall see myself out.' By rights she should have pursued a career on the stage. She left the room with a sweep of her skirt and a glance over her shoulder as she closed the door behind her, leaving Mrs Trotter standing, feeling unaccountably stupid, behind her great desk.

As Trixie descended the stairs she remembered the delicious surprise she had in store for Miss Craven and stopped short of the front door, opening and shutting it with an energetic slam as if she had left. Looking around furtively she pulled a fresh herring wrapped in newspaper from her coat pocket and silently crossed the hall to the drawing room. Peering round the door she saw her at the bureau under the window. She had her back to Trixie and was searching for something, opening and shutting each drawer, somewhat irritably, stirring their contents with a bony finger. Trixie shrank back behind the door, watching through the gap between its hinges. Presently Miss Craven seemed to find what she was looking for; she stopped scrabbling and held up a small brass key, shook her head and tutted loudly to herself.

'That wretched *woman*!' Trixie heard her spit, and stifled a burst of laughter. She was clearly not the only one who made a hobby of vexing Miss Craven. The 'wretched woman' could only be Isobel Craven's nemesis: one Miss Rosalind Pinch. Miss Pinch held the position of Mrs Trotter's personal secretary so the two were constant competitors for seniority within the household, daily treading on each other's toes, interfering in each other's responsibilities. They had been sworn enemies for so long now that neither could remember why exactly, but kept up their mutual hatred as both had invested so much effort in it already. Trixie watched as Miss Craven unlocked the bottom door of the bureau to reveal a squat iron safe. She stopped for a moment, key in hand, apparently in thought, before placing it in another drawer. So, hiding the key was a household game! Then she seemed to feel she was being observed — she stiffened, and lifted her sharp nose as if to sniff the air.

Miss Pinch's voice floated down from the room above. Trixie could not make out what she said but it seemed she was reprimanding some poor soul, who was no doubt imagining the pleasure of killing her in her bed. Miss Craven seemed satisfied that she was alone, for she turned back to the bureau and, reaching above it to the picture hanging there — a small Canaletto if Trixie was not mistaken, very fine and surely original — she took another key, from behind the gilt frame, and opened the safe.

Trixie never bothered to leave the herring up the chimney. She forgot it altogether, in fact, until she was halfway home with a small ensemble of hungry cats behind her.

★　★　★

Mirabel Trotter sat at her desk for a full ten minutes after Trixie May Turner had flounced out, in deep thought, which she was not good at — after which things were no clearer. Failing to decipher what this strange visit had been about, much less what the truth might have been, she decided to give Trixie's intelligence the benefit of the doubt, just in case. She would wait till tomorrow and turn the girl out on the street, with a crown for her trouble. Kidnapping was becoming a precarious business. She resolved to confine her attentions, for the time being, to more reliable concerns: extortion, running the older girls, a little smuggling. And there were new interests to pursue: ventures involving the workhouse mortuary at Whitechapel and a surgeon at the London Hospital, whose recent acquaintance she had made at one of Mr Worth's parties. Dead people, she surmised, with solid reason, would be easier to steal. This was becoming more apparent every day. She bellowed loudly for Miss Pinch, making the pictures jump against the wall, and ordered her carriage.

★ ★ ★

Annie Atkins was not woken for work the next morning but allowed to remain in bed. The other girls set to, airing the upper floors of the house and sweeping the rugs. She woke to the sound of Nina crying, footsteps running down the stairs. She sat up, wondering why she was still in bed and if she was in trouble. It was quiet again so she dressed quickly and crept down the narrow stairs. As she reached the next flight a dreadful commotion struck up downstairs, making her jump, a banging and thudding as if someone was throwing furniture. The door of foul Mrs Trotter's room swung open across the landing. Annie stopped still, shrinking into the corner.

The racket seemed to involve Miss Craven and poor Maureen O'Dowd, who had thrown herself into a cupboard to escape the lashes of Miss Craven's stick — an unwise move, for now she found herself locked in and, terrified of small dark spaces, was hammering on the inside of the door and howling in panic, to the sadistic delight of her glass-eyed jailer. Most importantly, it brought Miss Pinch out of the Trotter office where, no doubt, she had been fixing the books in her own interest. The commotion had startled her; she was jumpy already from poking her fingers in while the boss was out, and she came raging out from behind Mrs Trotter's desk, forgetting, in her haste and fury, to lock the office door. The windows were open inside; a gentle breeze ruffled the curtain. Miss Pinch flew down the stairs like an angry dart and Annie Atkins took her chance.

She crossed the landing and stepped gingerly inside the lion's den, stomach turning as she crossed the threshold, her breath rattling like an old woman's teacup. The room was huge and stern; the furniture seemed to watch her.

When she looked down from the window she saw why it had not been fitted with bars as every other. There was a sheer thirty-five-foot drop to the paving below, the wall stretching away without a ledge or any other feature that might serve as a foothold or grip to hang your life upon, save a thin drainpipe running straight down that you would not trust with half your weight, even if you had the bottle for the climb. She stared at this prospect, dumbstruck. She only noticed that the commotion downstairs had stopped when the stair creaked below the landing, and again: another step, coming towards the open door. She found herself climbing out, legs first, gripping the sill, swinging a foot over to meet the pipe, grasping it with white knuckles. She flattened herself to the wall as someone inside closed the window. The urge to scream welled in her throat and she swallowed it, trembling like a dry leaf.

The drainpipe held fast enough till the first floor, when a part came away from the wall above her, as it had threatened, with creaks and groans, all the way thus far. She pushed away as it started to give, landing in a laurel bush on the far side of the garden wall. She opened her eyes slowly in case there was something terrible to see — an impossibly twisted leg, or a bone sticking out through her skin. Finding only scratches and a bruise or two she thanked heaven, then untangled herself from the shrubbery and ran.

Downstairs the commotion raged on and

no one noticed she was gone. Misses Craven and Pinch vented their mutual loathing, full force, like valves shooting livid steam, with poor Maureen O'Dowd still locked in the cupboard, her desperate screams ignored. The butler and cook came up to watch and found themselves restraining the combatants, and soon the whole household was involved.

Once the fuss had died down the staff busied themselves tidying, and attending to minor injuries sustained in the excitement. It took the rest of the morning to restore order. Annie was only found missing when Miss Craven, at Mrs Trotter's bidding, came to find her at noon to set her — reluctantly — free without question. Cursing herself for not having locked the harlot into her room, she turned the house over, raging all the while, the other girls trying to hide their delight.

Mrs Trotter suspected immediately that Trixie May Turner had had a hand in it. As the girl was leaving them anyway it mattered none but put the devil's fury up her all the same. She took it out on the unfortunate girls who were left behind, making them scrub the chamber-pots with soda till their hands bled, and waking them at half past five on Sunday morning to make ready her bath and her boots, in the event that she might ride that afternoon — which she had done only twice in her life. It had been an unsuccessful exercise on both occasions, horses seeming to have an instinctive dislike of her. A bad humour settled upon the house in Shoreditch where it remained for several weeks.

* * *

Annie found her way back by those faculties that are employed only when one is left to survive all alone. She fell through the door into the arms of Charlie and Grace, and was presently tucked up in bed, attended by Daisy and Kate, who fussed over her every need for the rest of the day, tiring of servitude the next.

* * *

Mirabel Trotter reviewed the security provision at her Shoreditch premises and, concluding it was watertight, laid the blame — to Miss Pinch's relief and delight — on Miss Craven's head, which was not strictly fair, though Miss Craven dared not say so. She was happy enough to escape with a most severe warning. The slightest error was intolerable, Mrs Trotter told her. It had taken her many years and a great deal of personal sacrifice to build up her business. She simply could not run the operation with less than completely dependable associates and would consider any slipping of standards to be a personal affront. Miss Craven bit her tongue and said she would make it her utmost endeavour to ensure that no such thing would happen again. Mrs Trotter said that indeed she hoped it so.

Thereafter she left the Hammer family and their house-guests alone, and they, in their turn, avoided Dorset Street, Thrawl, or Flower and Dean, to which they had no call to go anyhow, and settled the next week into a reasonable, though cramped, state of play. The girls made themselves helpful and things were tidy enough; but Grace sat down after all were in bed and thought hard about their prospects.

★　★　★

The next day she sent the girls with Charlie and a fruit cake to visit the Cherrys, a sweet, decent couple in Cannon Street Road. Mrs Cherry used to watch the boys when Jake was just a baby. She was a kindly woman, always smiling, and devoted to Mr Cherry, a smart little man with clean cuffs who worked for the railway. They had lost their own children two years before to influenza.

Grace had hit the nail on the head. The very next day Mrs Cherry came to visit Bell Lane. She took tea and admired the girls' animal drawings, and their pretty hair, marvelled at how big and handsome Charlie had grown, the clever books Billy read, Jake's beautiful manners (which had never appeared before), how charming their home was, and what lovely moss roses. Then she took Tom on to her lap and cut to the chase. She could see that Grace was doing admirably for them all — and she took her hat off to her for it — but had her hands full indeed, and not an inch of space to spare, while she and Mr Cherry fair rattled around in their empty house. Might the Atkins children come to stay with them? Grace accepted this gracious proposal without hesitation. Daisy, who had been eavesdropping, considered it rather more intently and had a few questions of her own: where did Mrs Cherry live, was Mr Cherry nice, and how were her lodgings? And — before Grace could stop her — how old was she? Mrs Cherry answered Cannon Street Road, yes, he was, and that Daisy might come and see for herself if she liked. And she was as old as her tongue and a little older than her teeth.

Billy had to take Tom over and settle him

in, as he cried without him, having grown attached these last two weeks. He came back with red eyes, visiting again the very next morning to see that Tom had slept all right.

★　★　★

Trixie May sat with her feet up on the silk chaise, alone in her rooms on Wilton Square. She sipped her pink gin and contemplated recent events. She had come a little too close to Mirabel Trotter's business for her own liking, these last few days. It was something she usually thought nothing about and now she felt ashamed for she found it distasteful indeed. She resolved to distance herself from Mrs Trotter for the time being. Perhaps she might spend some time in Hampstead with friends she had neglected lately. Or take a few days in Surrey. It was just the weather for riding out.

12

The rain does not wash London clean, not East London anyway. It gathers in filthy puddles among the spewing rubbish, bringing up the smell, filling the gutters, painting the streets slick and grey. It drips off the edges of every filthy roof in thick gobs of dirty water, pooling at your feet, seeping in round your collar, unseasonable enough even to keep the Irish indoors.

It was chucking down in bucketfuls as Grace took refuge in the Britannia. There was Mary Kelly, pretty thing, sat at the bar, unusually sober for that time of the evening. She spotted Grace and smiled radiantly. Save for a purple bruise on her cheek she looked right enough.

'How's tricks, Miss Mary?'

'Oh, I can't complain,' she replied sweetly, in her County Cork accent, as if she had stepped off the boat last week.

Off she went to prowl her usual spot, across the street outside the Ten Bells. Grace watched the rain run down the window in little rivulets, like turgid veins, and wondered when she might see Jack next. After their visit to Limehouse he had disappeared and she had been too occupied all week to think much about him. She made a dip, an elderly gent who mistook her for a brass; she let him ply her with gin, then relieved him of his wallet and melted into the street as he visited the bar.

The rain had slowed to a fine drizzle, whipping around in the thick night air, poking her with clammy fingers. The street was thick with people, chattering and pointing, children running, moving like a tide down towards the docks. She caught a wisp of smoke in the air, a dark smell as if it was November. A little unconscious, she drifted with the crowd down Leman Street. In the distance a thick orange glow spread against the night sky, drawing them on, like a spell. At Cable Street they could hear a rumble, ominous like Judgement Day, growing louder, roaring down Dock Street. An acrid scent blew on the breeze like a ghost; waves broke in Grace's ears and she was running through the village again, past the juniper bush, up the lane, watching herself go. Licks of flame escaped and blazed into the dark. London Docks was a raging ball, scorching their dumb faces.

An explosion split the air, drawing synchronised gasps from the crowd, bursting like fireworks over Grace's head — belching heavy black smoke from the warehouse on Spirit Quay, which houses the East India Company's fine brandy and, under cover of darkness, our handsome Jack Tallis. Her heart seemed to shrink and drag down through her guts, as if she were back on the Big Wheel.

People were turning out from Garrick's, and the Pavilion, pushing in from the back. Sally Ann's vacant face bobbed up a few feet away. The drunken theatre mob would have been tempting to dip any other day but Grace didn't spare it a thought. She watched in horror at the gates as the warehouses burned to the ground.

★ ★ ★

Of course Jack wouldn't be at the docks at this hour! He'd be drinking in the Queen or the Saracen's Head. She stopped off at both to put her mind at rest. He was at neither, and no one had seen him since six o'clock, when he had been spotted leaving the Camel, lurching off in the direction of the river in need of a lie-down. Michael Robinson poured her a gin and told her he hadn't seen Jack since yesterday, which Grace knew was true. Michael Robinson has handsome hands, dependable, that look as though they make things and as if he tells the truth — which, indeed, he always does, though he chose not to divulge his suspicion that Jack might be entertaining a lady friend.

Assuring herself that this must indeed be what he was up to, she walked home, sunk in her own thoughts. At the corner of Cable and Cannon Street Road she came upon Nelly Holland. Nelly was a good girl. She kept herself clean and sober for the most part and looked after her ragged friends. She was searching for Polly Nichols, who had been thrown out of her lodgings the day before and had been seen that very afternoon, blind drunk, in a brand-new bonnet. Nelly was worried and wanted to put her to bed. Grace said she hadn't seen Polly all week and they parted company. Not five minutes later whom should she come upon, staggering, clutching the wall?

'Polly!' she said, gripping her by the shoulders, trying to penetrate her glassy eyes. 'Nelly's out looking for you. You must go back to MacMurphy's. She's a bed for you there.'

Polly Nichols struggled to focus upon the apparition before her, trying to make sense of what she was saying. She got Grace sharp for long enough to recognise her — though she couldn't have told you her name — before she saw two of her again, and laughed helplessly, a private fit, making sense impossible. Pointing her back the way Nelly had gone, Grace watched her weave down the road, cackling at nothing.

She listened to her own footsteps for another hundred yards or so, her brow knitted; told herself again she mustn't fret about him, he'd be safe somewhere. If only he would turn up. She was sure she wouldn't sleep until she saw him.

Drawing near to the lights of the Frying Pan she picked out a silhouette, unmistakable through the steam on the window, and stopped on the kerb. He was laughing, in his charming way, flashing his beautiful teeth. She saw him leaning in close to the girl, slipping an arm round her waist. Grace held her breath, frozen to the pavement, quite, quite foolish.

★ ★ ★

The London Docks raged until midnight when the blaze began to die down. There were scattered fires still as morning broke; the usual crowd formed, to see if there would be work today clearing the wreckage. They pressed their faces to the gate, staring in at the smoking ruin.

Some twenty-three miles away, resting his stout legs by the road and peeling an apple with all the meticulousness of a surgeon dissecting a rat, sat Mr Horatio Blunt. He was on his way into London to settle an ancient score, and meant to be there today. Now Mr Blunt might be an altogether crooked man, remorseless and greedy, but the very worst part of his character was the bitter grudge that he held, hardened with time, and he longed for the sweet taste of revenge. He might look from a distance a jovial sort of fellow — being large and ruddy — but if you'd asked him for directions you would spot the ugly glint in his eye. He crushed a small beetle underfoot before hoisting himself upright, and pressing on towards London.

13

The very first view that Grace had of London looked like a great grey cloud laying low across the horizon. As she saw it she wondered if she really wanted to go any closer. But she did, and was swallowed into a tangle of streets where the colour drained from the scenery, dim as if some giant had put a lid on the sky. Grey walls towered in the gloom at every turn, damp and rotting; rats and sewage ran in the alleys; dark and desperate people lurked in the streets having nowhere to go.

She spent the first night in Bermondsey, having encountered it almost directly. Our Grace was a resourceful woman. She could learn to fit with anybody and blended into the scenery. She kept the necklace next to her skin for the first week until she had found lodgings and connections. She meant to sell it, but she knew she'd have to wait. It wasn't the sort of thing you might shift in a week or two.

And then she read about it in the paper — or rather, a page of the *Echo* that was wrapped around the pudding she'd just bought: 'the centrepiece of Lady Stanhope's fine collection,' it said; ' . . . thought likely to have been taken overseas,' it said, ' . . . sure to surface on the international market in time'.

So down it went, under the floor again, and there it stayed. Grace was chased through her nightmares by Mr Blunt, and worried — at quiet moments — whether he was out in the dark somewhere, hunting her down. But the days passed without a sign of him, and little by little she stopped looking over her shoulder. A million people lived in London. She took a job at the market and, after a month, was breathing easy again.

It was in Bermondsey that she learned her trade under the most thorough instruction of one Harry Tate, whom she met in the Cherry Tree one dark evening as she took refuge from the cold wet world. She was in the habit of sitting face to the door so she saw him come in. He stopped short and stared at her, on account of her fresh country face and that she was in his seat. They got talking and hit it off straight away.

Harry was a fine professional thief and in a very short time Grace acquired new tricks: her natural criminal talent was smoothed and perfected. They worked different patches around Southwark Park or the Old Kent Road. Grace watched her back but not for Mr

Blunt any more. She thought of him less and less, swallowed in the great black city, dense warren of streets and brick, of tunnels and bridges and squares, with train tracks cutting over the buildings and the silver river snaking through its dark heart.

Blunt did make several fruitless attempts to find her: indeed, he was not satisfied. He seemed to hear his stolen treasure call to him at night, flashing red rays through his cloudy dreams from far away, and he would wake tormented, bilious with rage. The closest he came was Wandsworth, at the edge of the city. Though he knew she had come this way he saw plainly that there were a thousand places to look and his heart sank. He pressed on for a while, but within another mile London seemed bigger still. He drew his poor horse up, then turned away, vowing to return.

When he arrived at his gloomy home he sat brooding in his armchair, plotting his next move, his furious retribution. Presently a knock on the door revealed Ivor Squall, with intelligence regarding their next venture, gathered through the daily running of his accountancy firm — which, although small and somewhat mean, like Squall himself, had several considerable clients, providing him with invaluable scraps of information, details he exploited to their greatest effect. He acquainted Mr Blunt with the latest, and then listened, patiently enough — though he really had no choice, much less interest, in the matter — to the tale of indignation that followed, which he had heard already. He failed to understand quite why Mr Blunt was seething so — why such a rage over a silver tankard, even if it had belonged to his dear late mother? Though the girl would seem certainly to be a most insolent type.

★ ★ ★

He comes creeping through the dark, under the door in Bell Lane, towards the bed — as he does maybe once a year now — a malevolent shadow approaching. Grace struggles awake, swimming up through wet concrete. And she is fearful of closing her eyes again and fights sleep till it overwhelms her. Tonight she finds herself rising from her bed, haunted by a red shining light. Peaceful breathing fills the room. Her mind wanders down a crack in the floor, behind the stove, among the rubble and into a secret corner that only mice and cockroaches know, to see the deep red beauty, sparkling to itself in the dark.

She hasn't looked for five years or more. The thought that it may not be there makes her want to laugh out loud, or vomit. She stoops and prises up the short board. It groans sharply but the children don't stir. Placing it delicately aside she reaches under the stove, gingerly, as she is not fond of spiders, fingers searching the rubble. They close on cold hard stone and she pulls it from its grave and holds it up to catch the chinks of light from the street, forgetting herself, scarlet rays dancing on her face.

14

First thing the next morning Mr Horatio Blunt came at last to his destination, after ninety-nine long miles and seventeen years of waiting. He was in a filthy temper, having entered London the day before to encounter, almost immediately, roadworks at Wandsworth, which had delayed him — with bitter regret and loud cursing — late enough to miss office hours, even supposing he had not found himself lost at Nine Elms and again at Victoria. Kicking his horse, he had gone growling east to find a room — which had fleas.

He stopped outside 133 Oxford Street, and rang the little brass bell marked 'Squall.' After some moments shuffling footsteps were heard within and a pockmarked youth with shoes several sizes too large opened the door. His mouth hung open stupidly and he wore a threadbare dark suit he had outgrown two years ago, giving him the overall appearance of a lost and rather shabby penguin. He stared dumbly at Mr Blunt.

'I am looking for Ivor Squall. Is he within?' demanded Mr Blunt, glaring at the dull boy

— he hated slow-witted people. The spotty youth stepped aside to let him in and indicated the staircase, his mouth hanging open all the while. Mr Blunt took this dumb gesture to mean that Mr Squall's offices were situated on the upper floors of the building and ascended the stairs.

'Who is that idiot?' he enquired of his accomplice, once they had greeted each other.

'My nephew. He's slow.'

'Indeed.'

With rather mean glasses of sherry in hand they settled themselves into Spartan arm-chairs by the grey window, and Mr Squall began. In great detail and with considerable embellishment of his own central role, he recounted how he had single-handedly tracked the target to her very door, this last point somewhat let down by the absence of a specific address. 'I know for certain they reside within two streets either side of the hay market,' he said hopefully. 'I have made further enquiries around the district,' this was a barefaced lie, 'and can pinpoint a very particular district with some confidence.'

His confidence was waning fast, in fact, under the relentless pressure of Mr Blunt's stare: blank but somehow expectant, as if he was still waiting for the part he wanted to hear. As Mr Squall had already told him everything, he dried up, his voice trailing away weakly, and was possessed of a completely unanticipated sense of failure. He felt small and weak — which indeed he was, but now in his very own office! Though he had business with Mr Blunt from time to time, it was never in person (indeed the best way, he mused to himself ruefully).

He had certainly not remembered Mr Blunt to be quite such an intimidating figure. He seemed to cast a shadow over the room: the furniture seemed small suddenly; the desk had lost its meagre authority. Had he foreseen this he might have thought twice about bringing this beast of a man into his private office, to invade it thus, grunting quietly and staring into space, as if Mr Squall was not there! How dare he? It was in Mr Blunt's own interest that he had been good enough to invite him there in the first place — quite apart from the prospect of a decent reward. Indeed, he had banked on something handsome in it for him — which he was not so sure of now, as he sat on the edge of his chair, feeling as though he was made of matchsticks.

Mr Blunt continued to stare for an interminable two minutes without speaking while Mr Squall wondered where he should look, thought of a few possible things to say, which he quickly decided against, and remarked to himself how loud the clock ticked. At last Mr Blunt rose from his chair, Mr Squall stumbling up beside him, seeming to have shrunk since he last stood up.

'You can show me there now,' said Mr Blunt, 'while the iron is hot.'

'I am afraid I have some extremely pressing matters to attend to this afternoon, appointments that have been fixed for some time that must be seen to without delay,' ventured Ivor Squall, timidly. 'Would five o'clock be convenient for you?'

This futile assertion was met by another granite stare as Mr Blunt made for the door, Mr Squall dripping in his wake.

★ ★ ★

If you have ever woken to find that the ceiling seems too close, the cracks and dirt all too clear as you open your eyes, and instead of getting about your daily business, protected under the collective illusion that what we do matters at all, you want to spill hot tears at the hard world, and for time lost, and for how wrong you have been and just how sharp everything feels, you will know how that Wednesday morning was for Grace. She covered it well by bustling around the fire and generally busying herself with chores.

Jack was all over her thoughts and she was dismayed to find that she missed him. She saw now what a tricky position she might be in. Already it seemed she had gone too far to avoid heartache and she kicked herself for indulging in such a nonsense, becoming lost in its charm. She felt as if she had been cheated at cards. When one is miserable, she reasoned, one cannot mope about the house: one must do something simple and useful or jump in the Thames and be done with it. She went out with Daisy for apple fritters.

* * *

Not five minutes after they had left, Jack Tallis happened along to knock at number twenty-eight. He had woken that morning with Grace in his head and come to find her as soon as he had swallowed his breakfast pint. He was met by Jake, who pushed his grubby face out of the door to say that he didn't know where his ma had gone. She had told him but he had not been listening. He slammed the door before Jack could leave any message, not out of rudeness but an urge to finish his marble practice before she returned to shout at him for not sweeping. Jack considered the outside of the door, reflecting on how he seemed unable to find her when he wanted to.

★ ★ ★

As August was fair and quite warm, so September was a dark, heavy blanket. The sun struggled through the cloud as if it was going out. The dark air seemed fitting for the dreadful news. Nelly had not found Polly Nichols in time to take her indoors to bed. She turned up, all right, on the front page of every paper. It was difficult to avoid the ghastly details — they were thrust in your face, shouted on every corner.

'What happened, Ma?'

'Don't worry about it, darlin'.'

'Is it a murder?'

'Let's go and get cake.'

★ ★ ★

Ivor Squall took a hansom cab to Whitechapel with Mr Blunt — reluctantly. He made it as plain as he could that he really must get back to his desk by twelve. One o'clock at the absolute latest.

★ ★ ★

The Hammer girls wandered along hand in hand and ate seed cake, looked at pigeons and sat on the bench by the churchyard, like matching gloves in different sizes, watching the local girls go round.

The wide Whitechapel Road was full as usual, populated this morning with relentless haycarts and country bumpkins, fat and swarthy, with their arms like great hams. Grace didn't dip farmers often, they always had dogs for one thing, but one particular turnip did take her fancy, sat on his cart, large as a barge. A ragged knot of brasses had gathered at his feet, hung on his every word, as he supposed, with awe and wonderment, as he related details of his farm, two hundred acres — so he said — with trout in the river and plums on the trees. He had plainly used the trip to the city as an occasion to drink himself stupid before nine o'clock and did not feel the eyes fixed on his pockets. Grace had robbed him not a month before. She watched as he barked at his cowering dog, clocked his wan-faced daughter sitting on the cart in her thin dirty dress that may have been pink once. They crossed the street towards him.

'Watch your toes under the cart, darlin'.'

Grace and Daisy drew in and joined the circle, waiting for the group to break a little, some distraction or movement. It happened

171

presently. The farmer made a grab at the heaving female flesh in front of him and caught a handful that happened to be Lucy Fear's breast. She slapped him hard.

'Dog face!' cried the drunken farmer, and a small riot broke out, scuffling and slapping between him and the girls, screeches, and shouts — 'I'll put your eyes out!' 'Stick that, you filthy cur!' As they struggled, Grace threw herself against him, as if she had been shoved from behind, and lifted the farmer's wad from his waistcoat. Daisy, with her little eyes at pocket level, saw everything, lightning fast though it was. This was the first time she had noticed her mother dip somebody's pockets. Being a clever girl she knew instinctively not to say anything just then, but Grace was in for it after.

'Ma, why did you take that man's money?'

For the first time in her long life Grace was dumbstruck. The only sensible response she could muster: 'Do you think I shouldn't have?'

'No.'

'Never mind it now.'

★ ★ ★

Ivor Squall became nervous as they approached Whitechapel, knowing with dreadful inevitability that what he had to show for his bluff would be inadequate, and seeing no way out of this imminent difficulty. He tried to cover this by talking a lot about the area as they went along, most of which he made up as he did not know it well.

Horatio Blunt's face was stone, not remotely impressed or, indeed, giving any visible sign of having heard a word. He looked out of the window at the slurry of East London: puddles of horse piss, wretched children, sleeping bundles of rag. Somewhere in this pigsty he would find that bitch and take his revenge. 'Are we nearby?' he barked, cutting quite across what Mr Squall was telling him about the local vegetable market — which, to be fair, was not interesting.

' . . . they really are very good with cold meats or even . . . Oh, yes, quite near, quite near now, yes, we are.'

'How near *exactly*?'

'Just another half-mile or so,' stammered Mr Squall, peering down the road.

★   ★   ★

The foul air had not dissuaded the crowds from Petticoat Lane, tramping through the filthy puddles, with fine drizzle dampening their clothes and their lungs like cold steam; the Hammers poked about the market

173

unconcerned. The boys ducked about in the fog but it was too early for their sort of mark to be out. They never stole from traders — they were hard-working people who deserved every penny, and if you were caught fleecing one you were in boiling water. Grace and the boys were so tidy that most of the locals never knew how they got along — they supposed she ran a brothel in Wentworth Street.

They stopped and bought chestnuts and hot tea. The baked-potato man leered at Grace, which put her off buying any. He was handsome enough but a touch grizzly and she'd had a bellyful with Jack and couldn't be bothered. Daisy wanted to warm her hands by his cart so Billy went with her. Potato Man offered her a slice of toast, which she accepted graciously.

Spitalfields seemed to drip with gloom that morning, damp and filthy, in mourning it seemed for poor Polly Nichols. Grace didn't want to think about her. Or Jack, though she knew full well he had been carrying on. She wished she hadn't seen him at it.

'Come on, Ma,' said Daisy, pulling her down Goulston Street towards the sweet-shop. Ten yards behind her a dark carriage rolled past. Its occupants: a wild boar of a man and a woodlouse. The back of her neck prickled; she shuddered as she might sucking lemon drops. The black clouds crowded overhead; a curious breeze caught her.

'Let's take a trip,' she said.

'Where?' said Daisy, after cheering loudly.

'To the Crystal Palace,' said Grace.

★ ★ ★

The carriage crawled along the kerb as the traffic stuck up Whitechapel Road, attracting several girls, reaching in at the window, smiling, thrusting their wares and then cursing them as they drove past. Deciding they were attracting too much attention, they alighted and carried on by foot, Ivor Squall reluctant, yet tempted by the prospect of more creeping about. Mr Blunt strode along behind him, stamping to hurry him up. He wore a cruel sneer upon his flabby face, which repelled everyone in his path. They reached the corner where Ivor had last seen the Hammers. He slowed and wondered how best to proceed. It took Mr Blunt not a moment to realise that he was engaged in a wild-goose chase and he was not favourably impressed.

'Am I to take it that this is where your information falls short?'

'This is the very spot where I saw them

175

last.' Ivor tried to make his voice sound authoritative. 'They were heading in that direction.' He pointed down Osborn Street, boiling with carriages and crowds, bargaining, shouting, drinking, a great din rising in the gloom, a thousand voices chattering. Mr Blunt gave Ivor a look that turned his last shred of good hope to stone.

★ ★ ★

Daisy was impressed with this ready answer, though she knew nothing of such a place. A crystal palace! Why had Ma not mentioned this before? It sounded like something from a fairytale and she was wondering if she had heard right.

This proposal was a stroke of genius on Grace's part. The Crystal Palace being not a figment of fantasy, but the vision of a divine lunatic made manifest, as solid as you like: a confection of steel and glass so colossal that one must stand a mile off to see it all at once, as if, having drawn up the plans at its conception, a rabid frenzy had seized the architect, inspiring him to triple its every dimension. A magnificent, superfluous creation, it was built for no other purpose than to house its vast collection of wonders and to take one's breath away. No practical necessity troubled its invention. So was cricket born, and mountain climbing, art and seed cake. All that we are that is special and precious and extra.

To be pedantic the palace is not truly crystal, and houses no royal personage, but it is magnificent beyond one's wildest dreams; fit indeed for the Queen. The surrounding park counts among its attractions life-sized representations of the dinosaurs that were supposed to have walked the Earth before men — paling a little perhaps in comparison to the palace, but certainly worth a look. Everyone was eager for such novel sensation and fairly clamoured to visit; they washed their faces and put on their best hats. By eleven o'clock they were on the train.

★ ★ ★

The hands crawled round the clock for poor Ivor, dragged on a tour of the district, from pub to pub, into the afternoon. One o'clock came, and then two: his feeble assertions — he really must get back to his books as a matter of urgency, catch the post, the paper would be piling up on his desk — were swatted aside; by three o'clock he had given them up. Mr Blunt drank and glared at the company; he said nothing, but spat odd words under his breath. Ivor couldn't make them out but it made him jump and unnerved him thoroughly. He glanced at the ogre, brooding silently into his jug.

★ ★ ★

In the Princess Alice the Wilson girl — she of the hatchet clan — spotted them. She had an eagle eye for a new face and pointed them out to her boyfriend, who was a member of the Wilson gang and went by the name of Dog Brown, on account of his thick neck and pointed teeth. From time to time he ran errands for a particular lady (if we might call her that for now) in Limehouse.

They were a strange-looking pair, sitting in the corner side by side. Few words were exchanged between them; the little rat-like man wore an expression of utter despair. His brutish companion sat staring ahead, gulping rudely at his ale. A cloud of menace hung around him. The rat man twitched in his shadow, eyes darting here and there. Dog Brown wondered what they were after and if he might help.

★ ★ ★

The dinosaurs most certainly did not disappoint the children, or Grace for that

178

matter. They crouched in the park, in shallow pools, with spiny backs and grey-green skin, big mouths full of teeth, frozen mid-roar, in perpetual attack. Large aquatic beasts with elongated jaws devoured the smaller ones, their children, so it appeared.

'Look at that duck,' said Jake.

'Did they have ducks then, Ma?'

'No, darlin', I don't think so.'

'Well, they didn't have people,' said Jake, with some authority.

'No people?'

'No, not even one.'

And there was the Crystal Palace, tall above them, a million sparkling panes, spectacular enough even to knock Grace out of her black mood. The weather had cleared — although it might well have been raining still in Whitechapel — and sunlight twinkled at them, caught in the glass. To Daisy this constituted a real princess's castle and she stood below it in awe and wonder, gazing at this vision, better even than she had imagined it from what Billy had told her on the train. (She was somewhat disappointed not to find a princess's bedchamber or throne, though there were very many other things that compensated for this oversight.) The fountains and cascades that lined the walk gave way to wonders inside; they stopped as they came through the grand entrance and gazed around them at the great hall, spacious beyond their imagination, shining with light. Displays of every modern endeavour were here, every marvel of the industrial age, treasures from every corner of the Empire. The boys looked at machines, the girls preferred the stuffed animals. They wandered through the Greek court, the Renaissance and the Alhambra, taking in the fountains, the statues and the exotic plants; they looked at silver and brass and brocade and spears, and as they came through the Indian jungle there were jewels, sparkling at Grace on silk cushions in shining cases, sunlit through the great glass ceiling high above her head.

'Look!' she said. 'An elephant!' complete with howdah and a stuffed monkey on his back. And just when they thought nothing could top that, the aquarium! They sat down to take refreshments in the Palm Court, eliciting snooty looks from a well-dressed couple at the next table. Grace gave them the dead-eye and Daisy bestowed her sweetest smile upon them. Fancy cakes came, and sandwiches with the crusts cut off, on a tiered stand with paper doilies.

Grace clocked Jake sizing up their neigh-bours as they dropped sugar lumps into their tea with silver tongs. 'Jake. Don't you dare,' she said.

'Dare what?' said Daisy.

'Dip that macaroon in your cup.'

He looked at her with his eyebrows up, feigning innocence. 'Yes, Ma.'

* * *

Little Jake Hammer had noticed that Grace has not involved Daisy in the family line of business as yet. He had asked her why but had no satisfactory answer. This confused him, as he could see no reason why Daisy should not be allowed to join in, and he felt a little sorry for her. He had started to learn the family trade at four, and he was sure Daisy was older than that now. Maybe girls were a little stupid, he surmised, and came to things later. Though Daisy could read already better than he. He decided he might teach her himself, so they could surprise their ma one day.

* * *

When the Hammer family could eat no more buns they wandered away across the grass, looking back every few steps, the autumn sun shining out from behind the clouds, tingeing their edges with gold. Grace and Daisy held hands, the boys laughed and dodged around them, wrestling each other to the ground.

They took the train home once Grace had sworn they would came again, and before too long. At Aldgate they stopped to buy pink spray roses from Lily Dixon. Lily Dixon has a sharp little face with huge eyes, spaced far apart, like the creatures children see at the bottom of the garden. She sells only one variety a day, but always beautiful, fresh and properly conditioned. If you changed the water every other day they would last for a week, a tip she would have been better not giving her customers.

'Hello, Charlie!' she said.

Charlie went a bit pink. The family made faces at each other.

'Hello,' he mumbled.

'Why are you shy?' said Daisy, to her poor brother, who grimaced at Lily and went a good deal pinker. Matching the roses, in fact. The family stood around in an expectant circle, making no sign of small-talk among themselves.

'Let's get these home and put them in water, then!' said Grace, to his relief. Lily said goodbye sweetly to everyone and on they went, Charlie trudging along trying not to look at anyone, the others trying not to snigger. Down Commercial Street they came upon Sally Ann Dunn who was upright at least. Daisy gave her a rose and an apple dumpling, which she dropped in the road. When they got back, there was handsome Jack Tallis on the doorstep, with nothing but a saucy grin.

★　★　★

As she watched him fast asleep, like the king of the bed, Grace marvelled at how this circumstance had come about and how she had not managed, though she had promised it to herself, to field the little tricks with which he had edged his way back in, to resist that smile, the silver tongue. He was just too damned charming. Even as you knew it wasn't true. He had made no mention of where he had been and Grace had not asked. She was sure she did not want to know. He had an angry cut above his eye, maybe three days old, and another across his cheek. He always looked like trouble coming. She slid under the blanket, musing on what it was that made such a man so attractive and how he looked so innocent asleep.

★　★　★

Ivor Squall got away from his imposing new companion as the clock struck eight, which was good going but seemed not a moment too soon. He could feel Blunt's blank stare on his back all the way down Folgate Street as he skittered away. Round the corner he collected himself, breath rattling alarmingly in his delicate lungs. Mr Blunt was a difficult customer. Dread set in Ivor's empty belly. He had stirred up something indeed. Much more than he had bargained for.

★ ★ ★

Mr Blunt returned to his fleapit lodgings, after letting his disappointment be thoroughly known, and sat on his infested bed with his head in his hands. He ground his teeth together, made fists in his hair, raged to himself inside at the impotence of his efforts.

★ ★ ★

Ivor Squall went to sleep in his office, which he liked to do on occasion: it made him feel safe. Peacefully, curled up under his desk, next to his precious stationery.

15

When the family woke up, faint sunshine was creeping into the room. Daisy made a beeline for Jack, jumping up next to him. 'Hello,' she said, with a savvy little smile, delighted to see him but keeping it reserved.

'Hello,' he said back, playing the same game.

Then they sat and beamed at each other. Daisy proposed first: 'Do you want to play?'

'What should we play?'

'Wolves.'

*　*　*

Mr Blunt woke to the sound of traffic, with a fresh feeling of urgency. He lay still for a moment, staring intently at the ceiling. The rage that had kept him up till late had subsided enough for him to think. He would comb the district methodically, street by street. Within a day or two he would surely come up with something. First he must call upon Squall, just to keep him on his toes, though he did not plan to enlist his help today, useless as it was. He rose, dressed and consumed a large breakfast of eggs and sausage.

He caught Ivor skulking from his office, surprising him.

'Argh! Good morning, Mr Blunt!' he grimaced, dropping the packages he was carrying. 'Did you sleep well?'

'I did not.'

'Oh,' said Ivor, scrabbling around Mr Blunt's great feet for his parcels. 'I am sorry to hear it.' Gathering them together at last, he drew himself upright, tentatively, into view, withering under Blunt's stare, along with several nice begonias in the window-box behind him.

'I shall be abroad in East London this morning,' said Mr Blunt, 'expecting satisfaction. We shall see.' And, with an ugly smirk, he turned towards Whitechapel and stalked off into the crowd.

★ ★ ★

'Ma killed this man once, you know. I saw her.'

Something so matter-of-fact in the tone of Daisy's definite little voice, stating this information as if it were not so very different from any other noteworthy topic, breathed a chill up the back of Jack's neck. It came

186

smack out of the blue, into the middle of a game of Snap. He wondered what in hell had set such a thought in motion. He knew it was surely true and couldn't find a word to say.

'She hit him with a bottle. Bang! And then he fell down and she hit him again. Don't tell because she doesn't want anyone to know.' Jack fixed on a corner of the carpet. It had a faded blue leaf pattern, the intricacies of which he had never fully appreciated, and a hole he had not noticed before. Then, from Daisy, not to reassure him but because it was the next thing that occurred to her: 'He was trying to steal us.'

'Oh,' he said.

'Do you want to do drawing now?'

'What should we draw?'

'Well, I don't know, do I? Let's get the paper and think of something.'

And so Jack drew dinosaurs, glancing at his clean clothes and wondering how soon they might be dry.

★   ★   ★

At the end of Bell Lane Mr Blunt was commencing a thorough search of the area in its tiniest detail. He drew himself up determinedly and even sniffed the air. He knew that Grace must dwell within a stone's throw of where he stood. On the corner of Commercial Street stood a couple of local girls. He thought he might ask them first. 'Good morning,' he said.

'Good morning to you!' said Mary Kelly, pretty thing. 'You're a nice rosy gent, aren't ya?'

'I'm looking for a woman. Perhaps you know her,' began Horatio. 'I — '

'Special, is she?'

'Is it a special woman you're after?' They cackled loudly. 'What's so special about her then?' Mary leaned down and tugged up the edge of her skirt; he caught a flash of her thigh under the black stocking, soft and luminous, lily-white, like the light of the full moon.

★ ★ ★

He thought of that white thigh again, several unsuccessful hours later, as he came back round to the same spot. Mr Blunt had never encountered such a labyrinth of alleyways and ramshackle dwellings as made up the East End of London. It had seemed a good idea to divide his map into sections and do without Squall's help; he saw now that he had underestimated the task altogether, having covered just a crumpled inch or two, which, furthermore, did not seem to correspond entirely with the tangle of streets before him. Lost and thoroughly irritated, he resolved to drag Squall along with him tomorrow and retired to ease his worries for a short while in the Britannia, situated on the next corner. Solace from the wretched stinking hard world. In he went and ordered a pint of ale.

Now, sitting in the Britannia was a wise old man who could spot a scoundrel through the back of his head, and he clocked Mr Blunt directly, having not seen him about before. I wonder who he's after, he thought, for it seemed perfectly obvious to him the fellow was missing something. His drink stood neglected upon the table — from time to time he cast his eyes wildly around the room, settling on nothing. His cheek twitched of its own accord, he ground his teeth, his fists clenched as if they longed to strangle someone — he fairly brewed inside, boiling some awful grudge. The fellow evidently felt the attention for he stirred and looked around the bar again. His eyes settled contemptuously on Mr Byron Stanley, travelled from his green felt hat to his drink and away without interest. Then he drained his jar and rose from his seat to leave. The old man resolved to follow, though he was not usually given to interfering in other people's business. He had an ominous feeling about this restless fellow, what with the recent attacks. As Mr Blunt vanished into the street Mr Stanley slipped out after him.

He followed him to the edge of the City, where he watched him vanish down Barge Street, from the shadow of the Tower.

★ ★ ★

Mr Blunt made straight for Ivor Squall's office, where he rang the bell as hard as he could. Ivor, who was expecting a late delivery, answered the door himself, recoiling with horror when he saw Mr Blunt, glowering at him in the darkness.

'No joy?' said Ivor.

'I am not happy, Mr Squall.' A heavy gloom seemed to gather round the porch; the air grew cold, Ivor quaked in the doorway. 'Well, it is early days yet, Mr Blunt.' Oxford Street was ghostly quiet. 'Do forgive me for not inviting you inside. I am about to leave the office myself, you see,' he said, in his slippers. Blunt grasped him by the collar and pulled him up until poor Ivor's feet were barely touching the floor. He whimpered, shrivelling under the hot breath.

'I shall call on you every day, Mr Squall. You may be sure of it. Every day until I am satisfied.' He dropped Ivor on his doorstep and strode away into the night.

★   ★   ★

Across the city Charlie popped out, his hair combed, to see his new girl again, deaf to the queries and taunts of his merciless family, who assumed he was off to see Lily Dixon. He let them think so as it was better than having no privacy at all. He picked Elsie Brown up at the door of her lodgings in New Street and they went to the Oriental, where he spotted Jack Tallis in the smoky crowd, his arm round a woman, laughing his wide laugh, drinking beer and gin.

★   ★   ★

Stripe Wilkins entered the room so silently Miss Emmeline Spragg could swear he'd blown in through the window.

'The woman with Jack Tallis,' he said. 'She lives in Bell Lane with four children. She operates a family concern. Her name is Hammer. Grace Hammer.'

16

One might have imagined that the carnival of horror parading across the front pages every day now, fresh in the newspapers each morning, was some novel new entertainment for the delectation of the hungry public, such was the lurid detail and melodrama with which they competed for the ravenous audience. The *Illustrated Police News* ran a full three pages on the recent murders, including several pictures, depicting the grisly scenes of discovery, for the apparent purpose of their vivid imagining. What on earth will they print tomorrow? thought Grace. As if there wasn't enough sensation already for people disposed to such things, if not on their very doorsteps then surely a short ride away from their perfumed gardens to the scrag-end of their fair city. Grace was haunted by her last sight of poor Polly Nichols, in her brand-new bonnet, weaving down the Whitechapel Road into darkness. Once or twice she had dreamed of running after her, only to find she was gone.

★ ★ ★

Ivor Squall hid in his office for three days, breaking cover only to scurry home — very early or very late — while Mr Blunt scoured Whitechapel, loitering at street corners, engaging the locals, making what he hoped were casual enquiries, without any luck at all. This infuriated him on many counts, the least of which was that he loathed the district, though he suited it well. It beggared belief that of the very few who thought they might know a Grace Hammer, none was able to be specific about where she lived, or any more informative than to enthuse about what a lovely family the Hammers were. He felt himself sicken as he smiled along, keeping up whatever long-lost-relative story he had invented. *Where was she?* Had she given him the slip? Waiting and failure were feeding his viciousness. He felt he would grab her by the throat when he found her and shake her like a rat.

He stopped at the end of Church Street and clenched his fists. He would catch Ivor Squall before he left his office tonight. Outside the Ten Bells Mary Kelly was basking in the lamplight.

She took him down Red Lion Court, rather than to her room. She didn't like the look of him. Down the dark alley past the heaving shadows, white thighs in black stockings. He was rough and his hands felt damp. After soiling poor Mary's skirts he felt not soothed but rather stoked; he strode down Brick Lane, growling at the evening, and fuelled himself in the Frying Pan. Mr Byron Stanley watched him go from under his green felt hat.

★　★　★

Ivor Squall was tidying away his stationery for the night, with difficulty — he had taken to working in the back room (which was more of a large cupboard) so that his candle would not be visible from the street, and nothing was in order — when the bell rang. The sound shrilled up the back of his ears and tugged at his scalp. He froze, with his precious envelopes clutched to his chest. He need not ask himself who that might be. Trembling, he crept upon his hands and knees to the front window and peeped out. Below on the step was the dread shape of Mr Blunt — unmistakable even from Ivor's curious aerial view — grunting and cursing at the door. Ivor cowered below the sill and listened to his own heart thumping until he heard the heavy steps retreat, rumbling east.

★　★　★

A knocking, weak but urgent, brought the goblin to her door, cursing the absent fellow she had posted to answer it while she took stock upstairs. Ivor Squall was lurking on the slick stairs, undulating.

'Good evening, Emmeline,' said he, with a glutinous smile, little rodent hands clenching as if he was counting invisible money. 'I wonder if you might spare me a moment.'

It was most unusual for Ivor to call upon Miss Spragg at home. She looked him up and down, shrinking him a good foot further as he writhed on the step.

'Why, of course, Mr Squall. Do come in. I've some sausages cooking. Perhaps you might eat with me.'

'How kind, thank you, but no,' said Ivor, who never ate in company.

'Now,' she said, settling herself into a bundle, poking at the rancid frying pan, 'what brings you to Limehouse, Mr Squall?' She knew it was something desperate. 'An unexpected pleasure indeed!' She beamed with such glee at Ivor that he quite mistook her meaning and the awful notion flashed through his mind that she had taken a shine to him. He wanted to turn tail and run but he was, indeed, desperate.

'There's a woman I'm looking for,' he said, surprising himself, and Emmeline Spragg, with his boldness, 'by the name of Hammer.'

She looked inside his head with her black eyes. 'Hammer,' she said. 'Hammer.' The sausages hissed in the pan. 'I'm afraid I shall disappoint you, Mr Squall. I know no Hammers.'

Ivor seemed to deflate as she said this, the weight of the world on his shoulders.

'Is it very important Mr Squall?'

She never seems to blink, he thought. 'Perhaps,' he said, carefully. 'She is wanted most urgently on the business of a special client. Most urgently indeed.'

'Evidently.'

Miss Spragg took a sausage from the pan. Brown grease dripped down the fork on to the putrid wool of her gloves.

'Won't you sit down and make yourself comfortable, Mr Squall?' He did so, touching as little of the chair as was reasonably possible. 'I expect your special client will be offering some reward. On such important business!'

'Well, yes, perhaps, I expect so, yes, they might.'

'So, who is it wants to know?'

He found he was quite unable to sit up straight, much less look Miss Spragg in the evil eye. 'Ah, ha ha ha ha!' was his best effort.

Her eyes twinkled black at him. 'Are you

not at liberty to say?'

'Well, exactly the point I was coming to, Emmeline,' he said. 'Most regrettably not.'

'Regrettable indeed.'

Ivor Squall is a tiresome little man, thought Miss Spragg, after he had scuttled out — with a little sympathy perhaps for his predicament: he seemed so very agitated. She was human, after all. She cackled at the very idea, black blood oozing through her veins. Tiring of this whimsy she turned her villainous thoughts to the woman Hammer — such a private creature — and why the business had thrown Mr Squall into such a frenzy. He would crack for sure, eventually. She might keep a special eye on the Hammer family.

17

Mr Blunt had spent a fruitless week in Whitechapel. Grace was known to most in the district by her first name only, being a secretive soul, and he had had no luck so far. He was a changed man — indeed, a different colour altogether, the country bloom fading in his cheeks. He had been tempted down several dark alleys and enjoyed the local female company, which soothed his temper in short bursts. At night he stalked the district, a great looming shadow, glowering and muttering to himself. He growled at people on street corners; women felt afraid and crossed the road. Grace heard talk of this sinister fellow; she didn't pay it much attention. She felt glad she hadn't come across him.

Blunt does not know that on Saturday he walked past Jake playing marbles in Brushfield Street, and on Thursday he would have come face to face with the entire family at the market, if he had kept on down Wentworth Street instead of ducking into the Princess for a quick one. He had missed Grace again just that morning outside the butcher's.

All the week, as he pursued his task, Mr

Byron Stanley — who could spot a scoundrel through the back of his head — traced his every move, from under his green felt hat. More than once he was almost discovered.

★　★　★

'So! How's Lily?' said Grace over Sunday dinner, in the way that mothers do, which makes you want not to tell them anything. Charlie cringed. A blush started but didn't bother past his ears. 'She's keen on you! I saw her by the pawn shop and she asked after you. Told me to give you this.' She presented him with a red rosebud from Lily — clearly a wicked sort, given to teasing.

'She's not my girl!' he protested.

'Do you think she's pretty?' This, of course, from Daisy who was fascinated by the strange adult world of courting and secrets, having recently become aware that sometimes things were going on to which she was not party. She knew how to flirt as all little girls do, and loved handsome men, but knew that there was some other mystery attached just for grown-ups. She wondered what it was that made them laugh that way, and knew she was not in on the joke. However, this is the way of things for small children and, equipped with cast-iron perseverance to deal with their daily ridicule, they are hardened to it. So, instead of feeling left out, she pursued her enquiries.

'Did you kiss her?'

Everyone laughed and she wondered why it was quite that funny. Charlie thought he had dodged the question when Jake dived in.

'Well, did ya?'

'Not Lily!'

'Elsie, then!'

'Which one's Elsie?'

'I might 'ave.'

Daisy wondered how he didn't know.

'He did. He did! He kissed her!'

'Leave him alone!' said Grace — a fine thing for her to say since it was she who had started it. The brothers jeered on for a moment or two. Daisy watched intently, with her serious button face.

'All right, it was Elsie and I did kiss her.'

Further riotous enjoyment was had from this admission, only Daisy fully retaining her composure. Incisively she cut straight to the next relevant point. 'Can we see her?'

'No!'

'Why? Is she ugly?'

'No!'

'Where does she live?'

'New Street. St Philip.'

'Oh.'

Daisy had not reckoned on getting an

answer to any of her questions and had no idea where New Street was anyway so she was flummoxed into silence. For a moment.

'Which house?'

The whole room laughed again; someone touched her hair; she waited patiently for them to calm down. She was formulating her next line of enquiry when there was a sharp knock at the door.

They opened it to find Nelly Holland, red-faced and breathless with news. 'Grace they've found another one this morning! In Hanbury Street. With her heart torn clean out of her chest!'

Jake was already halfway out of the door. She grabbed him by the scruff. 'And where are you off to, young man?'

'I want to have a look.'

'I'm sure you do, but you'd only be satisfying your nasty curiosity.'

'Oh, Ma!'

As she turned away from him, to catch Daisy jumping off the table, he slipped out through the door, just too quick to catch.

'JAKE!'

'Don't worry, Ma, I won't be long!'

'Oh, Charlie, sweetheart, will you go after him?'

* * *

Miss Annie Chapman had lost her two front teeth courtesy of a customer in a dark alley. Now she was hanging by a hook on the mortuary wall having her photograph taken, for it was she who had perished in the back yard of twenty-nine Hanbury Street, discovered by poor John Davis, who was still reeling from the shock. When the boys reached the scene of the crime they found the landlady selling tickets by the passage door to enter and see the bloodstains. They didn't go in, though Jake was ready to lift the sixpence.

★   ★   ★

'I've seen him lurking about by St Mary's lately. You want to watch out for him. He's that smart type who likes to slum it — coat tails, stick, all that. Most of the girls have shied well off and so should you. He's a nasty fucker. Mary Kelly entertained him last week. God knows, she'll consort with any piece of scum for a shiny coin. Though she barely remembers a thing after eleven o'clock any day, she said she wouldn't have him the next time — she couldn't say why. Just that he was cruel. I asked her what he'd done and she said nothing in particular, just that he'd made a very strange proposal, something she didn't want to repeat. Well, what that could be if

202

Miss Kelly doesn't want to repeat it you can't imagine, can you? He comes from Belgravia, she says. I'd stay well away from him, and so should you.'

Nelly Holland leaned back against the wall and sighed, wondering if any of this was going into Sally Ann Dunn's stupid head. The gentleman to whom she referred had been seen about a few times of late and had given one or two of the girls quite a turn. He had grabbed Busy Liz from behind in George Yard, stepping out from the shadows. As she struggled free and fled, he laughed her down the street — a sickening laugh by all accounts, varying from brutish to inhuman with the storyteller. Though Grace had managed to escape the finer details, she had heard he'd asked Mary if he might wrap his hands round her throat and squeeze just a little while he was about his business. As many of the gentlemen slummers made unusual requests this wouldn't normally be worth a mention, but in the current chill wind it cloaked him in suspicion, along with every second man in the street.

Sally Ann Dunn cared nothing for what was round the corner but her next drink. She wasn't one to fret about troubles ahead or hope for better luck next time — it never came. This much she could count on. She had never had a present or a surprise that she could remember and didn't want to start now. The hollow girls who haunt the alleys, clutch at straws, lost each in their own world kept her company: making desperate alliances, loud threats, and sleeping where they dropped, fights breaking out round their blissful heads.

That evening she was conscious still, it being barely seven o'clock. She had done well that day, having earned two shillings and drunk but half of it. Now Nelly was intent on telling her about poor Polly Nichols and this monster on the loose and she didn't want to think of it. She was careful enough anyhow, she reckoned; you could tell a strange fellow by the look in his eye. She stood up to get another drink, the blood rushing to her feet, the tiles spinning round her.

★ ★ ★

Ivor Squall had managed to give Mr Blunt the slip that afternoon, or so he thought, which made him feel rather clever. In truth, his usefulness had been exhausted now that Mr Blunt could find his own way around Whitechapel and he had not tried particularly hard to locate him for the last couple of days, or even drop by his office to torment him further. Ivor had been asked so many times if he was quite sure it was Grace he had seen that now he was not. That evening he had anticipated a visit and left the office early, and was at that moment on his way home to enjoy a nice piece of boiled beef he had left over from yesterday. He prefers his food simple and holds no truck with fancy seasoning, though he likes a bit of mustard. He twisted his wiry mouth into as much of a smile as it would go at the satisfaction of being alone for dinner, and rubbed his rat hands together, again.

★ ★ ★

Mr Blunt, too, was dining alone in the Britannia, on steak and kidney pudding, which was sufficiently delicious to have distracted him from all else. Lucky for Grace, though she knew nothing of it, except for a shiver that ran through her — as if someone was digging her grave. As Mr Blunt was lost in his gravy she passed right outside the window: if he could have reached through the glass he might have touched her head — though it was up in the clouds, thinking about Jack Tallis: who else? Grace had met him that day and had a drink or two, and more besides to remember him by; she found an idiotic grin on her face, as she had at intervals all afternoon. She'd been keeping Jack away from the house: Charlie had given him a frosty reception at his last visit and wouldn't say why. Grace wondered idly what he knew but she was sure she didn't want to ask. She drifted down Commercial Street, in a wistful bubble. As she neared the corner she felt someone skulking behind her. He hung back, measuring his steps, and quickened his pace as she did.

She turned left deliberately, away from home, and crossed the road heading for the Ten Bells. Sally Ann was inside the door, leering at a dusty bricklayer. He turned away from her broken grin back towards the bar, leaving her hazily forlorn. She spotted Grace coming in and latched on.

'Evening, Miss Sally,' said Grace, glancing behind her. Sally Ann started on the story of her latest misfortune. She's getting tiresome, thought Grace. She'd better not ask me for money today. Grace's shadow came in behind her and she met him with a hard stare. He was tall and well dressed, with greying hair and a groomed moustache, and looked not the slightest bit brutish or sinister but, rather, returned her look with startled embarrassment and averted his eyes. She watched him all the way to the bar and slipped out as he ordered a pint of ale. As she looked back through the door, Sally Ann was lurching after him, spilling someone's drink.

Red Lion Court was pitch black and quiet, save for the bestial grunting of two or three brides and their clients. Trying not to hear she made her way through, glancing behind her as she reached the bend. No one was following; just the dark shapes of the couples moved slowly behind. Grace Hammer had not carved out a decent life for herself among the flotsam of East London by waiting for someone to bite her first. Her safety after dark was secured by the clear head she kept on her shoulders and the razor that lived in her pocket.

Sally Ann took all of a minute to discourage the mystery gentleman from staying or buying her a drink, with her missing teeth and her Hell's breath. Outside the door he looked this way and that, wondering where Grace had gone.

Grace came out into Hanbury Street and kept to the shadows all the way down to Brick Lane where she turned right, then right again at the church, heading for home. She was halfway down White's Row when she heard footsteps and looked behind to see a tall figure marching briskly towards her in the gloom.

'Excuse me, Miss,' he said, in a smart accent, not six feet away now. As he closed in, she swung round and smacked him in the face with a furious fist and before he could catch his breath she followed it with the other, bloodying his nose all the way down his starched shirt-front. Then she took off down the alley, grasping the razor in case he gave chase, which he did not.

In fact, he was a gentleman of unusual tastes, who was rather shy and had been hanging around the district hoping for satisfaction. He had seen Grace earlier in the day and mistaken her for a lady who might help him, choosing her largely on account of her kind, direct face. This seemed ironic to him as he knelt in the street, blood dripping from his nose. He was sure he would find it amusing one day.

★ ★ ★

At home, Daisy and Jake were wide awake though they were not supposed to be, in the back room, whispering. Billy had fallen asleep in front of the fire and Charlie was out. Jake was showing Daisy new games — magic tricks: how to fan the mark, brush against them to find the wallet; how to sandwich, distraction, sleight of hand.

* * *

Mr Blunt finished his dinner and shoved aside his plate, belching soundly.

Across town Ivor Squall finished his also, and washed his plate and cutlery fastidiously in his tiny sink. After tidying his desk, he sat down to enjoy the peace and quiet.

In the Britannia Mr Blunt stared into his beer, fuming silently at Squall's disappearance, plotting to catch him the next day. Such an air of simmering rage surrounded him that no one sat near. Into the pub fell Miss Lucy Fear. She had been thrown out of the Ten Bells after baring her tits for the customers' delectation. Staggering by the door she surveyed the bar, which was swimming before her, and made a beeline for the stranger by the window.

'Hello, love, buy a girl a drink?' she slurred.

Blunt glowered at her from under his eyebrows. Without a word he rose and struck her hard across the face, one way, then the other, and left her on the floor of the pub, the landlord gaping after him like a drowning fish.

18

The Hammers did so well on Monday that they knocked off early and bought a chicken. They had gone home and got it roasting and Grace had run out to get potatoes. On her way back she was crossing Commercial Street, thinking about browning chicken skin — and there he was. Just his head and shoulders through a pane of glass as her eyes wandered across the road, unmistakable, ominous, mean as a prize pig. She gasped and almost pissed herself, right there in the street. Horror ran up her back like a swarm of ants, crawling through her hair. He was sitting at the window in the Britannia, and who should be across the table from him but Jack. If they had looked out at that moment instead of lifting their beers to their greedy gullets they would have seen her, frozen to the spot, narrowly missed by the brewery cart. As it rumbled past, Jack glanced up and saw her. He did not wave or smile but widened his eyes, staring urgently at her for a second. Then she turned about-face and walked away.

★   ★   ★

The first thing she did, as if in a dream, was to look for the children. She ran straight home where Charlie was keeping an eye on the bird.

'Where are they?'

'Somewhere about. What's the matter?'

'Go and get them in.'

He came back with Billy and Daisy just as the secret board behind the stove was back in its place.

'What are you doing, Ma?'

'Nothing.' They looked at her funny, she thought.

'Where's Jake?'

'He's gone again,' said Daisy, rolling her eyes as if she was his mother. Grace told them to pack useful things for a short trip and their favourite toy, and not to ask questions for now. Then she flew to the Frying Pan to speak to Horace Daley.

★ ★ ★

Mr Horace Daley is the sort of man with whom you would entrust your very head if you had to leave it somewhere. If you had some extremely valuable item that you did not want to lose, a fine piece of jewellery, for instance, you could wrap it in rag and string and hide it in his cellar, in the sure knowledge

211

that it would be there when you wanted it next. You could even be sure that not only would he keep it safe, but also that if you put it into his hands he would not unwrap it to see what he was hiding, though you could hardly expect such restraint.

'Horace, I must leave London today,' she said, in the privacy of the back room. 'If anyone asks for me in the next week or two, tell them you never heard of me.'

'Right you are,' he said, clenching his red hands.

'And can you keep something for me?'

'Is it something special?'

'Very special indeed.'

'You can put it downstairs.'

* * *

In the back room of the Frying Pan, under the carpet, is a trapdoor which leads to the cellar. Down in the far corner a low passageway runs under the next building. Without a lantern you cannot see your hand in front of your face. If you cared to crawl with your head down to the end of the tunnel you would come out into the cellar of the house across the street, which connects to the shop next door and from there all the way under Brick Lane to Whitechapel Road. You have to squeeze through parts of the tunnel so it is not for the faint-hearted, or the fat, but you can stay down there, all right, if you don't mind a spider or two. It is said to have been used by Dick Turpin himself. No one bothers with it much any more. It is, however, a fine hiding-place: Grace makes use of it now and then, reckoning it the safest place in all the maze of London Town.

So down the stairs she went, under the trapdoor — while Mr Daley saw to his customers — trying not to touch the damp bricks.

As she kissed the beauty goodnight she fancied she heard it breathing, pulsing in time with her blood. And then, a sigh — or a rustle — behind her: a mouse! Or perhaps the edge of her skirt, brushing the wall; and she looked sharply into the darkness, into nothing and felt foolish. For now she could hear her own heart beating, and her own breath. Silence.

Then she bricked the ruby, still warm, into the wall.

★　★　★

'Where are you heading for?'
'I don't know yet.' She hadn't thought further than getting away. 'Wherever the first train goes.'

213

'From Whitechapel?'

'No.' Her hands were still trembling round her brandy glass. 'Liverpool Street's safer. Or St Pancras.'

Horace Daley regarded her quietly for a moment as if he was reading her mind. 'The railway system is a marvellous convenience,' he said at last. 'Busy, too.' He sipped his ale delicately, like a lady taking tea, setting the jar down as if it was a china cup. 'Why don't you take one of Big Roy's boats? Who would think of that?'

The idea hit her like an anvil falling from the sky. The river! Who *would* think of that?

★ ★ ★

Roy Harman is the nearest thing to a giant in the real world: you have to crane your neck to get a proper look at him. At the last count he stood seven foot two in his size-sixteen boots, and half as wide across. He had started growing in earnest when he was two, outstripping his big brother the following year — people thought him stupid as they assumed he was the elder. He topped five foot as he turned six and earned a man's wage at the docks by the time he was twelve. He'd done well for himself: the boats that Mr Daley mentioned were a fleet of lighters and

214

barges that unloaded cargo for the East India Company. Roy was handsome enough but had had only one woman in his life, on account of his sensitive heart and her being the only girl big enough, at six foot three, to consider taking him on. It was fortunate indeed that they made a perfect match, still standing sixteen years last week.

* * *

As Grace left the Frying Pan she skulked along the street, uncomfortable as if she were naked. She hurried home. Outside the Ten Bells were Sally Ann and Mary Kelly, who shouted greetings to her as she passed — they were in good spirits, having had no money for gin the night before and just earned the first that evening. She tried to wave inconspicuously, hurrying away as they called after her down the street.

They were to leave under cover of darkness that evening — Grace spent the rest of the day indoors with the curtains drawn. When Daisy asked her why she would not come outside she replied that she was spring-cleaning the house and enlisted her help. Never had the hours ticked by so slowly for Grace, who looked at the clock every seven minutes. By two they had swept and dusted everything and made the beds and Grace had to feign exhaustion as an excuse to stay in and read the paper. She avoided looking at the clock for as long as she could bear it in the hope that the time would pass more quickly but it did not. They folded the laundry, played rummy, sat on the bed. Daisy grew bored with Grace and ran outside with Billy to play, with strict instructions to stay where Grace would see them if she put her head outside the door.

Happily, she had no intention of doing so. Not ten minutes later Mr Blunt turned the corner from Wentworth Street and started up Bell Lane. He was in an uncommonly good mood, having caught up with poor Ivor Squall that morning and left him a gibbering wreck. This was the third street in his section for the next day — his search had begun again, a little wider, and he was getting ahead of his schedule as his enjoyment in prowling the neighbourhood grew. It tickled him to give people a turn in the gloomy alleyways at dusk, pulling his hat down and glaring menacingly from under the brim as he went past, revelling in the ominous sound of his footsteps, heavy and slow, imagining he heard feet skittering away before him, like nervous animals. And so his search had become less tiresome and more thorough. He had walked up Bell Lane just two days ago, quite early, and it had been much busier. Today there were just a few grubby children in the street and one or two old women on their doorsteps.

Though Mr Blunt had never doubted before that Grace Hammer's likeness was burned into his memory and that he would know her anywhere, his conviction had begun to waver. He had looked at too many women — his head spun with faces; they blended into each other. Once or twice he had thought he saw her, only to be confounded. Sometimes he could not picture him: which frightened him: he felt he was losing pieces of his mind, breaking up and drifting away from him like Madeira cake in a stream. He prowled up the street, scowling, past the little girl with the blue ribbon. She watched his feet approach, frowning at him as if he was a stormcloud, his bulk casting a gloom over her game.

★　★　★

Across East London Ivor Squall wrung his handkerchief, twisting it round his spindly hands, dabbing it against his bursting head.

'He is a most persuasive man. Imposing.' Here he shuddered from his shoulders to his restless fingers and back again. 'A *most* imposing man. He has called upon me again only this morning, without announcement. He really is most insistent.'

Miss Spragg eyed the sweating brow and the jittery hands. 'I only wish I was able to help you, Mr Squall,' she said, 'but certainly I shall keep my ears to the ground. Will you have an egg?'

'Thank you, Emmeline, no.'

'It is a shame indeed that you must keep your client secret.'

'Why, Emmeline, I am sure you must understand,' slimed Ivor Squall. He was going on to suggest that he was acting out of personal integrity but stopped short with a feeble laugh. 'I really must protect my own interests, you see. Of course, for the right information I should certainly cut someone in for a share of the benefits. If only someone knew where to find this cursed Hammer woman.'

'If only,' said Miss Spragg.

'I shall certainly not let go of it, you see.'

'Indeed.'

★   ★   ★

At seven o'clock the Hammer family left their home, managing somehow to elude the watchful eye of nosy Mrs Jacob, who was giving her twitching curtain a rest. Grace set a brisk

218

pace and kept her head down. The pubs were full and most people merry, paying them no heed. They looked as though they had been evicted from their lodgings that evening. Grace carried Daisy for some of the way as she was tired and wanted to go nowhere and the boys carried the luggage: Charlie blankets and clothes, Billy their personal things and Daisy's scruffy dog, and Jake some cheese and bread, and the roast chicken, trickling warm grease down his chest.

Never had she felt so conspicuous than on that walk from Bell Lane to the Eagle Wharf, Wapping, as if she was spot-lit: people seemed to look at her strangely as they went by, as though they knew something. The children, except Charlie, had no idea that anything might be wrong: she had told them they were taking a surprise trip and that they were to ask no more questions, a ploy that had worked a treat so far.

Every step towards the river seemed to take them further into a foreign land. The buildings loomed higher, warehouse blocks climbing as Whitechapel vanished behind them, their steps advancing into darkness. At Cable Street they crossed the edge of their patch. How we live in the same square mile every day, she marvelled. What village idiots we are, though we may live in the sprawling metropolis! She kept straight on down Dock Street, wondering at the relief that started to fill up her lungs, walking into this exotic world as though she no longer had command of her feet. Out of the inn before them, springing out of the gloom like a light-house, piled a bunch of Chinamen. At the front of the group was Genghis Khan, roaring at the night, baring his teeth. His hair sprang in a thick dark plait from the top of his head, shaved all around like an island. Daisy clung to her hand, and they hurried past in a tight little bunch.

The next corner was Smithfield Street. Billy was struggling so Charlie took one of his bags and they stopped to get their breath, sitting on their luggage on the kerb. Grace cast her eyes over the moonlit street. Just across the cobbles was the spot where she and handsome Jack Tallis had kissed, that first night, on their way down to London Docks. She pictured herself, caught by the waist on the corner, in his strong arms. She got to her feet.

'Let's keep going.'

'Where to, Ma?'

'You'll see.'

★ ★ ★

Mr Blunt was back in Bell Lane. Unfortunately he had spent some of the afternoon in the company of a friendly but rather stupid girl named Molly Whelk, who visited an aunt in Bethnal Green every Thursday, much to the old lady's irritation, and enjoyed a port in the Princess Alice after. She told him quite innocently that she did remember a very nice Grace who lived on the Aldgate side of Commercial Street: she thought her name might be Hammer — on Goulston Street, perhaps, or Middlesex. Or Bell Lane.

It was dark now and lights had appeared in some of the windows. The sound of chatter floated out as Blunt stalked quietly past. No one else was in the street. He stopped by one of the dark houses and peered through the letterbox. All he could see was a bundle of laundry, or what may be a corpse. He moved past. Someone came running down the street. They slowed as they saw him, then hurried past. The next house was quiet and dark. He looked in at the window. Up the street ahead of him a dark figure knocked at someone's door. No one answered. They knocked again, and waited, then turned away.

★　★　★

Nightingale Lane was long and dark, warehouses on either side, dwarfing the family, casting them into gloom. At the feet of

221

the great walls huddled dark shapes, in bunches, a small fire here and there, prehistoric figures in flickering relief. Grace's imagination tortured her as they went past, the sound of footsteps behind them, dark shadows lurking ahead. She could see Blunt's face, leering at her. As they neared the bottom of the street they caught a glimpse of the river, shining like the light at the end of a tunnel. It vanished between towers of brick as they turned into the high street, the smell of it following them, lurking on the other side of the warehouses that lined the way, strange and enticing. As they came out on Wapping New Stairs the Thames opened out before them and they stopped still and held their breath.

The grimy buildings had fallen away, and sparkling water stretched away at their feet; the air hung clear around them. Lights on the opposite bank glittered like stars. For a moment nobody made a sound. Then they started pointing at things floating by.

'Look, a crocodile,' said Daisy.

'It's a dead person', retorted Jake.

'No, it isn't,' said Grace.

Sure enough Roy Harman was there. The children, deducing that they were to go on a boat, were consumed with excitement. They had never been on one before, never mind at night. Roy helped them in — it was sturdy but, as he put it, not too bloody heavy to row — settling Daisy with her dog in the stern, which had a little bench with a back to it so that she could make a nest with the blankets. The boys piled in and jumped about until Roy told them to sit still. He gave Grace directions, and wished them all the best of British luck.

'If you go east you'll have the tide with you till about one but you'll get more traffic, and bigger ships, which are a risky prospect, and you'll have to take a turn at Canvey Island before it grows too wide and the currents get tricky. If I were you, I'd go west.' He gave Charlie a friendly slap on the back that nearly knocked him overboard. 'You can row for your ma, you're a proper lad.'

They pushed away from the stairs, Charlie trying the oars, sculling away over the river, waving at Roy as he disappeared into the dark.

★   ★   ★

As they slid past Eagle Wharf a lonely figure on the quayside watched the boat glide away. From the shadow of the warehouse wall the goblin Spragg remembered the woman with the green ribbon. The mean eyes tracked the boat down the river, heading west.

19

'That's it, there.' Billy pointed. They peered into the gloom at Bermondsey on the south bank, gliding by on their left. Was that port or starboard? thought Grace absently, missing what Billy was saying, her attention brought back by noticing how intently Daisy was listening.

'He took himself there when his ma died.'

'Who?'

'Tommy Hanley.'

'Where?'

'To the Bermondsey casual ward.'

'What did she die of?'

'Drink.'

'Oh.' She digested this, wishing she had been listening, trying to remember who Tommy Hanley might be. 'How do you know where it is?'

'I went.'

'By boat?'

'No!'

'You went through that bloody tunnel?' exclaimed Grace, so that the boat rocked slightly.

'Yes.'

'What tunnel?' enquired Daisy.

'It's a tunnel under the river, darlin'.'

'What's wrong with the tunnel?' piped up Jake.

'It's under the bloody river! What if it leaks?'

'It's perfectly safe, Ma,' said Billy, patiently.

'Never mind that. So what were you and Tommy Hanley up to in Bermondsey anyway? How d'you know it so well?'

'Nothin'! I don't! I seen a map of the river! We're just going into the Upper Pool, see, that's Fountain Dock there, and once we're through that and past London Bridge we'll go west till Waterloo, that's about two mile away, and then round the big bend south, down past Westminster, right next to the Houses of Parliament, then Lambeth and Vauxhall where it bends west again, on towards Battersea, Wandsworth, Putney, Hammersmith and so on.' The family gazed at him with wonder.

'No flies on you, are there, my Billy?' Grace found nothing more to say, and marvelled at how her brilliant son could see London in his head as if he had grown wings and flown into the very sky above the Thames. 'So after Hammersmith what comes next?'

'Barnes and Chiswick, then Kew.'

'You're a good lad.'

'Thanks, Ma.'

'Don't you be going to Bermondsey any more, son.'

'Why, Ma?' he said, as if he didn't know.

'I'm sure you know very well.'

'Why shouldn't he go?' demanded Daisy.

'Because the people are unfriendly and most likely dangerous, my beautiful girl.'

'It's not as if we live in Mayfair ourselves,' observed Charlie.

'None of my children are to go to Bermondsey or in that bloody tunnel,' said Grace, loud and firm, sealing the subject shut. She remembered very well what a pit it was, unpopular even with gentlemen slummers. In fact, it was no rougher than parts of Spitalfields, but Londoners must always have some district they imagine to be worse than their own. She watched Jacob's Island drift past, notorious decaying rat-hole. Faint cries and shouting came from the rotten maze of timber, crazy world the colour of Thames mud.

* * *

Charlie did well at the rowing, though Grace was sure he had not done it before. They slid past the docks, sheltered in the dark. Odd lights in riverside windows and the faint glow of the moon through the grey paper sky lit the way. Daisy and Jake were mostly speechless, but Billy had plenty to say, keeping up a helpful commentary on the passing landscape: how the cranes worked, the new bridge, half built, the Tower of London.

'That'll never be a bridge,' said Charlie, as they passed by the Tower. 'The sides are going up too high.'

'It's a bascule bridge,' said Billy. 'It goes up when a tall ship comes in.'

'How?' said Daisy, razor-sharp as usual.

'I believe it's something to do with hydraulic power,' he replied, hoping to confuse her as he did not fully understand the idea himself.

How does he know all these things? thought Grace. There was traffic on the river but no police. Just past London Bridge she took the oars.

'Can I row the boat?' said Jake.

'Can I?' pleaded Daisy, chiming in straight away.

'Not now,' said Grace. 'Maybe tomorrow.'

'Will we go on this boat tomorrow?'

'Well, who knows?' she said mysteriously, confounding the little face.

They passed quickly under the railway and then Southwark Bridge, the wall high beside them, dwarfing the boat. They stared up at the ironwork arches, vast above them, stretching out to great stone piers that rose from the turgid water, and the river seemed huge now, stretching across to the other bank like an ocean, a great surging grey serpent writhing under them. Even Billy was quiet for a while as they pushed on.

Grace Hammer had a peculiar gift for rowing, which was just as well because there was a long way to go. Bridges followed — Blackfriars, Waterloo, Hungerford, Westminster — each a monument to the miracle of man, a soft creature of flesh without claws or significant teeth or strength, who commanded steel girders and great blocks of stone. The family fell each into their own thoughts. As they slid past Big Ben towards Lambeth the great bell struck ten. An uneasy feeling crept up through Grace's belly and settled in her chest — she felt small, a matchbox person in a tiny boat, under a giant eyeglass. The children were craning their necks up to the clock; they had forgotten their cold feet. She wondered when she ought to tell them that they were not turning back.

'Let me take a turn Ma,' said Charlie.

Daisy fell asleep first, of course, after crawling on to Grace's lap. She covered her with a blanket and stroked her warm head.

When he saw this Jake huddled next to her and fell into deep slumber not ten minutes later. Billy fought it for a while and gave in. Charlie rowed on into the night.

★ ★ ★

In a nook in the damp wall, warming her twisted hands before a poisonous fire that crackled and hissed with mouldy wood, sat the goblin of Blight Street, contemplating the events of the day. She had spent it well, being out for most of the evening on business down by the docks and as happy to return home as a scorpion might be to scuttle back to its carcass-strewn nest. But Miss Spragg did not savour its comforts: she crouched in the dark, musing upon the little group on the river. What a curious business. Such an hour to take a pleasure cruise! She would wager Jack Tallis knew nothing of it. There is something at stake indeed, she thought. She must squeeze Mr Squall yet harder for the name of his private client.

These musings were interrupted by a knocking downstairs — four slow knocks, a pause, two fast and two more. Dog Brown was at the door. He was expected.

After their business was concluded Dog assumed his best air of mystery. 'Something's come up that may interest you,' he said, pausing for effect. She waited, poker-faced, for him to get on with it. She was sure that what he had to say would be a disappointment. Dog Brown was not famous for his brain.

'The gent I saw last week in the Princess Alice, imposing fellow, you'll remember me mentioning him.' Indeed she did, and glared at him to save him telling her about it again. 'Name, he said, was Belmarsh.'

Another tedious pause.

'Will you finish this tale today or will I beat it from you?' she growled.

'Well,' said Dog, triumphantly, 'I happened upon him in the Britannia this afternoon, drinking by himself, muttering and staring out the window, a proper madman he looked. Anyhow, I got talking to him and he's frantic to get his hands on this woman he was asking about before — Hammer, her name was — and did I know of her, he asks me again. Well, I'd still never heard of her, I told him.'

Miss Spragg's ears pricked and a curious nerve twitched in her neck. She maintained her air of indifference as Dog Brown blundered on.

'He wouldn't let it rest. And I was wondering who she was and what he was after, thinking it must be a matter of life or death the way he talked about her, eyes bulging — popping out of his head, they were. Never seen nothing like it. Life or death or a lot of money.'

'And then what?'

'Well, I'll tell ya. As he's got up to leave this paper's fallen out of his wallet. And I've had a proper look at it and it turns out he's not Mr Belmarsh at all.'

'There's a surprise,' said Miss Spragg.

'He's a Mr Blunt. Horatio Blunt. And I thought, Don't I know that name from somewhere? And then I remembered . . .'

Dog Brown droned on for several minutes more but the goblin was not listening. She herself had never made Mr Blunt's acquaintance but she knew exactly who he was, through the tentacles she spread over the south. Little wonder Ivor Squall was keeping his private client to his chest. Every top-rate fence knew the name: his reputation went before him with his bulging stomach. He was known for the superior quality of his merchandise — most particularly the fine jewellery in which he specialised, his area of expertise over the course of a long and distinguished career, for he was a lazy thief and would rather not run about the countryside with heavy silver if he could help it. Mr Blunt is renowned for carrying the very best pieces: flawless diamonds and purest gold. She kept this from faithful Dog Brown for the moment, disappointing him with her lack of excitement at his revelations.

'Could you find him again?' was all she said.

★ ★ ★

After Dog Brown had left, Miss Spragg sat very still for several minutes, like a crocodile watching its supper, as the pieces of the picture started to fit. Mr Blunt's urgent business must be something special indeed. Something very shiny.

Now, Miss Spragg was not to know that Mr Blunt had lost his pretty prize seventeen years ago and, supposing it long gone, was merely seeking his revenge. She assumed, reasonably enough, that the goods were knocking around somewhere, most likely in Grace Hammer's pocket. And knowing Ivor Squall quite well, she assumed, reasonably enough — but barking up entirely the wrong tree — that he meant to find the treasure and side-step Mr Blunt. Miss Spragg fairly boiled with curiosity: what fine rare things might tempt Ivor Squall to cross such a fellow? Her imagination ran wild in her head, flashing diamonds in her black eyes, sparkling treasures in her greasy claw.

And so she decided, reasonably enough, to go after the treasure herself. And perhaps the reward as well, if she played her cards right. She would find Mr Blunt tomorrow, and hear what he might have to say.

Emmeline Spragg made her way out, slipping like a dirty vapour through the broken landscape, plotting the chase. She would send a man on horseback: he could go ahead to Hammersmith Bridge and watch for the Hammers' boat. She stopped off at the Queen to see who might be about.

★   ★   ★

Grace took the oars again after Chelsea Bridge, settling Daisy gently into her blanket nest and giving poor Charlie a rest.

'You've done well, son,' she said. 'You know I couldn't manage without you.'

He moved next to Billy and shut his eyes. 'It's all right, Ma,' he said. 'I like rowing.'

Chelsea went by on the north bank, rows of clean houses, ornate like jewellery boxes. As they approached Albert Bridge Daisy woke, with a little animal noise, as if coming out of hibernation, and lifted her tangled blonde head to see a vision before her, coming closer, shining in the moonlight like a birthday cake.

She gazed up as they passed beneath. Grace thought she was making a wish. She watched the lamps shrink into the distance for a while, then laid her head down again. They started round the big bend towards Battersea.

'Ma, where are we going?' said Jake.

'Up the river, son.'

'Are we in trouble?'

'Only if we get caught.'

Billy stirred in his sleep just then, talking nonsense, making them laugh and letting her off the hook. Charlie tucked the blanket round his brother and gazed out over the water. 'It's pretty, isn't it, though?' he muttered, before he fell asleep.

★　★　★

Jack Tallis visited the Hammer family home that evening and found it quiet and dark. He stood in the street for a while, wondering where they could be, if not here, at half past eight. It seemed very strange. He thought of the country gent he had met that morning in the Britannia, who had asked after her, and an uneasy feeling turned in his stomach. From the moment Mr Belmarsh had struck up conversation Jack had thought it fishy. He had been minding his own business in the corner when he had noticed the fellow looking over, so he had given him a nod, out of courtesy, which the fat country gent seemed to take as an invitation to sit at his table. And it was odd how quickly he had divulged a good part of his life story while managing to ask a great deal of questions. He had long-lost family in the area, he said. Jack had been surprised when he mentioned a Grace Hammer, though he had covered it well and pretended complete ignorance of her. Grace had never told Jack her family name, leaving him to find it out from Nelly Holland, who could tell you anything about anybody.

When Grace had appeared outside the window not two minutes later he had nearly choked on his beer. She had stared at Mr Belmarsh for what seemed an age while Jack struggled to distract him with chatter. When Grace saw Jack at last he managed to throw her a look and then she vanished. He bombarded his companion with local information, trying to divert him — even volunteering himself as a guide for the afternoon. This offer was declined, to his relief, after a lengthy pause during which Belmarsh showed no sign that he had heard this generous proposition, but ground his teeth, and rocked slowly, staring at a spot on the wall. Jack had thought to call on Grace, once he had moved along. In the event he was distracted by a pretty thing who came in a few minutes after Belmarsh had left.

Suddenly he missed her, wistfully, as one does with something elusive. He turned away from the cold house and wandered forlornly down the street.

* * *

After Battersea came the railway bridge, then Wandsworth and Putney, sliding by ghostlike, faint through the silver mist that clung to the banks. It seemed easier now, as if the river had decided to help, carrying them along. Maybe the tide had come in. She cast her mind back to where she had come from, tried to count the miles and gave up. No rest for the wicked, she thought. Not in a lifetime. She rowed between the trees, standing tall and dark, rustling in the night breeze, breathing the fresh air, heading west.

As they passed up the river away from London it began to narrow and what little light there had been to guide them had faded away with the city. The full moon cast a silver halo on the water as they glided soundlessly towards Hammersmith Bridge. It seemed through the gloom to be a mythical creation, as if it had stood on the earth since the dawn of time. The tops of its four grand towers were lost in the mist; the suspension curved down in a huge iron sweep to the centre and back up into the cloud again. She looked up along the great pillars into the night sky, to the pointed tips of the very top of the bridge, then down to the great feet in the water, as they passed beneath, missing Miss Spragg's watchman, who was relieving himself in the undergrowth, having a touch of the runs and being unable to wait any longer. Only Charlie opened his eye a chink and blinked at her. The air grew cleaner with each new breath, keeping time with the dip and the splash that propelled them onwards. Grace went to sleep in a clump of bulrushes towards Richmond, falling down next to the oars, arms aching as if beaten by the devil.

★　★　★

Mr Blunt slept fitfully, pictures turning in his head. He dreamed of the girls by St Botolph, their sticky white thighs, and of Grace Hammer — kissing her, slicing her throat.

20

Daisy opened her eyes first, to see the branches of a great beech tree spreading above her, twinkling green with a million leaves. She wondered where on earth she was, then remembered the day before and that she was on a boat. She tugged at Jake's sleeve to wake him, as excited as if it was Christmas.

Beyond the bank of reeds and bulrushes a green meadow sloped up towards an enormous house, bright white against the trees, the windows sparkling clean. The landscape rolled away in waves like none they saw in London, not even in Victoria Park. And the air! It was fresh and clean; it slid through the lungs like sweet ether, pure, intoxicating. Charlie woke with sore shoulders. He lay for a minute listening to the little ones chattering, and wondered what on earth they were doing in a boat far from home.

Soon the whole family was alive and exclaiming at fishes and dragonflies, and other country wonders. The boys splashed at each other, unable, as boys are, to stay dry. Sunshine lit the water, the children laughed at something, and a fearless spirit took hold of Grace again. The prospect was thrilling! Up the river to who knows where! She laughed at her sore arms, feeling a trifle mad, watching the dancing light on the water as she rowed the boat along.

After a while her arms hurt unbearably. 'Who wants to row?'

'Me!' shouted the young ones. So they bounced from bank to bank for a while and ate cold chicken. A mile on they came upon Teddington Lock. Now Grace, though she was a country girl, could not remember having been through a lock in her life. She had seen them and thought she knew how to work one but she didn't want to ask the keeper for fear of striking up conversation.

Thank goodness for Billy, who knew exactly what to do, though he had only seen one in a book.

'Look, Ma, Teddington Lock. Can I wind it?'

'Yes, darlin'.'

★ ★ ★

After a seemingly interminable wait, Miss Spragg's errand boy decided that they must have eluded him in the small hours when he had nodded off for a minute or two. He was making good progress up the river, gaining on the Hammers, having called already upon Miss Spragg's associates in Brentford and the ferry near Isleworth. He was heading for Hampton Wick now, trying to stick by the river as much as possible and to keep his eyes peeled for the family, as he had been ordered to do. This last part he found difficult since much of the water was teeming with traffic, most of it families in rowing-boats, enjoying the sunshine. He felt unsure of what he was looking for.

Just five miles up the river, in Kingston, Grace bought provisions. They ate buns and cheese as Hampton Court glided by.

★ ★ ★

Miss Spragg had intelligence, not yet cold, that Mr Blunt was enjoying a drink in the Commercial, and within minutes she was on the corner, sneaking a look through the window. There was Archie Simmons, talking about the damp at his lodgings, no doubt, Big Roy Harman, Busy Liz and a small crowd of children from Dorset Street. A solid red man was swatting them away with heavy hands. He wore dirty brown tweed, just as Dog Brown had said: a solid man, no hat and a bright angry boil on his brow. This was surely Mr Blunt. And there in the very next seat, popping up like a rash again, was Ivor Squall. He was telling Mr Blunt something urgent, in a state of some excitement, waving his arms; or — indeed more animated than she had ever seen him. Up to something, for sure. And he looked to mean business about it.

In fact, poor Ivor was only trying to extricate himself from the whole affair, pleading, in effect, for mercy, which was why he was waving his arms more than usual.

What to do about Mr Squall? she thought, watching him through the glass. He is making a good deal of nuisance. There will be no easy way round him. And intent as he is on this business, she thought — barking still further up the wrong tree — there'll be no shaking him off it. Lurking at the corner Miss Spragg considered how far Ivor Squall might cramp her interests, and how much that might weigh against his merits.

★ ★ ★

She found him later at his offices, peering nervously from a chink in the top window. 'I can see you, Mr Squall. Let me in.'

Ivor came to the door in quite a state, wondering why his fortunes had turned so, these last weeks, and why he must endure so many gruesome visitors.

'I've seen her,' she said, once she was through the door and all the locks were fast again, which was quite a procedure. Had Miss Spragg called by just an hour before, his extravagant precautionary system would have been quite useless to him, for she had planned at first to kill him there. The cruel absurdity of his big bunch of keys and his safety ballet would surely not have been lost on him in his final moments. But he was luckier than he felt, for now: she had abandoned this plan as careless, and adopted another.

'Not an hour ago,' she lied. 'By Wapping Stairs. With all the children.' Ivor almost dropped dead upon the mat anyway. 'On the river they were, heading east.'

He took some time to recover his breath. 'I must contact my client,' he stammered at last, wondering how he might do so without Miss Spragg's involvement. He groped for a ploy to excuse himself, scraping around the inside of his head.

'Never mind that for now,' she said, relieving and confounding him in equal measure. 'She won't be far. We'll go and have a look first, just to make sure of it, eh? I'll arrange horses. We'll leave at four o'clock.'

Perhaps it was sensible, thought Ivor, twitching quietly to himself behind his bony desk, worrying it all over. It was best to make sure. He didn't want to lead Mr Blunt up the garden path, after all. Indeed, he decided — generosity flooding his delicate heart at the happy prospect of closing the matter for ever — if Miss Spragg had her woman she could keep the reward.

★ ★ ★

That day the Hammer children saw a great many things they had never laid eyes on before: fields of wheat, apple orchards and hop-pickers at work glided by. The boys swam — or, rather, Charlie swam while Billy and Jake clung to the side of the boat. Daisy wanted to go in but Grace wouldn't let her as they were in the middle of the river and she didn't want to go in herself. She could swim all right but she didn't like to be wet afterwards.

They stopped by a bank so that Daisy could paddle. The light came down in ripples through the leaves above, dappled on the water and the children, casting sparks around them. They caught tiny minnows and frogs and beetles like shiny buttons. At Sunbury Lock they were passed by Miss Spragg's errand boy, though he failed to spot them. He had become half-hearted in pursuit of his task and was more interested in riding as fast as possible to his next port of call, having several visits to make before Windsor where he was to turn back. He thundered past the lock at breakneck speed, thrashing his unfortunate mount. The family rowed on serenely, past the small island in the middle of the river.

'Do people live there?' asked Daisy.

'Yes,' chimed Charlie and Billy. 'Little tiny ones,' added Charlie.

'With webbed feet.'

'Where are they?'

'In the bushes,' said Charlie.

'Or asleep,' said Billy, knowing she wasn't that daft. 'They sleep in little houses under the ground.'

'Do they, Ma?' she asked, hoping for a straight answer.

'They might.'

Daisy scanned the trees intently. 'A lot of ducks live there.'

'That's what the little people eat.'

'Do they, Ma?'

'Most likely ducks and berries.'

'Berries?'

'Yes. But don't you go eating berries, you ask me first.'

'Why?'

'Because some of them are poisonous.'

'Where are we going Ma?' said Jake.

'You'll see.'

As the afternoon mellowed Grace turned her thoughts to where they might sleep. Charlie must have read her mind because he said, 'Ma, when are we going to stop?'

'When we get somewhere nice and quiet, son.'

The river wound on, past a field of sheep, a great weeping willow, past Shepperton, where the children clamoured to stop but were refused. A couple more locks appeared to entertain them until they reached the next town. A perfect row of riverside gardens slid past, then a long stretch of mooring. Behind it they could see a road, lined with shops, another inn, people walking along the riverside, enjoying the warm afternoon. It seemed too busy, and in spite of the children, who pleaded to get off the boat, she kept on past, ignoring their protests. The houses thinned behind them; the day began to fade.

'Are there lions in the country?'

'No, darlin', only cows and horses. And sheep, too.'

'And bears,' offered Jake.

'Stop it, Jake.'

'Are there bears?'

'No, darlin', there's no bears.'

They rowed quietly along for a while.

245

'Or wolves?'

'No wolves either.'

As if to prove the point, a couple of cows floated by, looming on the banks, mooing gently to announce themselves.

'Do you think we'll find a house to sleep in?'

'Perhaps an inn,' said Grace.

'A nice one?'

'Now that I don't know.'

'Hm. There are nice houses in the country.'

'Yes, darlin'. You shout when you see one you like.'

'How many days will we go on this boat?'

'Are you tired of it already?'

'No. I think we should go on it every day.'

The light was fading in earnest now.

'We could build a shelter,' suggested Billy.

You bloody could, too, thought Grace.

Daisy proposed the building of a house, which Grace explained would take too long and, although a fine idea in principle, was further hampered by their not having any bricks. A couple of riverside inns had been passed and she suggested stopping at the next. Everyone watched the banks intently, to be the first to spot the new scene of adventure. It didn't appear for some time, after all the children, save Billy, had grown bored of the anticipation.

'There it is,' he said quite calmly. They all scrambled to look, rocking the boat.

Their Nirvana was a small stone cottage, set back from the river behind a charming garden — like a picture on a chocolate box, from the fluffy smoke coming out of the chimney, clean and white like cotton balls, to the roses round the door. Foxgloves fringed the path that led down to the river and an old lady, rosy like an apple, was cutting pinks as the sun set. The scene was unbearably quaint. She is surely a witch, thought Grace, as she waved them in.

★　★　★

Miss Spragg arranged for horses at four and Ivor Squall joined her reluctantly, being thoroughly uncomfortable with animals in general but horses in particular. He was keen to get it over with. Steeling himself — as much as he might with his poor constitution — he resolved to hold on tight and hoped they would not go too far or too fast. Perhaps it might be worth his while, after all. Having recovered from his heady flight of generous fancy, he had revised his position, allowing fair shares with the goblin — an even split, should there be profit. He was happy enough thus deluded. Ivor Squall was not usually so far behind the game. He was a wily fellow and could make a great deal of nuisance. He wondered idly if his goodwill had been tallied in the great Book of Judgement and if it counted in his credit, being given so grudgingly.

Another thing he couldn't hope to know was that his horse, which looked neither too big nor too frisky, was the devil's steed in disguise. His stable boys called him Lucifer and swore blind he understood English. Indeed, he seemed to — he made no noise at all, stood still in his stall, casting his sharp eyes around as if he was thinking human thoughts. He needed a fierce hand to ride him but kept his temper mostly in check, finding good behaviour paid — balanced on a tight string, ready to tip, with the right provocation. Miss Spragg had chosen him especially for Mr Squall.

'I have word they stopped off at Deptford, not an hour ago,' said she, as they made ready to leave. 'We can cut across the bend, by West India Docks, and head them off.'

Though she looked an unlikely tangle of rag she mounted her horse robustly and took its head with a firm hand. Ivor was not so assertive. He did not feel in control at all, and though he made a fair show of it, Lucifer the devil horse knew it straight. So poor Ivor had lost the game before he started; he struggled upright in the saddle, remarking to himself how much higher it seemed from this vantage-point, and took the reins as if there was a rabid dog at the end of them.

The first mile went by tolerably well, he thought — he managed to hold on all right and keep up with Miss Spragg. They were cutting across by the West India Docks now, the houses and shops dropping away, dusk falling, the docks closing. Presently he saw the river, winding back to join them, black and shining — looking, he thought absently, quite remarkably like Indian ink. He thought wistfully of his little desk. So absorbed was he in matters of blotting-paper, pencils and stamps that he barely noticed Miss Spragg drop back, and thought nothing of it until she was behind him. He felt suddenly uneasy. His delicate stomach slid round his ribs and curled into a ball.

'No sign of them yet, then,' he twittered, through the dark.

'No, indeed,' she said.

Ivor was wondering what he should say next when Miss Spragg struck, jabbing Lucifer hard with a sharp stick just below the tail. He kicked out and took off like a thunderbolt, snarling, which he alone among horses could do. Ivor clung on desperately, losing his stirrups and his hold of the reins, grasping handfuls of satanic horsehair. Miss Spragg watched from a distance as Lucifer hurled Ivor from his back on to the bank with a good crack as he landed on his head. He wasn't moving, as far as she could see. She trotted up to have a look.

Ivor was certainly not moving unless you counted his desperate face, and the fluttering of his hands as he tried to reach for help — perhaps he thought she might save him! Blood pooled on the ground beneath his skull as he stared, crazed and hopeless, at her, like some wretched dumb animal; in fact the Book of Judgement had swum before his eyes and he was wondering if his account was in credit — he had not anticipated dying today and felt unprepared. And terrified. She stood patiently for a whole minute but still he stared, writhing a little as he tried to sit up. Miss Spragg had had enough. Grasping his useless arms she dragged him to the river's edge. Then she took him by the hair and pushed his head under. She held it there for a good two minutes, enjoying the view and the fresh air until he was still.

★ ★ ★

'Why didn't we come before?' Daisy wanted to know.

'Because we didn't know it was here.'

'Do you think Mrs Robertson was here all the time?'

'Yes. Lucky for us.'

'We're lucky, ain't we?'

'Yes, darlin', we are.'

'Do you like this bed? It's made of feathers.'

'Very much. Do you?'

'Yes, I like everything.'

I hope that keeps up, thought Grace. Daisy's attitude was comforting: she slept a beautiful ten hours in the clean feather bed.

Grace's head was uneasy on the pillow. She dreamed Blunt was coming down the towpath that followed the river. His face was indistinct, just a space in the dark shape that advanced towards her. She found herself unable to get out of bed, even to move or scream. She woke with a struggle, sweating and gasping for air.

★ ★ ★

In fact, Miss Spragg was much nearer Grace's tail than Mr Blunt. She had sent word to a number of acquaintances along the river: the lock-keeper at Penton Hook, and Chertsey, and various innkeepers, and should they have information she would hear of it soon enough. She sat by the greasy lantern in her lair in Limehouse, awaiting developments.

★ ★ ★

Mr Blunt, meanwhile, prowled the noisome streets of Whitechapel, finding himself back in Bell Lane again. As he paused by the darkened windows of number twenty-eight a curtain twitched across the street.

21

Madeleine Robertson had been married a long time ago, to a man she loved with all her heart; he had loved her back for twelve happy years until he disappeared into the sunset with a milkmaid who had started work at the farm not three weeks before. Maidie had never bothered having another man, though she was a handsome woman and could have wed again. She simply never considered it. She was in love with Mr Robertson and that was that. She did not wallow in her miseries for long but sold the farm and got on with a good life by the river.

When the Hammers woke up to the sound of birdsong, she had a handsome breakfast ready. Though they ate well in London they had never had breakfast like this, with eggs and bacon and sausage all at once, and the children were silent, fixed on devouring it. Maidie Robertson chatted sociably to Grace, showing an interest without being too nosy.

'So you came from London, you say?'

'That's right. We live there.'

'I've a sister in London. I went once to see her. She lives in Brixton — do you know it?

It's dreadfully busy. You can't hear yourself think for the chatter and the carriages. I saw a fire engine there, all the bells ringing and people jumping out of the way, such a commotion! Still, I expect you're used to all the hustle and bustle.'

'You do become accustomed to it, it's true. That doesn't mean we don't like a bit of peace and quiet.'

'We like the country,' interjected Daisy.

'Do you, young miss?'

'Yes. We like it very much.'

'You're a good girl. Would you like to feed the chickens?'

They trooped out with Billy and Jake in tow, trying to get in on the chicken-feeding. Charlie and Grace washed the dishes.

'So, what are you up to, then, Ma?' he asked her, as if he expected a decent answer.

Go on, then, and tell him, he's big enough, she thought. 'We're getting away from someone in London.'

'Who?'

'His name's Mr Blunt. I knew him before you were born. I stole something from him, years ago, something very precious, and he has found me out after all this time. You go along with me in everything, in trust, as you always have.'

'I know, Ma.'

'Do you, though?'

'Yes,' he said, solid as a brick wall. 'Don't worry, Ma. We'll be all right. He won't get past Daisy.'

They were laughing as the troops came back into the kitchen.

'Why are you laughing?' demanded Daisy, straight away. They laughed more then, and she shot them one of her hard stares.

After roast lamb and potatoes and a look at *The Water Babies*, Grace felt the itch to move and on they went, packed into their trusty boat, laden with food. They waved until they had rounded the bend, entreaties to return at any time and to take care ringing in their ears.

The day was not as bright as the one before, and it seemed that the moment Mrs Robertson's cottage was out of sight it began to rain, as if encouraging them to turn back. Grace struck up a chorus of 'The Fireman's Dog' to raise flagging spirits. They pushed on for a while, taking shelter under a huge willow tree some half a mile on as the day grew wetter. Under the branches was a green kingdom, enchanted and dry, the leafy roof curving round them. They waited for the rain to stop.

★ ★ ★

Jack was nursing a pint in the Ten Bells, wondering where Grace had gone. He had been busy the last day or two with some casual work and various unexpected but pleasing female distractions. Now that these were finished, and he was bored, he was annoyed to find her unavailable for entertainment. With complete disregard for his own comings and goings the last week, he mulled possessively over where she could have gone without so much as a nod in his direction, and whether she had another fancy man. How could she! He felt, with a stab, that hard truth, that you can't have your cake and eat it.

★ ★ ★

Many miles away, tucked under a tarpaulin in the rain with her children, Grace suddenly thought of him. More a picture than a thought: his hands, his jaw, his melting grin. She felt a pang of sadness until she remembered he was no good.

★ ★ ★

In a lonely house in Shoreditch Mirabel Trotter sat before the fire in her darkened room, counting the days since she had seen

Trixie May Turner; she reckoned it at eleven. She sensed something was up — there had been not a word — and she missed her. She calmed herself by having a little brandy, and then another. Her burly sons were downstairs but she didn't want their company. Mrs Trotter poured herself one more and swallowed it straight, listening to shouts and laughter below. Staring into the fire, she saw blue dragons, devil-heads, burning buildings.

22

The footsteps came from behind, as the ones that you notice do. She remarked to herself the moment they began to follow that they rang dull in the ears, flat and sinister. They stayed close behind in the shadow, neither overtaking nor falling back, and she gripped the neck of the bottle in her pocket, squeezing Daisy's hand, keeping her eyes on the end of the street. Her tormentor hung behind them another twenty yards, another fifty. Just the soles of his shoes and a soft, wheezing breath, which she caught as she strained the very nerves of her eardrums.

Just as she thought she could bear it no longer she heard the footsteps quicken, and as time slowed she marvelled at how he had still surprised her, though she had been poised on a nerve string. She turned as he leaped towards her, pushing Daisy aside, and swung the bottle, still half full, into the side of his head. It shattered into pieces that flew through the air, a shower of glass and gin, catching the gaslight, twinkling and falling to the ground, leaving a vicious jagged dagger in her hand. As if in a trance she heard Daisy scream, looked round to find her crouched by the wall and gathered her up. They glanced back at him once, staring dumbly at them, mouth hanging open, blood running down his face into the puddle of gin.

Grace came to with a start and a little gasp, knuckles white on the side of the boat. The family were sleeping. She took in the reeds, the birds, the chirping riverscape.

The family woke early and cold fingers of sunshine fought through the canopy. Billy rowed them into the weak morning sun. Charlie broke out breakfast — rolls, butter, cheese, ham. He gave the first roll to his sister. And on they went. Whitechapel seemed far away. The sky grew blue, the children spotted sheep, the birds sang. It was all very nice but she knew they made quite a picture: they must keep moving. Maybe they should get off the river soon.

They stopped past the next town, and tied up the boat. After they had tidied their few effects, prompted by Charlie, and eaten, they sat on the riverbank and tried to catch fish with long switches and a line they found in the bottom of the boat, though Daisy was content to imagine hers. Their eyes fixed on the water, every ripple and splash. Within five minutes Daisy tired of this. Grace and she walked up the bank to the lane at the top and over the bridge.

'I know a good game,' said Grace. 'You get a stick and drop it in the water, then run the other side and see whose comes out first.' Daisy found herself a fine stick and a large twig for Grace.

After Daisy had won four times, and lost two, and they were playing with blades of grass as the good sticks were becoming harder to find, Grace suggested a foray into the village, though Daisy wanted to play on. She was lured by the possibility of bull's-eyes and the promise that they would play sticks again on the way back. Though only once.

They took a little footpath that ran behind the town. As they wandered up it, Grace filled her lungs with the sweet, clean air and imagined how it would be to live in the countryside, spending every day among the rolling green fields instead of grey streets and human wreckage. Maybe in a little house like that one on the hill ahead, with its apple trees and its thatched roof. She pictured herself inside, baking, or making jam perhaps, the children running around outside, picking blackberries and apples. Daisy skipped ahead, plucking wild flowers from the hedgerow as if participating in this idyllic fantasy. And suddenly Mr Blunt, never far from her thoughts lately, swam into them again, spoiling the scene. She saw him thundering down the footpath towards them, breath grunting, coat tails flapping, heavy boots kicking up stones. She felt uneasy and looked about her, and though she knew he could not be near them, not yet at least, her nerves crackled, as if she was being watched. She remarked to herself then that the only way she could be free of this shadow was if Mr Blunt was dead and buried. A cold notion that dropped out of the sky on to her head. She was surprised she had not thought it before.

They came upon a winding road that appeared to be the main street. A sign said Runney Mead. The sky was blue between the billowing clouds, white like Maidie Robertson's feather pillows. Two shops huddled together opposite a miniature pub.

'What's mead?' said Daisy.

'Some funny old drink they used to have in the olden days.'

'Is it nice?'

'Dunno, darlin'. I've never had it.'

'Everything's so small, ain't it?'

They bought plums, bull's-eyes and sweet tobacco, and walked through the village, munching, lost in thought. A woman watched them across the square. As Grace looked over she lowered her head and went inside her shop. The windows all around seemed to stare like dead men. She hurried Daisy on.

By the boat the boys were talking about some girl with red hair they had seen in the last town. When Grace and Daisy reappeared they had given up fishing and were eyeing up a fancy skiff moored at the other bank.

'What are you doing?' Grace said.

'Nothing.'

★ ★ ★

All the way from Datchet to Boveney Lock, Grace sank into herself, the children chattering around her. They must leave the boat soon. Supposing someone knew they had left London on the river, and had merely to follow it along? She had felt sure before of their secret escape, now she was not. At Romney Lock the keeper seemed to watch them for all the time it took the water to fill. Grace could see him peering from his little booth as the boat came up.

Now, our Grace is a handsome woman and it may be the lock-keeper was merely sneaking a good look at her — he is a lonely fellow, and though he spends his days in this idyllic spot, with the birdsong all around, and eats fresh country eggs and ham every morning, he finds it interminably tedious and longs to see the lights of Piccadilly; so who knows how he whiles away the hours in that little booth of his — but the running and hiding and secrecy had drawn Grace tight as piano wire. She could hear the grass grow, smell fox in the hedgerow, see through skin, and this had quite skewed her judgement of everyday things, which is the problem, of course, with suspicion. So, he was not a lonely lock-keeper but a spy, piercing her with sharp eyes. She turned her back.

'Look, Daisy, a windmill.' Even that seemed to watch them, looming dark across the fields.

'Why doesn't it go round?'

'There's no wind.'

'What's it for?'

'Making flour.'

'Oh!' Flour was not something Daisy had thought much about; it came in bags and never troubled her. But she was pleased to know anyhow, and to solve the matter of windmills, which she had seen on china cups but never considered properly either. 'Can we wait until the wind comes?'

'No, we can't.'

They made a stop presently at Maidenhead, which seemed a bit risky, but the children were clamouring for food and they had none. They moored on the quieter side of the river, at the end of the landing.

'We're not stopping long!' Grace shouted after them, as they leaped out of the boat and ran down the jetty.

The children were hoping to find another Mrs Robertson and were cruelly disappointed by the surly fellow who was landlord at the Orkney Arms. They sat down to chops and boiled potatoes and were quiet for some time, the landlord scowling in the background, before Grace ventured conversation with him. 'Do you see many travellers around these parts?'

'No,' was the gruff reply.

Even Daisy did not melt his rude manner. 'May I have a cup of milk, please?' she asked him politely.

'Get your nasty hands off the bar, little girl,' he said, under his breath, so that her mother could not hear, which she did. Grace bit her lip.

They wolfed their food, making surreptitious faces at each other all the while, paid their bill and left. The landlord watched them until they disappeared round the next bend, staring intently from the upper floor of the inn, beard bristling as he sucked his front teeth — a habit he had indulged since childhood — which made his chin protrude, giving him a pugnacious yet ridiculous air. He stood on the small balcony as if it were the prow of a ship, imagining himself to be Lord Nelson, before he had lost his arm. He enjoyed this fantasy for a few moments, until his wife, who was even more disagreeable than he and bedridden with colic, shouted for him to empty her pot.

★ ★ ★

Where do you think you are going? said the tiny voice at the back of Grace's head — the one that spoke at unsure moments such as this. In the rush to escape London she had not thought past the end of her nose. When she looked at their prospects she felt that she had been labouring under a wishful delusion: did she imagine that he might simply abandon his search after a week or two and go home again? How stupid. You are sleepwalking! You knew he would come, the voice scolded. You have made a pig's ear of it.

They stopped for a nap not a mile on, concealed by a great bank of alder, and Grace went back and robbed Landlord Nelson while Charlie watched the little ones, who were sleeping peacefully as she came running through the orchard, night falling behind her, Charlie turning the boat to row back the way they had come.

She shivered in the night air, punting silently past the Orkney Arms. Charlie kept his head down and steered them away from the bank with the other oar. The river was empty; they kept to the shadows on the far bank and disappeared under the bridge. Grace would get her family off the river as soon as they woke, before Laleham and Maidie Robertson's cottage. If Daisy went there again she would never get her away.

★ ★ ★

Jack was turning away from the house in Bell Lane once more. They were gone for sure. It must have something to do with Mr Belmarsh. He had the uncomfortable feeling that he had failed her — a sentiment she might have appreciated, though there really was nothing he could do — and tried to content himself with the thought that she could get by nicely without his help. Trixie May Turner might know something.

It didn't take him long to find her. She was on good form, though precious about her recent exploits. They had several jars in the Britannia. She hadn't seen Grace since all the business with Mirabel Trotter, or so she said.

'Where do you reckon she is, then?' he asked, for the second time, possessed of the irrational theory that all women are part of some general conspiracy, as many men are, especially the ones who are up to something themselves.

'I've really no idea,' she replied again.

'Do you think something happened to her?'

'No!' She felt sorry for him suddenly, staring moodily into his jar. He needed diversion, perhaps a little venture. Trixie and Jack had a modest history of partnership in crime; certain occasions when an opportunity had presented itself. She needed help with a few tricky tabs that were owing. 'Don't sulk, Jack. Listen to this . . . '

★ ★ ★

Mr Blunt had taken to drinking in the Frying Pan lately, finding it the quietest place for a beer at certain times of the day. He has asked, of course, after his long-lost cousin, a Miss Grace Hammer: bringing solemn family news, most regretfully — and notice, on a happier note, of a financial nature — but Mr Daley, the landlord, amenable fellow though he was, could not attest to having heard of such a person. He did, come to think of it, remember some Hammers from years back — they lived west, he was sure of it, Hammersmith way. Mr Blunt was sure these were not his Hammers and ignored him. He wondered about the tunnel that was rumoured to run beneath the building, stretching under the street and beyond. The idea of this subterranean network appealed to his devious nature. He wondered how one might get in.

23

'I've seen your lady friend,' said Miss Spragg to Jack, the next time she met him.

He gave just the reaction she had hoped for. 'Where?' said he, trying not to look as if he wanted to know too much, but failing entirely upon showing that he knew whom she meant. Miss Spragg smiled hideously at him, baring a graveyard of rotten pegs, making him want a stiff drink.

She had asked Jack about the charming companion he had brought so carelessly to her private residence in Blight Street; he was not forthcoming, of course (being loyal to Grace in that particular at least), but she hardly needed him to be. There had been a sighting of the family near Maidenhead yesterday; she'd had word of it this morning, and was quite sure the information was reliable.

'I'm sure there must be something you could help me with in return,' she said. 'There are a great many services a fine lad like yourself could offer a poor old woman such as me, all alone in the world.'

It is true to say that Miss Spragg has

wide-ranging interests of a business kind. It is certain that many of these involve dirty work indeed. She has a good deal of use for a man like Jack, rough and ready, not too curious.

★ ★ ★

Maidie Robertson was thrilled to see the Hammers again and ran down the garden in her apron.

'We came back!' exclaimed Daisy, as if it was a surprise to her as well.

'Yes, here you are!' beamed Mrs Robertson. 'Come indoors and eat something.'

When the children had gone to play — 'Stay in the garden.' 'Yes, Ma.' 'Away from the river!' — the women sat down to talk.

'Now, dear, what are you up to?' said Mrs Robertson, sharp as a new pin.

So Grace recounted the whole story, omitting not the slightest relevant detail. 'And what do you plan to do now, dear?'

'Go back to London.'

'Whatever for?'

'To get shot of the necklace.'

'What will you do with the children?'

'Put them with a family I know in Harrow.'

'I think it would be best to leave them here with me.'

Grace thought this over in less than a

minute, looking at Maidie Robertson. Then she gave her Landlord Nelson's money. 'I will,' she said. 'Stay away from the Orkney Arms down the river.'

'Good luck, dear.'

And so it was that Grace Hammer left her children, who didn't seem to mind much, in the care of kindly Maidie Robertson early the next morning, kissing them on the way out, mist clinging round the boat as she glided across the water, oars lapping stealthily.

★ ★ ★

Two miles away, as the crow flies, in the charming Norman village of Halliford, Miss Emmeline Spragg was enjoying her breakfast alone in a private room at the Plough Inn. Chewing on her bacon she contemplated the day before her. When the plate was clean she pushed it aside and smoothed a tattered map upon the tablecloth. She reckoned on taking the towpath to Shepperton, to call in on the landlord of the Anchor, before cutting across country and up towards Maidenhead.

★ ★ ★

Grace had not been without the company of any, or all, of her children since the day she had had Charlie, and although she felt a pang of emptiness at the thought of them, she was surprised to find herself content to be alone. It was novel indeed to be so free, with no little voices asking for things, and she thought guiltily that she might not miss them as much as she had imagined — at least, not all of the time. A lonely moorhen regarded her, floating along like a tiny coracle a cautious distance away. With her mouth full of ham sandwich Grace's thoughts turned to London: shifting the necklace was a tall order in two weeks, never mind two days, which was all she planned to stay, three at the most. She must make some house calls. Suddenly the inside of her head seemed a vast and unfathomable place. Perhaps he was gone already. Perhaps she was getting in a knot about nothing. The moorhen watched her glide away, shrinking into the distance.

She made good progress, though the river twisted after a mile, writhing round innumerable bends. The boat was a lot bloody lighter without all the family but there was no Charlie to take a turn, so she tired after a few miles and slowed down, going with the current. As she drifted along, lost in thought, a ragged figure on horseback made its way along the towpath, coming towards her. The horse slowed and stopped. Grace recovered her arms and started to row again. As the boat slid by, two goblin eyes watched it go from behind a great bank of nettles.

Miss Spragg smiled grotesquely to herself, rubbing her spiny chin with glee. What a chance sighting! Grace Hammer, London bound. She noted with particular interest that her family were not with her. After a moment's pause she urged her horse on down the path, towards Maidenhead.

24

Grace drifted into London like a ghost as 16 September was dawning. The filthy Thames was swathed in mist and a cold blue glow lit the riverbanks, bearing no apparent relation to the rays of any burning orb. How hot the sun must be, she mused, to light our every detail through the blanket of cloud that covered London, settled on it like a giant sleeping animal, with the bustling hardy people beneath, damp like rags. She saw them as she drifted past, catching glimpses through windows of private scenes, flashes of the street in the gaps between warehouses and loading bays, in perfect detail but misty like a dream.

At half past six she pulled the boat in under Eagle Dock. A lamp was burning in the office window above. She tied up beneath the jetty and scurried up the harbour steps. A furtive knock upon the door at the top of the stairs brought forth Big Roy Harman.

He was surprised to see the family were not with her and pleased the boat had not sunk. They had hot tea in chipped cups in his rickety office.

'Listen Roy,' she said. 'You haven't seen me.'

She set off down Cable Street. The pubs were filling and the bustle made her feel safe. She even stopped at the Queen for a shot of rum. She would chance a little look up Bell Lane first and pick up a few things, if the coast was clear.

Commercial Street was just the same, going on as normal. She wondered what she had expected. She stopped at Betsey's bake stall to buy treacle tart. Betsey had not been asked searching questions by any suspicious gentlemen — perhaps Grace was making a great meal of nothing. She turned cautiously into Bell Lane; nothing looked untoward.

As she approached her front door her stomach turned over. It stood ajar, just a crack; the lock was broken. She stopped still. And her heart, and the traffic. The city babble seemed to hold its breath. She crossed the street, and pushed the door open with shaking hands.

As if in a dream, the wreckage of her home and possessions spilled across the room before her like a burst tomato: the contents of every shelf and drawer strewn round the room. The coal bucket was upturned on the bed; splashes of black dust defaced the sheets; books lay like dead birds across the scene.

And Daisy's best blue dress, torn like a rag.

The perpetrator of this chaos had withdrawn an hour ago, foul-tempered and bored of waiting, taking by way of compensation the pleasure of pissing on the wreckage and smashing her china as he left.

Grace took Daisy's dress, and the cricket bat, which Charlie had forgotten, being too busy helping the others.

★　★　★

It was Jack who had dropped her in it. Blunt had been suspicious when he had denied all knowledge of the Hammer family or, indeed, anyone who might help him find them: he had been rather too keen about it. And when he saw Jack again that very morning, knocking at a door in Bell Lane — which seemed to draw him back every day — he did not catch up and greet him, but kept a distance and went up after Jack had gone to see the door from which he had come. Through the window he spied a child's drawing on the wall: a ballerina, balanced on one pointed toe. The artist was evidently proud of her efforts — she had signed the picture with her name. 'Daisy Hammer', it said.

Jack, yawning and useless, with his

276

handsome face, had shambled to the end of the street to sit in the Britannia and never noticed a thing.

★ ★ ★

Shaking, Grace made her way to the Frying Pan to see Horace Daley. The shock was engulfing her now. She wept hot tears, trudging away in the drizzle, feeling further than ever from her children, sick at the thought of their broken things. Up Thrawl Street she went, kicking herself all the way.

As she rounded the corner she glanced in through the window of the Frying Pan. And who should be in her favourite seat at that very moment but Mr Horatio Blunt himself. She froze mid-step, struck by lightning.

He was fully engaged in constructing a sandwich from a slice of sausage and a crusty roll and did not lift his head to see the stricken figure through the glass not ten yards away. (Had Mr Blunt known that the interest he took in feeding his fat gut had foiled him for the second time he might have indulged it a little less, and done a good deal better but, of course, there was no one to tell him.)

Grace pulled herself together as he raised the sandwich to his mouth and slid back round the corner, heart shrinking, pulse banging in her ears.

* * *

Big Roy Harman was not in his office but she found him in the yard breaking rocks for ballast. He sat her on a crate with a bucket of tea and listened to the tale that unfolded. When she had finished, he picked up his hammer and put a big lump of flint in his pocket. 'Let's see if he's still about.'

She followed him out of the yard feeling like a small child, hurrying after his giant strides. Crowds seemed to part like waves before him as they made their way up Osborn Street into Brick Lane.

Blunt was gone. Grace felt a sudden irrational panic that he might pop up behind her. After a few deep breaths this subsided, leaving the feeling that comes when a big spider you have been tolerating on the wall has vanished from the spot it has occupied for the last day or two.

'There's been a gentleman asking after you,' said Horace.

'I know,' she said. 'I saw him in my seat.'

'He's a nosy fellow. Started on about a secret tunnel. Reckoned he'd heard it went through my cellar.'

'What did you tell him?'

'I told him it was a fairytale. Now, let's get you out of sight.'

In the back room, after a nip with Horace (to start the day properly as he put it), she sized up her prospects. She must get her skates on. First to Canning Town, to call on a gentleman who was known to deal in especially shiny things. She would come back for the necklace if he was interested. She wasn't about to go running around with a twelve-carat ruby in her pocket on the off-chance.

As she crossed Brick Lane she came upon Trixie, who took her straight into the Alma. Grace sat in a corner seat and had another gin.

'Someone's looking for you,' Trixie said.

'I know. What did he say?'

'I haven't seen him myself but he's been all over asking.' She watched Grace swallow her gin. 'Who is he?'

'A nightmare.'

'I could help you with that.'

★ ★ ★

Grace skulked from the Alma with her hat pulled down and her face buried in her scarf, which looked a little odd, as it was a seasonable day. At the corner of George Street she clocked an old man filling his pipe. He wore a little green felt hat; she could swear he was watching her. Perhaps she imagined it. She glanced back at him, feeling eyes on her back, but he was tucking his tobacco into a pocket.

At every corner she held her breath, expecting to see Mr Blunt. It seemed as if everyone she knew was in the street at once this morning, stopping to greet her and ask where she had been; she kept conversation short, eyes darting up and down. Crossing Hanbury Street she bumped into Lily Dixon, with sweet williams today, deep pink, purple and white, like little friendly faces. On the next corner she walked smack into Mary Kelly, whom she had not seen for at least a month, and was engaged in unavoidable conversation, Mary being delighted to see her and interested in all the family news, as the Irish generally are. As they chatted Grace felt as though someone was aiming a gun at her; people seemed to look at her searchingly as they went past. After they had talked about the children, and what a shame it was they weren't out with her — Grace trying to chat without telling her anything much — Mary went on her way. Going up past the Jewish club Grace saw Nelly Holland but thought better of saying hello. Nelly talked too much to everybody. Grace liked her, though, and felt deceitful as she hurried past with her head down.

Mr Rubenstein, the gentleman who dealt in especially shiny things, was unavailable that afternoon. She made enquiries after him but was told nothing more helpful than that he was up west and not about for business until tomorrow. He was a private sort so she didn't push it. As she skulked back to the Frying Pan her mind drifted down the dank stairs beneath the trapdoor — she would take a look this evening, just to make sure.

Unhappily the back room was occupied when she returned — a private card game in progress. Thwarted, she retired upstairs to wait. Ten o'clock came and went, then eleven and midnight. Evidently the players had deep pockets. She fell asleep at last, in a warm bed. A tap at the door woke her. She sat bolt upright in the dark.

'Grace,' came a voice through the keyhole. It was Jack. She threw open the door and pulled him in.

Once the door was locked he was greeted with a long, enthusiastic kiss. 'I missed you, Jack,' she said.

'Where have you been?'

'Never mind that. Tell me what happened in the Britannia.'

She quizzed him thoroughly about what Mr Blunt had said, and everything else he knew, giving him no chance to ask where she had been. She watched his mouth as he talked. She had made resolutions that hadn't lasted past the first crooked smile before. She remembered this later as they pounced upon each other, urgently, with their matching lips, moonlit: making butterfly love. It was then that she began to sense Jack Tallis was a bad bet. Just a feeling. Not in the charming way she had first been attracted to, but darker altogether, something she couldn't explain.

★ ★ ★

Three miles away, in Bethnal Green, Mr Stanley shadowed Mr Blunt, following his every move. He had gone after him into the Camel and watched as he drank beer and leered at unfortunate girls. Before long he had one on his knee and was buying her gin. She looked much the worse for wear, but had most of her teeth and was charming enough. She said her name was Sally Ann.

25

Miss Spragg's goblin fingers stretched far across the country. She had tracked the progress of the Hammer family as far as Maidenhead, and had come in person, on the hearsay of an acquaintance who ran the Orkney Arms and would surely regret it if the journey should prove fruitless for her.

She had slithered into his pub the day before, startling the regulars.

Landlord Nelson had taken her through to the back and spilled what he knew, keen to send her on her way. She was more fearsome even than when he had seen her last, which was four years ago if not more. Her face was withered with lines, her evil soul drawn on it for anyone who could stand to look at her long enough. Her eyes were mean, her mouth a cavern of foul tombstones. Her back had hunched still further, and though she had shrunk, her sinister authority seemed to have grown.

She asked him about the children particularly, how old they were, the colour of their hair. It made Landlord Nelson's skin creep a little but he was soothed by a generous tip.

He told her they had gone upriver towards Henley and that the bitch had stolen his takings practically from under his nose — the truth being that she had taken them from the drawer in his bureau, through the open window, and by the time he had noticed, it was the next day, given as he was to drinking alone after hours. They could be in Oxford by now, he told the goblin. He was keen to wring Grace Hammer's wretched neck himself.

★ ★ ★

For just a moment as she opened her eyes Grace wondered where she was. Her dreams had been busy and strange, playing the last few days over, twisting events in her head. She must take care of business and get back to the family.

And so under the trapdoor she went, trying not to brush against the damp walls. She set down her lamp and clapped her hands to chase away the spiders. The wall was dark and pockmarked with hollows and holes, black bricks stacked as if by some great subterranean insect. She counted seven from the corner, three from the top, and pulled one out. Then, telling herself she was a grown woman and ought not to take on so, she slid her cold hand in.

Her fingers groped blind into the dark space, crawled into the corners, panicked, frisked the bricks. She pulled them out and counted again, plunged her hand back into the hole, grasping at nothing.

In the back room, head in hands, she pieced together the awful truth. 'He must have come in at the other end.'

'No one's used that tunnel in fifty years,' said Horace, shaking his head.

'He was down there with me. I heard him.'

The blood seemed to stall in her veins, and then a strange current stirred it: like swelling poison, pumping through her magpie heart — and she knew she couldn't let him get away with it.

★ ★ ★

It took little more than a few calls upon various local acquaintances to find out that Mr Blunt had been enquiring after her whereabouts for the past fortnight or so, most often claiming to be a long-lost member of the family with news of a bequest to which she was entitled. Most of them, acquainted well enough to know that Grace had no distant wealthy relatives, had seen him off at the door. Mrs Crackit at the corner coffee house had been sweetly concerned that Grace might miss out, but had thought it best to confer with her personally before giving out her address. Grace reassured her that she had done right, and that there was no fortune, and tried to impress upon her as plain as she could that Mr Blunt was a dangerous man who was on no account to be entertained, if not in so many words. Poor nervous Mrs Crackit trembled visibly, eyes chasing over the door bolts, imagination running wild.

'Please don't worry yourself, Winifred,' Grace said, trying in vain to soothe her. 'He won't hurt you, he's looking for me.' Oh, God, that sounds all wrong, she thought.

At Mrs Jacob's door she felt a cold current. She told Grace that a Mr Belmarsh had called, but had nothing else particularly to say about him. She mentioned nothing about an inheritance. After an awkward pause Mrs Jacob asked after the children, affecting a casual air, betraying nothing. Grace left, wondering what she had told him and what enticement he had offered.

Now to call on Sally Ann. Sally would have seen him if he'd been about.

★ ★ ★

Back in St Giles Mr Blunt awoke from a deep stupor with a crippling headache. He had never had a hatchet buried in his head before but, he reflected as best he could, if he ever did it would surely feel very much like this. He could not recall coming back last night and had fallen asleep with his coat and hat on. There was blood on his cuffs, lots of it, dried in the fibres of the wool.

It took him several minutes to remember the events of the night before. As it flooded back to him he recalled the girl: her dress, her tattered bonnet; the pattern on the wallpaper; the ugly mole between her collarbone and her throat. When he had seen her he had wanted to take out all his rage upon her.

Sally Ann Dunn was the easiest target in the pub, if not the parish, born eager to please. She never turned a man down if he might buy her a drink. Adrift on that particular evening she had caught the piggy eye of Mr Blunt and it was not long before he had her full attention. Mr Blunt was not a charmer on his best days, but Sally Ann's perpetual stupor rendered her impervious to the dark cloud around him, his clenched fists and his furious contempt — boiling especially hot that evening. Sally had merely laughed as he raged drunkenly to himself, mistaking his growling for jest. She barely understood English, these days, if truth be told. Neither did she mind when he grabbed a handful of her breast or thigh, rough and spiteful, not once looking at her face. She had only grinned wider and leaned down for him to get a better view. It is no surprise, of course, that she took him back to her lodgings.

★ ★ ★

As they had left the pub Byron Stanley had drifted after them. He had last seen them on the corner of Commercial and Dorset Street, where he had vanished into the night, feeling suddenly afraid.

★ ★ ★

Once Mr Blunt had relived the full horror of the night before, he rose from bed and dressed, then proceeded to the nearest good coffee house where he devoured a cooked breakfast of eggs and bacon, with brown crusted bread and butter. He ate greedily, smacking his lips, spraying crumbs, as if he were at home by himself — causing his fellow diners to push their plates away and have coffee instead. He leered at the serving girl and goosed her when she came to clear the table. After settling his bill, he swaggered out. Luckily for him he never went there again, for she would certainly have seen him coming and spat in his gravy.

★ ★ ★

Grace found Sally Ann Dunn dead upon the bed, her throat slit. The blood had dried on the sheet to a brown-black colour and her body was pale and stiff. Grace stared for what seemed an age before she went near. Strange how shock is, she thought. Numb, like looking at pictures or through glass. She took a clean rag from the trunk and laid it upon Sally's dead face. Then she left quietly and went to sit by the riverside. She had known this would happen one day, and it seemed to her that, regrettably, death was in most instances a relief for the lost girl. She pictured Sally Ann's blue eyes, bloodshot and innocent, her rotten grin, and remembered the day she had broken her teeth on the kerb outside the Ten Bells, getting up without a care and, finding one still intact in the gutter, shoving it back into its bleeding socket and heading inside for a gin. Grace wished she could float Sally's corpse on the Thames and set it alight.

Daisy and Billy would be inconsolable. She would not tell them the whole awful truth and hoped they would not find out. Neither would she alert the police: she had been wily enough thus far in her career to avoid their attention altogether, unknown at the local station, a rare position for a London criminal. The children had followed her shining example in maintaining the clean family slate — no hasty risks must be taken. But there were no friends who might call by to discover Sally's corpse and raise the alarm, and she couldn't leave her until the landlord came on Friday. She decided to keep an eye open, and if Sally Ann was not found by Tuesday, she would drag her outside in the small hours of Wednesday morning and leave her in the street.

After reflecting on the harsh and comfortless life of Sally Ann Dunn, Grace rose from her spot by the river, where the mudlarks scratched through the stinking rubbish at low tide for any scrap they might sell. One had found a rusty trowel and was holding it up triumphantly for all to see, which was not what he might have done had he thought more about it. Several vagabond figures, flapping in ragged shirtsleeves like demented ravens, were making their way across the prehistoric landscape towards him.

As she turned down George Yard she saw the green felt hat again and marched straight up to him with her chin jutting. 'Why are you with me wherever I go?' she said.

'Are you looking for a large, ruddy man, with old-fashioned clothes and a cruel sneer for a smile?' said Mr Byron Stanley.

'I might be.'

'Come with me.'

The curious little man in the green hat proved to be divine intervention. He was a member of the Whitechapel Vigilance Committee, active since the murders had begun that summer. He had trailed Horatio Blunt all week and seen him break down her door.

They skulked to the White Hart and into the corner seat where he gave Grace full details of Mr Blunt's every movement and with whom he had spoken. Apparently he had spent the day drinking in Whitechapel before falling asleep on a bench in St Mary's graveyard. He had not called on anyone about business, or made any move to leave London. Grace shrank back in her seat. A cold hand crept round her heart. Mr Blunt might have his necklace but he was not satisfied yet. She made plans to meet Byron Stanley the next day, for further intelligence.

* * *

A moment of clarity visited her that evening as she drank tea at Mrs Cherry's table, with

291

Tom on her lap; he was much better now, and heavy. There is no way round it, said the tiny voice at the back of her head. You must kill Mr Blunt or the game will never end. Sally Ann's dead face swam before her. She knew who to ask as well.

Grace cursed herself for her weakness, the glitter in her stupid eyes. What had she made of her fortune? The ruby was a useless trophy, a forgotten thing under the floor — as good as if she had thrown it away. It seemed to matter less than Daisy's torn dress.

★ ★ ★

London has always been brown and grey, not least in autumn. In warmer months it wears the colours you could swear had never been there — purple, yellow and blue — in crevices and cracks, sprouting forth again to blossom in the city. From October until March, London Town is bleak and unrelenting, a gloomy place where the poor never get properly dry or warm. The sky is dark, the work is hard, the going heavy. And so life in Whitechapel rolls on, people battling against the elements, scuttling between the damp buildings, brick towers slick with rain, blank cracked windows staring. The poor witless souls who had caroused away the summer with their bar-fellows — as if the warmth and ease would last for ever — were caught without a bed, like last year, trying to keep warm without a coat.

Out in the countryside Mrs Robertson and the Hammer children ate apple pies, shot rabbits and read a great many new books. They taught Daisy to spell complicated words, such as 'octopus', which she would surely never have occasion to write but which were nice to know.

Down by the river, Mrs Robertson was calling Jake for his bath. She had a great tub of warm, soapy water waiting for him and had determined to wash him thoroughly. Daisy had been scrubbed already and was drying before the stove, savouring the aroma of rabbit stew, her maiden kill.

'Jake! *Jake!*' called Maidie Robertson, to no avail.

At the bottom of the garden Jake Hammer crouched in a space between the hedge and a gnarled wisteria that grew into the pear tree above. In his hand a twelve-carat ruby, swinging on its sparkling chain, caught the last rays of sunlight, flashing red stars across his face.

26

The next morning Grace went looking for Miss Trixie May Turner, and found her carousing in the Horn of Plenty, as she scurried in with her hat jammed down and her scarf round her face as if she was freezing. She grabbed Trixie and took her to the back room.

Of course, Trixie was ready to oblige. She knew just the man, she said, to help Grace with her difficulties. He was certainly experienced, and though he was not cheap she would pay on dispatch. And, yes, she was confident that he would have no trouble with the task in hand, notwithstanding the size and ferocity of the problem. Grace gave a thorough description of the subject, her account of his movements, and departed for the Cherrys', leaving Trixie to take care of the rest.

★ ★ ★

To Landlord Nelson's horror Miss Spragg had decided to make the Orkney Arms the base for her investigations, having no further intelligence, and had been with them now for two nights, with no talk of her departure. He began to wish he had never told her anything. Mercifully she was out for most of the day, returning at nightfall to disconcert his customers. He served her in her room, whenever possible, to the effect that he had become a slave to her every whim. His wife continued to bellow at him from upstairs, causing the company to feel sorry for him, though they did not like him much, and to wonder how an invalid might be so loud. Of course, his wife told Landlord Nelson that he should take the situation in hand and turn the goblin out, but how could he explain why he couldn't seem to do it? If she was on her feet, his wife told him, she would have seen her off by now. Why was he so weak and lazy? As she berated him he watched her lips move, hearing not a word, while he wondered how it was that he had ended in servitude to two witches, and wished that she were dead.

★ ★ ★

Miss Spragg detested the countryside and was unhappy to find herself there for longer than she had hoped. There was no word from London, and no sign of the children, though she fancied she could smell them on the breeze. Her colleague had made a definite sighting and he swore blind they had departed west. After searching some way up the river she had tired of horseback and the mixed welcome she was receiving at her door-to-door enquiries, and had decided, quite correctly, that they must have gone back beyond Maidenhead together. This enraged her, and made her saddle sores worse.

The next day she rode back the other way. Taking the west bank of the river she reached Bray, where she started her furtive enquiries again. The houses were fewer for the next hour and she made rapid progress.

It must be noted that Miss Spragg was unlikely to have much luck by this strategy, on account of her dreadful countenance, which made people recoil, some more visibly than others. One or two slammed their doors as soon as they saw her, or even screamed. No one claimed to have seen the family she described.

Emmeline Spragg knew they were along this stretch of the river — she had seen the mother near Laleham, with her own eyes, and all alone. She urged her horse onward with a vicious slap, making such good time over the next few miles that she resolved to push on to Chertsey and cross the river there, going back on the other bank. Little did she know how close this would bring her, scowling in the drizzle at the milestone.

* * *

Trixie sat at her dressing-table, brushing her hair. She had decided she was finished with Mirabel Trotter. She had managed to avoid her for two weeks or more and shuddered to think of her now. And she had hatched a tidy plan involving the office safe and the dancing key that she had seen at her last visit to Mirabel Trotter's grand residence. The problem was the need of an accomplice: she herself would have to be prominent somewhere else, in public, with a sound alibi — and she could think of no one who would dare to break and enter the Trotter house. It occurred to her now that this Blunt fellow might pave the way. Burglary was his trade, after all, and he knew nothing of Mirabel Trotter's reputation. Trixie might kill two birds with the one stone. Suppose Mirabel was at home, she thought, perchance with her sons, who knows what might occur? She might save Happy Harry Harding's fee for one thing — and if Jack could happen along after the rumpus had died down, to find the house unsecured, that would be most timely.

The very next day Trixie tracked down Mr

Blunt and was ready to meet him as he turned up in the Frying Pan. Acquainted most thoroughly with the facts, she recognised her target at fifty paces and affected appropriate nonchalance, positioning herself next to where he would land at the bar. It did not take her long to strike up conversation. Within ten minutes they had moved through to the back room, with the kind permission of Horace Daley. They smoked Havana cigars and just a little opium. She needed the help of a certain type of gentleman, as she put it to him over several gins and a hand of twenty-one.

The job seemed simple enough; indeed, he was wondering whether he would bother with it at all when Trixie said something that made him prick up his ears, not in connection with the business at hand but some chatter in which she knew he would have no interest.

She was not daft and knew perfectly well that she would have to bait him with something, and so, with the casual air of the born liar, she dropped her 'very dear friend' Grace Hammer's name. She saw the lights flicker behind his eyes, which had been glazing over just a moment before.

An hour later she had furnished him with certain information, pertaining to the layout of the Trotter residence at Shoreditch: how he might gain entry, where he would find the safe and the key.

★ ★ ★

Jack was sitting in the Saracen's Head when Trixie walked in with news. 'You'll never guess what I know,' she challenged him.

'No, but I'll wager it's something good by the look on your face.'

She sat down across the table from him, rather pleased with herself.

'Well?'

'I've a nice little job for you.'

They huddled into a booth and she told him what he needed to know about the Shoreditch house and its secret treasures. He was to go at ten o'clock sharp, Thursday next. On Thursdays the rent collections were made, rounds that stretched from Hoxton to the river, and from there to Mile End, and by evening the safe would be fit to burst. After scaling the back wall, he must follow the side of the building round to the garden door. He would find it open.

Jack was reluctant, to say the least. 'The Trotter house? You must be off your rocker. I'd sooner pull my own teeth.'

'Listen to me. Mirabel Trotter will be accounted for. Did you think I hadn't thought of it? You insult me, Jack.' Here she shot him a reproachful look, tinged with hurt, to show how wounded she felt at his faithlessness. 'Now, then. I've got a girl on the inside — her name doesn't matter. She'll leave the door unlocked and take care of the diversion. All you've to do is empty the safe. Don't you mind anything else.'

He was schooled thoroughly in the arrangement of the rooms, and where to find the safe, and the key. He assured her he could do without it in any event. He was taught to pick locks at his grandfather's knee. Then they drank gin as though they would die tomorrow and sang into the night.

★ ★ ★

Of course Trixie did not tell him the whole story. She did not feel the need to disclose the fact that Mr Blunt would also be visiting the premises that evening. With the benefit of her careful planning, she regarded it as an irrelevance. If Jack went at ten sharp, she reckoned, all attention would be elsewhere. She would meet him an hour later, at eleven o'clock, at Liverpool Street, whence she would get out of town for a day or two.

★ ★ ★

Out in the country Daisy woke from a bad dream and sat with Maidie Robertson by a low, glowing fire, listening to *Alice's Adventures in Wonderland*. As they turned the page a sharp knock came at the door. They looked at it.

'Go and get in with Charlie upstairs and bolt the door, Daisy,' said Maidie Robertson, very quietly. Daisy had heard her mother talk like this and did as she was told without question.

Mrs Robertson went to the front door and opened it, feigning sleepiness. 'Who's there?' she asked, blinking as if confused. The cloaked figure on the doorstep turned to the lamplight, casting a faint glow upon the creature inside the dark hood. Miss Spragg, the goblin creature, flashed her most hideous grin. Unsettling enough to behold in the broad daylight, looking as she did like a ghoul from a dark fairytale, never mind in deep shadow on the doorstep, she gave Maidie Robertson quite a turn; but she composed herself, and smiled politely.

'I am so sorry to wake you at this hour,' said the cloaked horror, in an oily voice, and it was as if a cold wind had swept in at the door. The hairs stood up at the back of Mrs Robertson's neck. 'I am leading a local search for a woman believed to be at large in this parish. She may be in the company of some unfortunate children whom she claims are her own, going by the name of Hammer. We are seeking them most urgently or any information relating to their whereabouts.'

There followed an impressive silence as Maidie Robertson looked suitably overawed, as she supposed typical country folk would to a city rat, but said not a word, as if dumbstruck.

Miss Spragg grew impatient and pushed for more. 'This woman is a dangerous criminal, holding them to ransom. Their poor parents are naturally distraught. May I ask if you might have seen any such party passing by this way?'

As she spoke her cold black eyes wandered into the cosy room. She had assumed that country people were simple creatures, used only to hoeing and reaping and other such agricultural pursuits, and did not suppose they would doubt her ludicrous story for a moment.

Maidie Robertson, of course, saw through her straight away. 'Well, goodness me, no,' she said. 'What a terrible thing. I've seen no one out of the ordinary. How many are they?'

'Four,' said the goblin. 'Three boys and a girl. The little girl has golden hair.' She looked along the top of the bureau, her eyes like mice crawling over each object, the china cat, the pansies, a teacup.

'No, I've seen no such family about, no one at all. But perchance my sons have. I could wake them if you'd like, though they've been working in the fields all day.'

Miss Spragg's eyes landed on a blue satin hair ribbon on the floor. 'No. That won't be necessary,' she said. 'Thank you kindly for your trouble.'

After she'd left Maidie Robertson made fast all the windows and doors, which she was unaccustomed to doing. She packed a carpet bag with a few clothes, Daisy's hairbrush, a bar of soap and a revolver, and put it by the door. She planned to rise at dawn with the family and call upon Mr Mullins at the farm, who would be up milking.

Miss Spragg rode directly to the next village where, though it was the middle of the night, she found a light burning and banged on the window. She brought forth a disgruntled farmer who quieted upon seeing her and duly obliged with a room till morning. After sleeping but three hours she rose and went out into the dawn mist, certain to find help in the form of a sturdy man, as everyone, in her considerable experience, had their price.

She happened upon him just ten minutes

later at the edge of the village, herding cows into the milking shed, a large dull fellow in a brown cloth cap. When she waved money under his nose he was interested enough to listen, though it required a good effort as he was quite stupid. Not fully understanding the finer points of the goblin's plan, but grasping enough to know that it did not involve murder and that he was to be richly rewarded, he found himself saddling a horse and leaving the cows to wander in their field. They started back towards Laleham, to the little house by the river.

27

Sneaky Jake Hammer woke early, and went about the house quietly on his own, as he liked to do when the opportunity arose, pretending for his own amusement that he had no family and was alone in the wide world. He pulled on his boots and ventured outside to look at the horses over the way. He had reached the garden hedge when he caught the sound of hoofs coming up the lane. They stopped some way off and he peered out cautiously. Two figures on horseback were talking: one pointed down the lane, a small withered figure in a ragged cloak — clearly a wicked witch — waving a crooked arm towards the house.

Jake fled back up the garden path, heart racing, flinging himself inside the door and slamming it as the riders approached the house. It was only as they drew level with the hedge that he saw them. And it was then that he saw Daisy, wandering down the path, picking rosehips. As she reached the end, beyond which she knew she wasn't to go, two horses stopped outside the gate.

Looking up she saw a surly man, and another creature such as she had only seen in nightmares, wizened and bent, with black eyes. Frightened, she backed towards the house and at that moment Jake opened the door and tore down the path shouting to her to run inside. She turned, and the man was off his horse, up the path and grabbed her. She did well to kick him in the shins with the heels of her boots, struggling as he hauled her up and away. Within a moment they were gone.

Maidie Robertson might have been an old lady but she was on the neighbour's horse directly, hard down the road the way they had left. Charlie followed her with the farmer not five minutes behind. They met at the crossroads, looking desperately for signs of which way to follow, and decided to split up and ride for two miles, then to turn back if nothing was found, converging again at the milestone.

Twenty minutes later they were all headed for Datchet, where they refreshed their horses. Mrs Robertson went into the inn to ask the barmaid while the men made enquiries around the square. Little did she know that Daisy was but a few feet away, through the floor. They had caught up with the goblin and her dull henchman, hiding in the cellar of the Bird in Hand.

Unluckily it was the landlady who had put up the strange party earlier that morning, before retiring to bed with a crashing headache, leaving the poor barmaid with all the cleaning to do and strict instructions not to disturb her on any account. Miss Spragg had presented herself alone, and while her visage had alarmed the good landlady at first sight, she would take anybody's money and so, although she had no decent accommodation left, she had offered the basement room behind the beer cellar, referred to among her family rather aptly as the dungeon, having been the object of threats made to her naughty children when they were young.

It was small and damp, with one tiny window that looked out at ground level on to the yard and admitted so little light that the room must be lit with a greasy oil-lamp that hung from the joists above, if the occupant was to see anything at all. She had expected the wizened creature to refuse it, but, seeming perfectly content with the arrangement — if such a thing could be expressed upon such a face — she explained that she had been riding all night and needed to rest.

Once installed in the dungeon she had

smuggled in her accomplice with Daisy, distracting the good landlady by requesting a clean blanket, which should have aroused her suspicion, but only irked her. She had gone upstairs to suffer in bed as her girl arrived for work and no one was any the wiser.

After exhausting their enquiries the search party moved on to the next village. Daisy heard hoofs above but didn't dare scream; she wondered if she would be rescued soon, if she might escape.

★ ★ ★

The search party were still out when a ransom note fell through the door of Mrs Robertson's cottage, brought expressly by a village youth who was happy to be woken by a strange hag with a sovereign, having recovered from the initial shock. Billy read the note. It demanded the surrender of the family spoils for the safe return of their little girl. No one but Jake had any idea what this might mean, though Billy was sure it had something to do with his mother. The old lady was to show herself, alone, at the crossroads at Hythe End, at precisely half past six that evening, to deliver the treasure. Until the matter was settled they would not see Daisy alive. They were urged not to play games or test the resolve of her captors.

Poor Jake fetched the necklace from under the wisteria. Now he understood what the game was about. He was sure that everything was his fault. Billy swallowed his horror as he was presented with the treasure, flashing in the sunlight; blood red stars across his face. They waited for news, together on the stairs, the door locked and bolted, the windows barred.

★　★　★

Daisy was bearing up well during her dreadful ordeal — she was a plucky little thing. Her captors had not hurt her but she believed their terrible threats and dared not shout for help. Luckily she had faith in her eventual rescue, trusting in divine justice, as small children tend to do, bravely, with no proof at all of such a phenomenon. The large dull fellow in the brown cloth cap paid her little attention, having chained her by the foot to the rusted iron bedstead. To Daisy's relief the witch had been out for an hour or more, leaving her under his watchful eye. So, there they lurked, in silence, behind the barrels, the little girl with her back to the wall, eyes wide, expecting the witch to appear again at any moment, perhaps from thin air.

Until that day Daisy had believed that such creatures existed only in fairy tales — Now she could see for herself that they lived outside the pages of Grimms' *Tales* and walked among us in the real world. She wanted to cry but dared not. The hours crawled past. If only Ma or Charlie would come.

★　★　★

Charlie was in a desperate state. They had had no lead of any kind, and he was beginning to grasp the futility of their efforts. At four o'clock he sent Mrs Robertson back to Laleham to see if the boys had heard anything, and pushed on for an hour or so with Farmer Mullins. At Slough he stopped suddenly. He looked as though he would throw himself upon the stones and cry his heart out. He knew he must turn back.

'Come on, lad,' said good Farmer Mullins, speaking his very thoughts. 'They can't have come this far. Let's go back by Wraysbury and search from there. You must eat as well or you'll be of no use to her.'

Indeed Charlie was weak with hunger, though he would refuse to eat until he found his sister. They started back along the road.

★　★　★

Miss Spragg's hired help was wavering in his resolve; in truth, he was not altogether comfortable taking young children from their mother, and the more time he spent with the woman the more distasteful he found her, especially now that she had returned and they were shut up in the same small room together. He could almost feel the chilly malevolent cloud that hung in the air, as she flicked her little black lizard eyes back and forth, smiling nastily every now and then at some dark, private thought. The girl, who refused to tell her name, was a sweet creature and he meant her no harm; neither did he want his wages now. He could see how frightened she was and tried to give her secret looks — though there was no chance she might trust him — wanting to cheer her a little.

Though he might seem to have had a good heart, he fell short of overpowering Spragg, as he could easily have done, and rescuing the little girl; he was a weak man who wanted no trouble with the law. The sentiment made him feel better about his part in the affair nonetheless, and so he watched her keeping quiet in the corner, praying for deliverance.

He had reckoned without Daisy's special resolve and, indeed, her new skills. She had forgotten nothing her sneaky brother had taught her and had already pilfered the key to the padlock that chained her foot to the bed. She had taken it from Cloth Cap's pocket when he brought her meagre supper — so neatly that he never suspected a thing. She tucked the key under the edge of the damp rug she sat upon and there it remained all afternoon. She kept quiet and resisted the urge to piss, as she would have had to ask Cloth Cap to unlock her for that. The witch had instructed him not to do so under any circumstances, but in her absence this morning he had taken pity and smuggled Daisy outside to spend a penny. This small kindness would prove to be his undoing, which would serve him right.

★　★　★

Charlie and Farmer Mullins had intended to return by a different route, thus widening the scope of their search, but the hand of Fate and the winding anonymous lanes sent them back again by Datchet, a circumstance they considered unfortunate, which, of course, was not so. They stopped to water the horses in the square and Farmer Mullins, a faithful companion indeed, persuaded Charlie to take a beer in the Bird in Hand, with a whisky to follow.

312

Now, the good landlady of the Bird had recovered her health and come down to the bar to make ready for the evening. As they had made their enquiries here already, it seemed futile to ask her but Charlie thought it worth a try. 'I wonder if you might help me, Madam,' said he, his face desperate, his voice shaking as she filled his jug. 'I'm looking for my sister who was snatched early this morning. She is a pretty little thing, just five years old, with blue eyes and fair hair. Might you have seen her?'

'You poor dear, how dreadful!' said our good lady, sympathy swelling in her heart. 'I'm afraid I've seen no children all day long. I've been upstairs with my lumbago, which gives me such distress. You must be frantic.'

'She is likely in the company of an old woman, a rather fearsome creature, if the truth be told. I haven't seen her myself but I understand she is short and wizened, dressed in ragged black and resembling, according to my young brother who is the only witness, a crone from Grimms' *Tales*, though you may allow for some exaggeration on his part.'

Now the landlady had never heard of Grimms' *Tales*, having no interest in books, but she knew immediately whom Charlie was talking about. Unfortunately she had more loyalty to Miss Spragg than to Charlie, having taken her money this morning with the promise of a handsome bonus if she was left in peace; this now served the purpose Miss Spragg had intended. Had our good lady actually seen the child with her guest she might have given Charlie a different answer, but as she had not, she persuaded herself that it could not be the same woman, after all.

'I'm afraid I've seen no such person,' she told him. Charlie sank into his beer, a picture of despair. Farmer Mullins put a strong arm round his shoulder.

'Excuse me,' piped up a sweet female voice. It belonged to a mousy girl named Alice Beakey, who had a habit of picking up on other people's conversation, which on this occasion would prove to be a virtue. 'I believe I have seen the woman you describe so vividly, riding out this morning. It gave me quite a turn to see her face! She was all alone, but I'm sure she must have been the one you're looking for. I don't expect there's another with such a fearsome appearance in the whole of England, or anywhere else for that matter. Is she a criminal? She certainly looks it! Might she be dangerous, do you think?'

Now, Miss Beakey is a lonely soul, due in the most part to her habit of talking too much, if given the opportunity, and asking rather too many questions. If she had looked hard enough at herself she would have found that her interest in disclosing what she knew had as much to do with involving herself in the affair as helping to find any lost children. Indeed, her information was of limited value, stopping short at the edge of the village, where she had been surprised by the goblin while picking wild celery. She had seen neither where the mysterious hag had come from nor where she had gone.

But her noisy chatter had prompted someone else's memory: a Miss Bunn had seen no fearsome crones, but had noticed a dull-looking fellow in a brown cloth cap this morning, with a small fair girl she had not recognised as being from the village. They had been behind the outhouse of the inn. He had looked about him in a rather surreptitious manner, she had remarked to herself at the time, and, now she thought of it, had definitely seemed to be up to no good. The question of why she had thought to do nothing more than watch out of the window and feel suspicious was passed over.

By now the blacksmith's wife had joined in; she, too, had seen the dull fellow in the brown cloth cap, though she could have sworn it was blue. It was possible he may have taken a room in the village, but certainly none of hers. She said she would ask about, and sent her daughter to see if the Beehive had taken in any latecomers last night.

★ ★ ★

Maidie Robertson was on her way to Hythe End, alone, as the ransom note demanded. She had no time to find Charlie and Farmer Mullins. She carried a twelve-carat ruby necklace and a Colt revolver, concealed in her skirts.

★ ★ ★

Downstairs the goblin had fallen asleep on the mildewed bed, her evil breath rasping in her throat. Daisy closed her eyes. She heard Cloth Cap shift in his seat. He sighed heavily, kicked at the chair-leg and scratched. Then, after a few minutes of huffing and fidgeting, he rose and approached the bed. Daisy peeped through her eyelashes, her heart pounding. He was standing over the witch, his face a picture of distaste, as if he were regarding a mighty spider on the wall. Daisy wondered what he was up to — afraid, yet glad of any disruption to her appalling circumstances. She felt as if she had been there, under the ground, for ever, though she

316

knew it couldn't have been more than a day.

In fact, he was not preparing to kill the witch in her sleep, as Daisy supposed, merely assessing the depth of her slumber. Her mouth hung open; he could almost see the poisoned vapour that passed for her breath, hanging in the air like a toxic particular. Her skin seemed flayed from a corpse, pale and dirty, as if she had been dug up from cursed ground. She was asleep, all right. He had been instructed to stay out of sight and to wake her at six, but thirst overcame him and he could not bear to remain in that hole a moment longer. He decided that one jar and a few minutes couldn't hurt. She need never know. A glance at the little one confirmed her asleep as well, so he removed his cap and combed his hair, in an effort to disguise himself, then crept out, locking the door behind him.

Daisy did not waste one second. She knew he might be back directly and that this could be her only chance. Her little fingers shaking, she unlocked the padlock and unwound the chain from her leg, slowly, so it made no noise, though she wanted to throw it off and run. The witch stirred. Daisy held her breath, her heart bursting in her chest. She freed herself at last and made her way on tiptoe to the tiny window. Silently, silently, she lifted the chair and put it below the sill, stealing a glance back at the bundle of rags upon the bed. As she stepped on to it, the chair creaked. She screwed up her little face, frozen, but the witch snored on. She reached up and tried the window latch. It wouldn't budge — having rusted together years before. She tried it harder, to no avail.

Daisy Hammer wanted to cry and scream but with an iron will she resisted this urge. As far as she knew there was no one to hear her: no sound came through the flagstones above — she wondered if the witch had turned the people to stone. She must save herself. At that moment she noticed that Cloth Cap had left his rifle behind. It was leaning innocently against the doorframe, as if waiting for an omnibus.

★　★　★

It seemed that the entire village had passed through the Bird in Hand, adding to the conjecture the possibility that Miss Trebor, who was due back from town at six, had taken them in, or that they were hiding in Mr Piggot's derelict outhouse. At the end of the bar skulked Cloth Cap, bare-headed, ears burning. He sneaked a glance at the boy, the farmer's arm round his shoulder: he looked as though he would drown himself in his jug. A guilty heartstring twanged in Cloth Cap's chest. Louder still was his self-interest. He was a spineless fellow, who would fail to redeem his sins on this occasion. Abandoning Daisy to her fate, he slipped away into the night.

Mrs Trent, the butcher's wife, arrived; after confirming she knew nothing of a dull fellow in a cloth cap, brown or blue, she offered the theory that the kidnappers were hiding in the woods behind the village. Lively speculation followed among the throng, which was perhaps fifty strong now. They were preparing a search party when the rabble was silenced by a gunshot from downstairs.

★   ★   ★

The last thing that Miss Emmeline Spragg saw was her small, fair-haired prisoner levelling a rifle at her head. She had been woken by the click as Daisy cocked it, and in the scant time she had to reflect before Daisy blew a fatal hole in her head she remarked to herself how well the child handled it — how inventive to have propped the heavy barrel upon the bedstead! — and wondered where she had learned such a skill.

Charlie was down there directly — Farmer

Mullins putting the door through with one good boot — and swept his little sister into his arms, where she cried as though she would drown him in tears. Wrapped in a blanket she went home on the front of Mrs Robertson's horse, as Charlie and Farmer Mullins scoured the town for the mysterious dull fellow, who had left his brown cloth cap behind him. He was never seen again, even though they traced him back to Canker Farm. He had simply melted into thin air.

Our good landlady was left to clean the goblin's brains from the wall, after which she barred the doorway, vowing never to use the room again. A week or two later she opened it once more to desperate guests, who found it impossible to pass the night there; they were woken in the early hours by a sinister rattling sound, accompanied by a curious smell.

28

In London Grace was blissfully ignorant of all the carry-on. She found herself hankering after Jack, having laid low in an upstairs room at the Frying Pan for the last couple of days. Trixie had seen him at the Commercial tavern and said he had asked after her, though Grace did not know if this was true.

★　★　★

Unknown to Grace, Jack the Lad was in St Giles, away from his East London haunts and the usual crowd, constructing his own plan for that night. Since Trixie had proposed the Shoreditch robbery, he had been wondering what the catch might be. No one in East London was honest: if they were, they wouldn't survive. Deceit was a way of life from Aldgate to Mile End, and no one held it much against their fellows. Surely there was something more to be had from this venture, he thought. This might be considered greedy or enterprising on Jack's part, according to one's point of view: the safe would certainly contain a tidy pile of cash on a Thursday evening.

Jack was going out to do the job, as intended, except that he had decided to leave an hour early. He had not consulted Trixie and he did not mean to share the proceeds. In fact, he planned to get out of town himself for a day or two, before she had a chance to catch up with him. He arrived at the house in Shoreditch and scaled the wall behind the magnolia tree.

After a quiet moment, listening, sheltered from view in the bushes, he crept out and crossed the lawn. Crouching below the level of the windows he sneaked a look inside, round the edge of the curtain, to see the darkened study, light from the hall leaking in through the chink in the doorway. He crept round to the garden door, taking a crowbar from his belt. To his surprise it was already open.

★ ★ ★

The clock had just struck nine when Mirabel Trotter heard the first creak on the stair. She had drunk half a bottle of cognac and fallen asleep in front of the fire in her drawing room some three hours ago. It sobered her immediately, as if a bucket of cold water had been thrown over her head. She gripped the poker that was still in her hand and turned towards the door. Someone was creeping very quietly up the stairs.

She rose from her chair slowly, crossed the room, graceful as a prima ballerina, and positioned herself behind the door. The footsteps reached the landing and paused. Not a sound but the clock. Then a tiny creak, directly outside, which made her jump. Seconds passed as the intruder listened at the door. Mrs Trotter held her breath. Then the handle turned slowly as somebody tried it, rattling softly.

Mrs Trotter gripped the poker ever tighter as a key turned in the lock and the door opened. A dark furtive figure sniffed his way over the threshold and was met by an iron bar, glancing across his head, followed by a small hatchet that she ever kept upon her person. She was not one to mess about and she realised immediately that she had never seen this person in her life before and was ready to swear to it. Her sons were downstairs, smoking and playing cards, but she hardly needed them. She laid about the intruder until he stopped moving. Then she wiped her face with the back of her butcher's arms and stood panting and sweating in the darkness.

The cries had brought the Trotter men

forth from the kitchen and hurled them up the stairs. They found their ma dripping with sweat and gore. She put down the poker. 'We'd best tidy up,' she said.

It took Mirabel Trotter, one of her burly sons (the other was faint at the sight of blood) and two men from the yard to clear up the terrible scene and restore order to the room. They took up the carpet and burned it in a brazier outside, an expensive silk carpet with an elephant-foot pattern, in deep red and black, that had come all the way from Afghanland. They took the dead man downstairs in a sack, with a cloth round his oozing head, and dumped him by the back door. Then they returned with a horse and cart and dragged him off to Canning Town, where they chopped him into several pieces with a bandsaw. Mrs Trotter rewarded them all with a handsome bonus.

The first London heard of the violent demise of Horatio Blunt was the baying of dogs as his remains were dispatched to the swine and the canine fraternity in Mrs Trotter's Mile End yard the next morning.

★ ★ ★

Jack had crept in through the open garden door and, finding the drawing room opposite, had ventured inside. He found the bureau without trouble and set to searching the tiny drawers. He found everything as Trixie had said it would be.

He had the key and was congratulating himself, before turning his attention to the safe, when the door swung open silently and in came Miss Craven, who was not afraid of bumps in the night. She held up a rifle as he swung round and pointed it at his head. He dropped the crowbar and put his hands in the air.

Miss Craven was the type who would kill an intruder without losing sleep at night. She would have shot this stranger without hesitation if not for the fact that the trigger had jammed. She braved it out, advancing towards him slowly with the barrel aimed between his eyes, while he wondered why she did not shoot and then concluded, quite correctly — though not in the way he thought — that she couldn't. In a second he was across the floor and had grabbed the gun by the barrel, swinging it round and down on her skull like a thundercrack. She fell to her knees and Jack hit her again, so violently that her glass eye popped out of its socket and rolled under the bureau, where it stared indignantly at his boots.

With his heart bursting in his mouth, he fumbled with the key, twisting it into the lock. A thick pool was forming around Miss Craven's head, stretching across the floor to his feet. His hands shook. He opened the safe door to see great wads of notes, rolled round with black rubber bands. At that moment he heard a dreadful wailing shout that shook the house and came so suddenly that he almost jumped out of his skin, heart pounding as if he was winning the Derby. It frightened him even more than murdering Miss Craven. He looked down at her — the blood had reached his boots, and the screaming had stopped upstairs. There was just a whimpering, like someone's last breath. Footsteps came hurrying up from below. Jack took to his heels and ran.

★ ★ ★

Rumours spread round the district of a double murder, but died as quickly as they had begun. There was no mention of such an event in any newspaper, no front pages with lurid scenes and sketches of the house with the murder sites marked, not even in the *Daily News*. The Trotter fiend had tidied her mess well away. Jack held his breath for a day or two, hiding out in Shad Thames. The company was gruff and evil: hyena people congregating in dens below the street to watch dog-fights, drink meths. Jack fitted into this scene well, much better than his mother would have liked. He took to smoking opium, played cards, started to lose his mind. After a week he had become the colour of Limehouse itself, forgetting a little more each day about the world above.

★　★　★

Trixie, of course, true to her name, was nowhere about while all of this was going on. She breezed into town a day or two later, as if she knew nothing of it. She was, of course, privately furious at Jack's betrayal but decided to bide her time, for she was sure he was stupid enough to turn up again when he had spent the money, having underestimated her regard for loyalty. One benefit of this unplanned turn of events was that Miss Craven was out of the way for good. Trixie sent word to Grace that the deed was done, then ordered rack of lamb and more champagne.

★　★　★

Grace went home to set it straight. She picked up the scattered papers and books, threw away the broken plates; it was dusk by the time she had scrubbed everything. She waved at Mrs Jacob behind her twitching curtain as she tipped her dirty bucket down the gully.

'Grace,' came that voice down the street, like a ghost. A cocky dark shape in the shadow, and there he was, like the King of Arabia himself — unbelievable! — coming through the rain as if he had heard her thoughts calling. He walked up to her, dripping, with his ragged grin, and she let him in. In the morning he was gone. Perhaps it was best. She left with a spring in her step to collect the children.

★   ★   ★

Some fifty-two miles away, in the picturesque seaside town of Whitstable, Miss Rosalind Pinch was toasting her success. She peeped inside the carpet bag again, just to see that the money was still there. She giggled girlishly, exactly as she had the last time she looked, then lifted the brandy to her lips, thanking the good Lord once again for her heavenly luck. She set down the glass and perused the map, planning her agenda for tomorrow. Perhaps she would take a carriage and ride down the coast to Brighton, or maybe see a show. She put her feet on the table before her, sighed contentedly and lit a large Havana cigar.

29

'I want to knock you into tomorrow and kiss you all at once, son.'

'Sorry Ma,' said Jake, hanging his head.

'Don't you sorry me, you tricky little bastard.'

'I won't do it again.'

'I expect you'll do as you please.' She wrapped her arms around him. Jake looked confused. 'What else are you up to that I don't know about. Eh?'

★ ★ ★

The family settled back as though they had never been away, but they talked of the country often and wrote letters to Maidie Robertson. If one of them came over quiet and gazed out of the window Grace knew they were dreaming of the riverside. One day soon they might move to the country for good, not so far, perhaps, from Mrs Robertson. She wouldn't tell them that for a while.

Charlie took his handsome face straight round to Elsie Brown's, his hands a little sweaty in his pockets, and they took up where they had left off. Daisy was happy to see her friends, though she wept for three miles after leaving her country home. When she asked where Sally Ann was, Grace said she'd gone home, back up north. Where was north? Far, she said — when she'd be back she couldn't say. It was hand-me-down Emily who told her, the very next day.

Daisy ran home with her little face tied in knots. 'Ma, Em said Sally had her head cut off. Did she, Ma?'

'No, my sweetheart, she didn't.'

'Is she dead, though?'

'Yes, she is, darlin'.'

* * *

It was back to business as usual in the district. Whitechapel had turned up no butchered women on its streets for three whole weeks, and started to breathe again, as easy as it ever did. Talk returned to hard luck and money trouble — even the papers had run out of things to say about the horrors. And then, at the end of September, just as the boys at the newsstands were shuffling their listless feet, two more were found, on the very same night.

The first was Busy Liz Stride, still warm, in

a yard off Berners Street, outside the Jewish club, stirring Gentile outrage to fever pitch. It seemed the fiend has been disturbed at work; he hadn't done the full job on her. The second was slit from belly to throat, sewn together at the mortuary with thick black stitches like Frankenstein's monster. She had been gutted, her nose slashed, her eyelids cut — in your ears at every newsstand, shouted loud in the street. Every man, woman and child of the rotten East End talked of nothing else. Every stranger was suspect, each shadow hid a fiend, and terror lurked in every doorway, especially now night came early. The women went about in pairs, which made business tricky for the brasses. None had thought too much about the uselessness of their patrol companion in the event of trouble, being dependent on the meagre spoils of their only commodity, and for the most part having a heavy drink habit to drown. Some chose not to care.

Grace went to see Busy Liz Stride into the ground, holding Nelly Holland to keep her upright as she convulsed in loud, drunken sobs over the chaplain's voice and then stared numbly past the headstones, as if lost, most likely thinking about her next tipple. Grace thought about Sally Ann, and Polly, whose meagre funeral seemed so long ago now. The

Whitechapel girls were disappearing one by one.

Grace was haunted sometimes by dark moments when she wondered if she knew the devil. Sometimes she dreamed of him coming, a dark shape at the end of a tunnel with the river behind him, and she tried to run, waking with a start. Not for the first time in her long life she counted the blessing that she did not turn tricks.

30

London clay makes yellow-grey bricks, the blocks that built the East End. If you venture to the finer parts of London you may find the Oxford clay, red and rich, moulded in intricate designs, floral patterns and curves; the houses stretch away in a straight matching line. How long will a brick last? A hundred years? Two hundred? Long after the building has bitten the dust if the mortar is not mixed right. To cut his costs, Mr Weevil of Norbury made his with too much sand, endangering the occupants of his cheaply built dwellings. It was a miracle indeed that those structures stood as long as they did before they fell down upon the sleeping heads of the people inside them. Mercifully they knew nothing of it, save old Mrs Tallis, who was smoking opium and did not care. Mr Weevil was chased out of the building game long ago and a factory stands on the site; and here, directed by a reliable friend, with a note of recommendation, Grace came to call upon a gentleman with the right connections. She stood at the back door, looking this way and that, chewing her lip as she waited for it to open, praying not to be robbed. Lady Stanhope's ruby necklace lay in her pocket, wrapped in a silk handkerchief.

Autumn had set in over London, the bitter wind was blowing, the time of year when inmates of workhouse or prison were most glad of the shelter. It was dark by five o'clock. People huddled together; less chatter was heard in the street. Everybody drank more than usual, claiming it kept them warm on the way home, crowding into the pub needing comfort and good cheer. They found a hundred reasons not to leave just yet: it may have started to rain outside, say, or someone had come in whom they must see about business.

If the ruby weighed heavy in her pocket on the way out, it was a lump of lead on the way back: now she knew what it was worth. Enough to move to the country, all right. She scurried down Whitechapel Road, beneath the great walls of the hospital, the rows of dark windows watching her down in the street.

The buildings seemed to drop away at the crossroads and the vista opened out before her, the wide sweep of the thoroughfare and the darkening sky, and she breathed in the night air, intoxicated, standing on the corner gazing down Whitechapel Road. Perhaps she saw trouble coming, or Polly's ghost, in her new bonnet — who can know these things? — for she decided to turn off, down Thomas Street.

The Union Workhouse loomed at the end, dark and forbidding, to discourage the downtrodden. She shuddered at its gloomy façade, scowling down at her as if it would snatch her up with a stone hand and pull her in through the barred windows. Grace was alone on the street and felt a prickle of fear. A gas lamp threw a warm sphere of light ahead; she gathered her nerves but quickened her step.

As she drew nearer the globe of light there was a rustle in the darkness. The back of her scalp contracted and she stopped short in the shadow and listened. It came again, from the side of the yard, near the mortuary; urgent whispering and cursing. It's Mary Kelly or one of the other girls working, thought Grace, and had turned to go when the voices rose and she heard they belonged to two men. Horror stories rang in her ears — she had an urgent feeling that she did not want to be seen. Holding her breath she moved closer to the wall, crouching into the shadow.

For a few moments there was silence and Grace wondered whether she should run for it. Then came the voices again, drawing closer. Panic swelled in her chest. There was muttering and the sound of something heavy being dragged along the ground — the men were exerting themselves a great deal. One must be fat: he huffed and puffed and had to stop for little rests, his accomplice cursing all the while. Did she know that voice? She held her breath, straining to hear. The gas light snuffed out, making her jump. Never was she so glad to be left in the dark.

She stood up cautiously — and ducked back down again: the men stood, with their backs half turned to her, not ten feet from the wall. They were engrossed in lifting what was plainly a fresh corpse, wrapped in sackcloth, on to a handcart. She peeped back over the wall. They were piling crates of rotten fruit on top. Crates of fruit! With a last shifty look round they made to leave, and as the taller man turned his head Grace glimpsed him in the moonlight.

It was Jack. Jesus Christ. Tin cans clanged in her ears — she could taste them like blood at the back of her throat. She had an urge to stand up and shout to him, but she shrank back against the wall, staring into a spot on the black paving, listening to the cart creak away.

★　★　★

Where would they take the corpse? she wondered. Who was it? She hoped he had not done such a thing before they were together last, watching the kettle boil, frowning at the stove. How could such a man have worked his charm on her? She felt shocked and stupid. The children noticed she was quiet and made her a card, with a bird on the front and paper frills they had cut from a picture.

★ ★ ★

Sure enough he came again, just a few days later, at two o'clock in the morning. He rattled the window stealthily as she sat reading and she knew straight away it was him. 'Go away,' she said, round the curtain, then shut it again.

He stood puzzled for a moment, watching his cloudy breath in the winter air, condensing on the window-pane; not sure what to do now that his charm had misfired. This was a situation for which he had made no provision. He decided, for reasons known only to himself, to knock again, at the door this time.

Grace appeared with a cricket bat in her hand, ready to batter him with it. The smile dropped off his face, making him look like a small child. She glared at him, familiar but strange. There seemed nothing to say. Jack shrank away into the night.

Grace put the bat down, kissed the sleeping children again and went back to her book. A little piece of her ran down the street after him, breathless, slipping on the cobbles, bursting with life.

★ ★ ★

After Jack left he wondered who had told her what. Or who she'd seen him out with. He was not surprised to find she hated him at last and did not blame her. Then he turned his thoughts to where he was to sleep that night.

On visiting a lady friend in Bow he discovered that the Metropolitan Police had been at her door, enquiring after his whereabouts. She had told them nothing, of course, but was not given to lying and could not be sure she hadn't blushed.

Jack reminded himself never again to consort with a girl just for her pretty face. He kissed her sweetly and went his way. Unfortunately he found the same welcome at Ruby Richardson's door when he called on her over in Cable Street. Ruby was a most voluptuous specimen of womankind, dark and mysterious, and one of his favourites. She painted her lips red and hitched up her skirt at the side into her garter, and was always pleased to see him, this evening being no exception, but she had the same story to tell. A detective from Scotland Yard, no less, had been asking after his whereabouts and she, a savvy lass, had told them he had gone to his mother's in Crewe — if, indeed, they were talking of the same fellow — and that she had not seen him since he had left. She had told them she would dearly like to get her hands on him too. She gave Jack a quick kiss and told him to be on his way.

The same story followed at every safe-house. He grew tired after a while, and went into the Prodigal Son for refreshment, where the landlord refused him, having been visited also, and not best pleased with the sudden attention for himself or his customers.

What Jack did not know was that Trixie May Turner, having been questioned by the police in connection with a certain murder, had pinned the ticket firmly on him. She had had them at her door before and they knew she always had something to tell. It was not for nothing that she kept her eyes peeled. She planned well ahead, saved people up for when she needed them most. She was loyal to her friends; it was a grave mistake indeed to cross her.

* * *

Mirabel Trotter enjoyed a sojourn at the seaside. Although the weather was unseasonable the air was bracing and invigorating and she had the opportunity to visit several colleagues and her sister, who was fat also. They ate many fine meals and watched the waves lash the pier. She thought fondly of Trixie, made plans to forgive her if she ever saw her again. This made her wistful and she stared out at the crashing sea through the rain on the window.

31

Newgate Prison is a bleak, dark structure, squatting like a giant anvil next to the Old Bailey, whence many of its wretched tenants have come direct. The heavenly dome of St Paul's Cathedral, rising above it, might serve to lift their spirits or inspire some repentance if only they could see it from the vantage-point afforded by the mean windows. The people who pass down Newgate Street, going about their daily business, carefree, laughing perhaps, or enjoying ice cream, have no notion of the despair just the other side of the walls they brush as they hurry past, within a spit of the hopeless souls locked inside.

Inside Newgate's walls the air seems to crush you, thick as you breathe it in; a heavy stench hangs in the atmosphere that reluctant visitors try not to swallow, hoping somehow not to draw breath until they escape. The cells are separate now for the most part and gone are the days when a prisoner could get a beer. For exercise they trudge in a circle, in a yard that was built to make a man feel small indeed.

Shuffling in this line Jack Tallis found himself — proud conman and dweller of night, a thin man. He would spend the rest of his days languishing in his cell, worn out like a rag.

'Will they hang him?'

'Yes, son. Don't tell Daisy.' It's a shame we can't watch, Grace thought, in a burst of spite. I wonder where they'll bury him.

★   ★   ★

Jack Tallis was hanged by the neck until dead on 6 November 1888, a day short of his thirty-fourth birthday, and an uncommonly fine one for that time of the year. He woke in his cell to the sound of the chaplain, who had several last rites to deliver that morning and was consequently in a bad mood, banging on the door. As he opened his eyes he remembered, like a lump hammer striking him full in the face, that he was to die today and marvelled at how well he had slept, then burst into terrified laughter. The Reverend Mr Cane, the filthiest rat ever to have been admitted into the ranks of the clergy, decided, upon hearing this private commotion, that he was too busy to be bothered with this irredeemable sinner and so passed by cell ninety-nine, abandoning Jack Tallis's soul without a care to the fires of hell for ever. Thus Jack found himself on his knees on the caked stone floor, begging God, in whom he had never previously believed, for forgiveness.

Over in Christ Church, Spitalfields, at that very moment Grace, who had never believed in God either and still did not, was on her knees before the altar, praying fervently for mercy on Jack's soul.

He must have heard her somehow for he thought of her suddenly and wished in that very moment, with all his heart, that things had been different. Overwhelmed with loneliness he sprang hot tears.

She wiped her face and went out thieving.

They came for him an hour later and found him peaceful, whistling 'I'm A Young Man From The Country'.

'Tell my mother I'm sorry,' he said, and spoke not another word.

★ ★ ★

The cold was vicious now, coming into winter, forcing itself through your clothes, sharp like a knife. Enough to make desperate girls do anything for warmth and comfort. And so they went round the church, praying for a crumb, entertaining anyone.

London life was shades of brown and grey. Brown and grey through the ages with a little red mixed in. Brown and grey endures for ever.

Epilogue

Life was sweet without the tell-tale heart, since Grace had found the man to deal with her interests. He had international connections, in America and Asia, and counted the famous Mr Worth among his associates. Grace trusted him as far as she could afford to. She waited for word to spread round the market. Sometimes she spotted Mr Byron Stanley in the Frying Pan and they had a quiet beer.

★　★　★

'So what will we wear to the Lord Mayor's Parade?' enquired Daisy, voicing her most important concern.

'I don't suppose it matters, darlin'. Everyone will be lookin' at the mayor. What do you want to wear?'

'A beautiful hat. With feathers. Can we go to Brixton?'

'We can go tomorrow.'

Acknowledgements

Thank you Vivienne Schuster, Clara Farmer, Juliet Brooke, the Chatto team, Jill Bialosky, Jane Gelfman and Keith Thomas. Also Gill, Derek, and everyone who put a penny in.

A TOWN CALLED IMMACULATE

Peter Anthony

It's Christmas Eve, and when bankrupt farmer Ray Marak saves the life of his friend and banker, Josh Werther, neither they nor their neighbours can imagine what the night will bring. Still traumatized by his time in Vietnam, Ray's world has shrunk — to the boundaries of his home town of Immaculate, and the warmth of his family: his sons Jacob and Ethan, and his wife Renee; Renee, the woman who waited for him during his wartime hell. But as the snow accumulates, so do the townspeople's stories, and the suspicions Ray has harboured for years start to resurface.

MILES FROM NOWHERE

Nami Mun

Thirteen-year-old Joon is a Korean immi-
grant living in the Bronx of the 1980s. Her
parents have crumbled under the weight
of her father's infidelity and mental illness
has rendered her mother nearly catatonic.
Deciding she's better off alone, Joon sets
out on a harrowing and sometimes tragic
journey, exposing herself to all the pain
and difficulty of a life lived on the
margins. Joon's years on the streets take
her from a homeless shelter to an escort
club, through struggles with addiction, to
jobs selling newspapers and cosmetics,
committing petty crimes, and, finally
towards something resembling hope.

JOHN THE REVELATOR

Peter Murphy

John Devine is an introverted, watchful, adolescent boy. He's stuck in a small town, worried over by his single mother — the chain-smoking, bible-quoting Lily — and the gregarious but sinister Mrs Nagle. He yearns for escape. When the charismatic Jamey Corboy arrives in town, John's life suddenly fills with possibilities — welcome and otherwise — and as he hides from the reality of his mother's ever-worsening health, he is faced with a terrible dilemma.

AN EQUAL STILLNESS

Francesca Kay

Born in 1924, Jennet Mallow grows up in an austere rectory in Yorkshire. Entranced by the act of drawing when young, Jennet moves to London on a scholarship to art school and meets the handsome and enigmatic painter David Feaver. The two embark on a tempestuous relationship that leads them into marriage and parenthood. Aware that David is becoming increasingly reliant on drink and tired of the dank house in which they live, Jennet agrees to a move to the brighter skies of Spain. But, as her career flourishes, her relationship with David grows sour — with potentially tragic consequences.

TRAUMA

Patrick McGrath

Psychiatrist Charlie Weir has tackled every kind of trauma during his years in New York City, but he's yet to resolve the conflicts within his own family, not least the bitter rivalry with his brother Walt. And he's never overcome the terrible blunder that lost him his wife and daughter . . . When Walt introduces him to the beautiful Nora Chiara, they quickly fall for each other. But soon, her vulnerability, which first attracted him, begins to sour their relationship. And as he probes at the source of her distress, something deep in his own unconscious mind arouses a horrifying suspicion . . .